THE
DIAMOND ROSE

A Sentinel 10 Novel

DANIELA VALENTI

Book One

Series Summary: Sentinel 10 follows the journey of Amanda, a powerful Sentinel who faces various paranormal challenges and struggles to understand the meaning of love.

Book Summary: A promising, young anesthesiology intern is suddenly imbued with the power to harness and control psychic energy, launching her into a secret world filled with danger and romance.

Distribution by Amazon KDP and Ingram Spark P.O.D.

Book Title: The Diamond Rose
Series Title: Sentinel 10
Names: Daniela Valenti - author

ISBN: 978-1-7774273-2-0 (hardcover)
ISBN: 978-1-7774273-0-6 (print)
ISBN: 978-1-7774273-1-3 (e-book)

www.sentinel10.ca

This book is dedicated to you, the reader.
Come with me, and let your imagination soar.
Welcome to the world of Sentinel 10.

Prologue

Amanda Griffith was trying to find her car in the hospital's employee parking lot. She had just finished her last day of medical school, and her shift had seemed days long. She was overworked and overtired. It was only the middle of the afternoon, and all she wanted to do was go to bed.

Her attending physician had been more difficult than usual today, tripping her up with incessant quizzing right as she was intubating a patient. Typically, Amanda was able to go head-to-head with her attending, but today he had worn her down. All of the anesthesiology residents in her year disliked the man. Amanda usually took a kinder stance, viewing the doctor more as a wise and formidable teacher, but her generosity extended only so far.

She held her hand over her eyes, scanning the lot for her car as the sun threatened to blind her, even through her oversize sunglasses. Squinting, she finally caught sight of it. She was making her way in that direction when—out of nowhere—the daylight vanished, as if a cloud had passed in front of the sun. But there wasn't a cloud in the sky.

As the darkness enveloped her, Amanda felt a charge. A shock wave coursed through her, like liquid electricity. She could feel currents running up and down her arms. Then a sharp pain pierced through her skull and radiated down her spine. Nausea and dizziness overtook her.

"Wow," Amanda muttered, as her brain started rattling off a running list of possible pathologies. Was she having a stroke? An aneurysm? Was this how it ended for her? But then, just as quickly as it happened, it stopped. Her symptoms disappeared, and the sun shone bright again.

Amanda squeezed her eyes shut and massaged her scalp. "I better get lots of rest," she said to herself. She was looking forward to the weeklong vacation she had planned. That would surely help.

In fact, she couldn't wait to get to her car. The trunk was already packed with suitcases, and as soon as her best friend, Lydia, joined her, they'd be dashing off to the airport for a much-deserved vacation in paradise—a week at a five-star resort in Panama. She could almost feel the sand between her toes.

What she didn't know was that the solar flare had irrevocably changed her life, in a way she could never have imagined. And nothing she'd learned in her intensive medical training had prepared her for what was to come.

Chapter 1

———◆◆◆———

Amanda stepped out onto the balcony of the oceanfront hotel suite. She was dazzled by the scenery before her: the lush green landscape as far as the eye could see, a perfect sunset filling the world with warmth, and the orange-dappled water lapping the beach, so close she could watch the cormorants riding the waves.

Lydia was stretched out on one of the lounge chairs, but her shoulders were hunched. She didn't look very relaxed to Amanda.

Amanda grabbed a mojito from the patio table and sat beside her. "Cheers."

Lydia nodded and raised her own glass. "Cheers." She was clearly trying to sound lighthearted, but Amanda could hear the sadness in her friend's voice. She surmised Lydia was thinking about Hank, her ex-fiancé. Hank had gotten drunk and cheated on Lydia two months before their wedding, and unbelievably, she was still mooning after him.

Amanda decided a distraction was in order. "So here we are, " she crooned. "Two single ladies at a gorgeous tropical resort!" When Lydia didn't react, she tried again. "So guess what I learned today—Panama has only three million people, but over twelve million cell phones. You know why?"

Lydia raised a quizzical eyebrow.

"Because having affairs is this country's number-two hobby! After watching telenovelas." Amanda laughed.

"Great." Lydia's voice was neutral.

"Oh, come on, it's funny! It got me thinking that if you really wanted to, you're in the right place to get even with Hank."

Lydia slid a hand through her rich chestnut curls. "I know you're joking, Mandy."

Amanda threw her hands up in the air. "Of course I'm joking! I wanted to cheer you up."

"Well, thank you."

"So . . . ?" She grinned.

Lydia shrugged. "No, I'm not going to have a revenge-affair with a Panamanian."

"Ha ha. That's not what I was going to ask. I was going to ask if you've decided what you're going to do about him."

Lydia reached for a mojito and stirred the ice cubes with her straw. "It's complicated."

The last rays of the sunset flickered across the sky before falling below the horizon. Amanda shifted on the lounge chair. "You're not seriously thinking of going back to him, are you?"

"I don't know. We were about to get married. That means something, you know?" She took off her sunglasses and gently pressed her hands over her eyelids.

"I get it," Amanda replied, but truthfully, she didn't get it. What was there to think about? Hank clearly wasn't the right one, and Lydia deserved better. Period. It was that simple.

Lydia was like a sister to her. They first met when they were seven, at some medical conference their parents had dragged them to. Neither girl had siblings, and they were both a little lonely. The bonded immediately. Unfortunately, Amanda and her family moved away a year later, when Amanda's father got a better position as a surgeon at a high-profile hospital. She had reconnected with Lydia when they ended up at the same medical school, and they had become like family since. Amanda had no real family. Not anymore.

"Hey, let's not think about Hank, okay?" Amanda urged. "Look, the moon is coming out. Let's head to the beach."

The girls walked along the water's edge, two slender silhouettes in maxi dresses. The sand was soft and damp, refreshing on their bare feet. Around them, warm rain sprinkled down—on the trees, on the sand, on the paved alleyways of the resort grounds—creating a peaceful hush. Late July was the middle of the monsoon season, and as soon as the sun went down, heavy clouds gathered over the lush island landscape. Every day, once the rain started, the resort quieted down. By seven in the evening, the beach was practically empty, and people congregated at the bar, the three restaurants, or at the café facing the Atlantic.

"Thank you for being here," Lydia said, taking Amanda's hand in hers. "It's nice to just *be* sometimes, isn't it? To stop worrying about what's going on at home and just chill for a while."

Amanda nodded, then faced the ocean. She was invariably drawn to it, yet something about it made her deeply uncomfortable. It was dark, forbidding, immense. Quietly powerful, invisible beyond a few dozen feet. "Doesn't it, I don't know, fill you with dread?" she asked her friend.

"What? You mean going back? Dealing with life?"

"No, this . . . the ocean at night. I always imagine it filled with monsters underneath all that black water." Surprising herself, Amanda actually shuddered.

Lydia nudged her with a small laugh. "But it's the same ocean we go in during the day."

Amanda nodded, but stayed silent. Her arms folded across her chest, she kept watching the water, its breath traveling on the back of the wind, its waves reaching the shore, forever trying to get a grip but always washed back, only to try again and again. Just like her . . . just like her whole life. Ever since she'd become an orphan, that summer when she turned thirteen and her parents perished in a mountain-climbing accident, it felt like she'd been trying to regain footing, in a way she couldn't quite define. It was like she kept trying to fit in, to belong to . . . something.

"What about you?" Lydia asked, seemingly out of the blue.

Uh-oh. She'd missed something her friend had been saying.

Lydia was looking at her. "You spaced out, didn't you? I was asking you about dating. Are you seeing anyone?"

Amanda grimaced and waved dismissively. "All the good ones are already taken." Amanda dated, a lot, but she'd never found that one special person. She'd never been in love. Her relationship, or rather, non-relationship, with her self-absorbed parents had left her with a hole in her heart she didn't know how to fill. That's not what she was going to tell Lydia, though. Faking a yawn, she stretched her arms, trying to look nonchalant. "I'm taking a break. I'm too busy with school now. I mean, we just started our residencies."

Her friend shook her head. "Just look at you. Those perfect eyes, as huge and as green as the ocean! Why didn't you find yourself a gorgeous dude, back when you were modeling?"

Amanda flashed to that year in her life, when her guardian grandmother had to be placed in assisted living, and Amanda was once again left to fend for herself. Though retrospectively, she felt very lucky for that glamorous year, full of photo shoots in exotic places.

"Thanks, but modeling dudes are wussies," she declared, hoping to close the topic.

Lydia scowled at her with fake disapproval, but her words were drowned out by a sudden sound—like the hum of high-voltage electric wires. Something moved on their right, and the girls instinctively jerked their heads in that direction.

Less than ten feet away was a figure unlike anything Amanda had ever seen. Merging into the twilight, semitransparent, was a column of thick, black smoke. It was hovering above the sand, oscillating, with something akin to lighting flashing within its core. It rippled and morphed into a vaguely human shape. She could feel waves of terror emanating from it, seeping into her, permeating the air. Raw, primordial terror. No . . . not terror. Waves of evil. It was made of harsh, inhuman evil. Even though her heart was thumping in her chest like a mad drum, she couldn't take her eyes off the black mass.

"Oh my God!" Lydia grabbed Amanda's hand. "What is that?"

The humming intensified. Then it made a move toward them.

Lydia let out a piercing shriek. They spun around and ran for the hotel. They stumbled across the sand and didn't stop until they reached the wide stone patio, pausing only briefly to weave past clusters of surprised guests. They headed for the glass doors leading to the hotel lounge. Amanda was afraid to look back. They erupted into the lounge, where a pianist was playing for a room of tourists hanging around the bar.

Unable to stop herself, Amanda ran headlong into a muscular man wearing linen pants and a form-fitting black T-shirt. Lydia, who was slipping on the marble floor beside her, grabbed Amanda's arm to save herself. In turn, Amanda grabbed onto the man in front of her with her free arm, and the three of them hovered precariously. Lydia made a hysterical hic-cupping sound.

Amanda suddenly noticed that the music had stopped. The room was dead quiet. Everyone was staring at them.

"Sorry!" Amanda flushed, righted herself, and stepped back from the man she had used to stabilize herself. To her dismay, she realized he was the most attractive man she had ever seen—which meant a lot coming from a woman who'd worked internationally with models.

"That's all right," he said. "I'm glad I could help." The rugged man smiled, but Amanda noticed that the smile didn't quite reach his gray eyes.

A young guy in ridiculously bright Bermuda shorts approached them. "Are you ladies okay?" He nodded to the man in the black T-shirt, who silently went around the girls and headed out toward the beach.

Watching him leave, Amanda felt a momentary pang of disappoint-ment. But she tried to focus. The younger man before her was looking at them with a worried expression. He had a chubby face, punctuated by a mustache and goatee that looked glued onto his skin. Amanda almost cringed at his tiger-striped shorts and the orange T-shirt that said, "Pan-amaniac!"

"Are you ladies okay?" he repeated.

Chests still heaving, she and Lydia glanced at each other. Her friend was fine. Amanda turned and examined the patio doors next. The presence, whatever it was, hadn't followed them. Standing there, in the air-con-ditioned upscale hotel lounge, the whole thing seemed utterly unreal. Amanda gulped and tried to regain composure. "Yeah, we just got scared," she said. "There are ghosts on the beach, you know!" She even tried to laugh, but it was too high-pitched to sound realistic.

Everyone was still staring.

"Just kidding!" Amanda quickly hedged. "Ha ha. We're good." She probably sounded nuts. She leaned in and whispered to Lydia, "Let's go upstairs."

As soon as they reached their suite, Lydia sat heavily at the dining table, her head cradled between her elbows and her eyes wide open in dis-belief. "What was that?" she said. "Is this what going crazy feels like? I am shaking, Amanda, shaking. It felt . . . I can't even describe it." She whipped her head up. "Wait, you saw it too, right?"

Still at the door, Amanda stood silent as Lydia stared at her, clearly dreading the answer. She tried to shake off her own shock. "Yes, of course, a black figure. I heard it, too. Did you hear it? Did you hear that humming sound it made, like something electrical?"

Lydia's eyes widened. "Wait. I can hear it now!" She turned to the balcony. "Oh God, Amanda, it's back!" She jumped to her feet, knocking her chair over. A hand over her mouth, she backed away.

Amanda saw it too—a dark shape on the balcony. It had found them. But how . . . ? Then, even as she was feeling grateful that they'd locked the balcony's sliding door, the black column was suddenly inside the room. There was no logical transition; it just materialized in front of them. The air seemed to change with its presence—it felt heavier, vibrating as if supercharged with electricity.

Petrified, Amanda watched as the blackness began drifting slowly toward Lydia, like a thundercloud. A black, flickering mass. It seemed to disappear for a few milliseconds at a time, as if going in and out of existence. As it approached, Lydia collapsed to the ground, unconscious. Then it turned toward Amanda.

In that moment, her head began to ache, and the strangest sensations crawled up and down her arms—like waves of electrical current mixed with nausea. As the black column loomed before her, the currents began shooting up and down her arms, faster and faster, synchronizing with her racing heart. She flashed back to the day in the hospital parking lot before she left for vacation, when the sun got dark and she thought she was having a stroke.

A polite knock sounded on the door. Before she could react, the door just flew open, narrowly missing her as it slammed against the wall.

The young man in loud clothing stood in the doorway. "Ghosts, huh?" He jerked his arm in the direction of the shadow, fingers fanned out, his face impassive, focused. Without any visible connection to his gesture, strands of blue, sizzling light suddenly engulfed the black figure, and it began dissolving.

The "ghost" was struggling. She felt it. She also felt the current get hotter in her arms, as if something was urging her to . . . use it. Tentatively, instinctively, she extended her arm in the direction of the shadowy mass and felt a deep pulse of energy escape her. Thin, nearly invisible blue flames erupted from her fingertips and the "ghost" instantly disappeared. Not a trace of it remained. Everything else was gone too—the nausea, the creepy-crawlies in her arms, the headache.

She and the man looked at each other. His grimace cracked into a smile. "Impressive," he said. "You must be our Sentinel 10."

Chapter 2

I'm a what? A sentinel?

She cleared her parched throat but remained silent, her mind still reeling.

The young guy started pacing around the room, rubbing his hands together, as if in anticipation. "Nice space," he said, stopping suddenly and taking in the suite with wide-eyed enthusiasm.

"Uh, *what?* You want to talk about our hotel room? Who *are* you?" Amanda glared at him, then hurried across the room, where Lydia lay in a heap next to the table. She bent over her unconscious friend and gently rolled her onto her back. With relief, she saw that Lydia was breathing. She took her pulse, which was steady. She had merely fainted.

Reassured, Amanda looked up to see a flush cross the man's face. "I know, I know, I have a lot of explaining to do. Is she okay?" Without waiting for an answer, he began pacing again, giving an impression of boundless energy. "You know, I'm so glad you kept your wits about you. This was a nasty little sucker; you have no idea. The most powerful one I've come across. Like, ever!"

Amanda couldn't comprehend his words, or his attitude. On the plus side, she noticed that Lydia was stirring back to life. Their jovial intruder sauntered over and crouched next to her. "Hello," he said to Lydia, peering into her face. "Let me help you up. You have such gorgeous hair! Love the color. Are you single? Let's go for coffee sometime."

Lydia gave him a confused look, then her frightened eyes met Amanda's.

The strange guy kept talking as if nothing unusual was going on. Either he didn't notice their reactions, or didn't care. Amanda surmised he must have untreated ADHD; he just couldn't stop himself from blabbering. He rushed on. "People can be seriously traumatized by these ectoplasmic manifestations. They don't perceive them like we do, of course. Not with all the visuals and stuff."

Lydia stood up and edged away from him. "Amanda, what's happening?" she asked.

"Ectoplasmic manifestations, apparently." Amanda sighed loudly. She righted the toppled chair for Lydia and pulled out another one for herself. Her legs were still shaking as she sat down next to her friend.

She took another good look at their guest—the apparent slayer of the supernatural, who looked anything but. He looked twenty years old, at most. He was average height, and on the slightly chubby side. His touristy T-shirt and Bermuda shorts made him look like a frat boy on vacation. But despite his over-the-top demeanor, he had pleasant features and friendly eyes. Amanda couldn't help but wonder what had happened to his handsome friend, who was such a stark contrast to the young man before her.

"I'm Matt, by the way. Matt Chadwick." He extended his hand.

"Amanda Griffith." They shook. His grip was a little weak. "Thanks for your help. What just happened to us?"

Lydia broke in, "And I'm Dr. Lydia Shelby. Can someone please explain how is it that I'm seeing ghosts? Are we all going mad?" She reached for the box of chocolates on the table, which she had been saving as a gift for her mom. Amanda knew that Lydia always reached for food when she was nervous.

"Nice to meet you both," Matt said. "It wasn't a ghost, it was a plasmid. That's, like, evil psychic energy that roams around trying to feed on people. You see, I was waiting for you downstairs. Well, I didn't actually know *who* I was waiting for; I was sent here to be on the lookout for the new Sentinels. Once you ran in from the beach, though, it was obvious. Ooh! Goodies." As if he had just noticed it, he plucked a chocolate out of the box. "I get so hungry after expending all this energy." He popped it into his mouth. "Mmmm. I'm going to get so fat with this gig. Not that I chose it! Not that any of us do. The gig, I mean, not the being fat part. Although, if people get fat—"

Amanda interrupted him. "Matt, can you *please* start making sense? What's going on?"

Lydia was looking at him as one watches a traffic accident. But as he reached for another chocolate, she frowned and silently pulled her box away. He looked dismayed.

"Matt. Hello. Focus," Amanda said, lightly clapping her hands to snap him out of his sugar trance.

"Okay, okay!" He sat down. "Sorry. I know. Okay, so here's the scoop. Do you know what a solar cycle is? That's the time it takes for the sun's magnetic field to completely flip. It happens every ten to eleven years: it builds up, then it flips again. But the cool part is that when the switch happens, it creates a solar flare that triggers a change in some people. It unlocks their hidden powers! It makes them capable of producing psychic energy. And, as I'm sure you've guessed, a flare like that happened two days ago."

Amanda's mind raced back to two days ago and the electric sensation she'd felt in the parking lot. She felt a surge of dread as Matt continued his explanation. Something had happened to them. Something big and possibly terrible.

Matt started drumming his fingers on the table. "From then on, they're called Sentinels. That's what I am. But I was inducted after a smaller flare three years ago; that's rare. Anyhoo. There's a few hundred of us around the world. What I just did back there is called an energy pulse. It's especially effective on supernatural entities, but it can be used on people too. Hurts like hell. Feels like your brain is burning. We can also use it to generate a physical force; that's called a power surge. It's like telekinesis, it moves things. It's really the same ectoplasmic energy, except a pulse is more, uh, sharp, and the surge is more blunt? It's hard to explain, but you'll see it for yourselves, because you're Sentinels too. Am I going too fast?"

The girls exchanged bewildered looks, but Matt carried on as if he hadn't noticed. "We all have the same powers, but to a different degree. There are eight levels of Sentinels, numbered three to ten. The higher the number, the stronger the powers. The Committee told me that two Sentinels would appear here, and one would be the Sentinel 10. Given how easily you disintegrated the plasmid, you are it, Amanda. Congratulations!"

As shocking as all this was, Amanda instantly understood. Something had indeed changed. She leaned forward. "Uh-huh. Let's say I believe you. Then, what level are you?"

He grinned. "I'll make you guess it." When the women rolled their eyes, he relented. "Just kidding, I'm a Sentinel 6. Each level is roughly twice as powerful as the next, so do the math. I really recommend you do the math, it's impressive—unless you hate math, then never mind."

"And me?" Lydia inquired. "I still think we're all insane, by the way. A case of *folie à trois.* I'll write a case report on it."

He laughed. "I don't know what level you are, but nobody's insane, Lydia. The Committee will know what you are. I have to say, though, you're likely at a lower level because the plasmid had such a huge physical effect on you."

"What Committee?" Lydia demanded.

"The Committee is a group of five people, they coordinate our activities around the world, pay us for the assignments, and provide protection. They're currently headquartered in Prague, in the Czech Republic. If you come with me now, they'll explain everything."

They stared at him in disbelief. "You think we're going to Prague?" Amanda said slowly.

He nodded. "Yup! A private jet is waiting for us." He paused. "If you don't come for the induction, more plasmids will find you."

"Are you out of your mind?" Lydia protested.

Amanda glanced down at her hands, remembering the energy that had escaped her fingers.

Clearly this was real, and it wasn't something they could figure out on their own.

Just then, a rattling came from the balcony, and Amanda froze. Not another one! The sliding doors opened, and Amanda's heart skipped a beat. The mystery man from the lobby stepped out of the darkness and into the room. He was stunning. A tentative smile played on his lips, and as he came closer, she noticed that he had a dimple in his chin, which was nearly obscured in scruff. His ruggedness gave him another dimension of sexiness that smoldered with his every movement. Amanda tried to shake herself out of her stupor.

Matt casually waved at him, as if it were perfectly normal for a hand-some man to climb up the side of a hotel and into their room. Though, based on the events of the past couple of days, Amanda surmised that nothing was ever going to be normal again.

"Ladies, allow me to introduce you to James Graves. He's a military pilot."

James made a tip-of-the-hat gesture, leaving both women silent.

"Wow, do you always have this effect on girls?" Matt joked. He intro-duced the friends to James. "And it looks like Amanda is our Sentinel 10."

"Pleased to meet you both," James said. He gave Lydia's hand a squeeze. When he took Amanda's, he held on a bit longer. His palm was rough and callused, and his touch ignited something within her, a spark she hadn't felt in a long time, if ever. This guy was going to be someone to her. Someone special. She was sure of it.

"Amanda . . ." he said, still not letting go. "You have really beautiful eyes." His tone was faraway. But then, he quickly shook out of his appar-ent daze and dropped her hand.

The women remained speechless until Lydia pinched Amanda on the arm. "Hey!" Amanda glared at her friend.

"So, our Sentinel 10 has at least one weakness?" James joked, flashing a perfect smile.

Amanda felt her knees go weak; she was glad she was sitting down already. "Um, it's nice to meet you, but what are you doing here? And how do you two know each other?"

Matt walked over to stand next to James. Their physical differences were almost comical. "James is one of us. He was the first new Sentinel I found. Like, one minute he was doing his air force thing, and the next"—he snapped his fingers—"a plasmid came right at him."

James shrugged his shoulders. "If it helps, none of this really makes sense to me either. One minute, I was on base gearing up for a sortie. The next, the sky went dark, and I felt like I was about to black out. But then I was fine, so I decided to go ahead with the flight. I did my sortie without any hiccups, but in the middle of my debrief, a black figure materialized in front of me. Then Matt appeared, and . . . well . . . you already know how it goes."

Amanda nodded in understanding. "Yes, that's almost exactly what happened to us. Except, the black figure didn't appear until just now on the beach."

Lydia closed the box of chocolates. "No," she shook her head, still chewing. "None of this makes any sense. I'm not buying this. How did you find us? How did your Committee know that 'Sentinels' were going to appear in Panama, at this hotel?" She put air quotes around the word *Sentinels*.

Matt raised his hands in a pacifying gesture. "That's another story, but I'll skip it for now. I know I tend to be a little all over the place. Let me call Basil, our adviser. He's, like, a hundred years old, and he knows everything. This is how it was supposed to go anyway: I find you. I call him. He makes you an offer you can't refuse . . ." At their expressions he added, "Oh, I'm kidding! Cheer up, why so serious? Ha ha! Okay, sorry, I know. I'm a little crazy. Here." Matt drew a phone out of his shorts pocket. He dialed, put it on speaker, and set it on the table between the two girls.

"Yes, Matt. Did you find them?" asked an older man's voice. It was warm, with a kindly tone that Amanda liked immediately.

"Hey, Basil! Yes, they're listening right now."

"Is James okay?" the voice asked.

"Here, sir," James replied.

"James, you don't have to call me 'sir.' I'm your adviser, not your CO."

"Noted, sir."

Matt broke in. "Okay, whatever. A plasmid attacked them. Can you tell them they need to come with me?"

"Do try to be more patient, please. Don't you remember what it was like for you when you first discovered your powers? It's overwhelming." The voice was soothing and dignified. "Try to put yourself in their shoes."

Matt chuckled. "Nah, it was no problem for me. I loved it! I thought it was hilarious. Anyway, fine. I'm a little hyper. I'm nervous, all right? Humor is the best way to deal with stress. Anyway, you tell them. One, two, three, go!" He swept his hands toward the two women as if Basil could see them.

"Hello. May I ask your names?" the voice asked.

"Amanda."

"Lydia." Lydia crossed her arms and leaned back in her chair.

"Pleasure. I'm Basil Blake. There's so much I want to tell you, but I'm afraid we may be interrupted. I'm sure Matthew told you that you are Sentinels, which means you have extreme psychic powers that enable you to condense psychic energy into an almost physical, usable form. And that currently, you are advertising your new powers around a fifty-mile radius, to any number of supernatural entities that may happen to be present?"

Lydia paused with another chocolate halfway to her mouth and blinked twice, staring at the phone.

Amanda's mind was racing. That last part did not sound good. "Wait, what?" she asked. "How are we advertising anything?"

"Ladies," Matt interjected, suddenly serious. "How do you think the plasmid found you? Our energy attracts them. You need training. If you don't learn how to shut off your powers, I don't know who or *what* will get to you next."

"Matt is correct," the voice from the phone confirmed. "Our jet is equipped with psychic protection. The most important task right now is to get you to our induction ceremony. Once you're there, we will explain everything you need to know." He paused. "You have these powers. Wanted or unwanted, they're yours for the next ten years. You need training to learn how to use them and how to shut them off."

"Hold on," said Lydia. "This is all crazy, okay? What powers—what the hell is going on? I don't have any powers. There was a black cloud that came into our room, fine, maybe it was a ghost or something, but the rest of it, look!" She stood up suddenly, shaking her head at the phone. "How can you expect a rational person to believe any of it, without proof? And just jump on a plane with Captain America and Mr. Funny Guy?"

Amanda understood where Lydia was coming from, but she'd seen enough to know better. "I think we should go," she told her. "Lydia, listen, things happened here while you were unconscious. I shot some . . . energy, out of my hands. And Matt did too. I saw it. That's how we disintegrated that thing. It's all real."

"It's true," James interjected. "I'm here to fly you gals out to meet up with others like us."

Amanda enjoyed the support of the hot pilot, but she tried to stay focused. "We need to know more. We can't deal with this on our own. We should at least see what they have to offer, get some explanations as to what's going on, okay?"

Lydia crossed her arms, giving her a hard look, and Amanda prayed that her friend would see things her way. As strange as this situation was, part of her was relieved; the story Matt and Basil relayed to them confirmed that they weren't crazy. She believed them. And she certainly couldn't leave Lydia alone, unprotected. The danger was real, so she'd drag her along if she had to. She could never let anything happen to Lydia.

"Also," she added, "we've got six days of vacation left, and I really don't think we should stay here. You saw the black thing. It was after us, whatever it was. Who knows if it's really gone, right?"

Lydia shivered and rubbed her arms. Finally she nodded and said, "So, did you say we're going to Prague? Fine. I'm game. I'll reserve my judgment until I have all the elements of the puzzle in front of me."

"I'm glad you agree," said the voice on the phone. "Time is of the essence. Matt can be a handful, but he'll get you here, and he will protect you, should anything try to get to you in the meantime. James, you're up for the trip?"

"Yes, sir," James said.

"Yes, Basil," the voice corrected. "James is a highly skilled pilot, and he'll be flying the jet to ensure top security for the flight. I'm looking forward to meeting you."

Chapter 3

"And that's our ride!" Matt said as a white BMW pulled up to the curb at the airport exit just outside Prague.

Amanda was impressed with the luxury they'd been enjoying so far. The private jet they had just taken had a full leather interior and large-screen televisions. And James flew the plane beautifully. After all the air travel she'd clocked with her modeling career, she knew a skilled pilot when she saw one. The takeoff and landing had been flawless.

She was disappointed to learn that James had some business to attend to before the induction. He said his goodbyes while the chauffeur emerged from the driver-side door. The chauffeur was impressive too, a real bodybuilder. Amanda eyed his toned form as he loaded their bags into the trunk. Despite the July heat, he wore a wool navy-blue suit. Amanda was thoroughly enjoying this continued VIP treatment, though she took care not to show it.

They had traveled about ten hours to get to the Czech capital. She and Lydia had slept sporadically en route, too emotionally on edge to rest properly. Amanda kept seeing the dark shape that had tried to attack them. She had so many questions, but Matt was fast asleep almost as soon as they took off, his seat fully reclined. When they climbed into the car, she and Lydia made a coordinated effort to sandwich Matt between them, so they could interrogate him on the way to their hotel.

Amanda went first. "So who's on this Committee we're going to meet? And what kind of protection were you talking about?"

Lydia piped up. "And what exactly was that thing that attacked us? You said it was evil energy? Like, what? You barely said two words to us on the flight! And where are we going?" She got more and more upset as she spoke, nearly hyperventilating.

Matt twirled his mustache with a childish air of self-importance. "Patience, my dear ladies, as Mr. Gioia—aka the big boss—would say."

He winked at Lydia. "I will leave all the explanations to him. We'll be at the hotel soon. You'll meet Basil, and he'll take us to the induction."

Lydia sighed. "Look, Matt, you're being very strange. We have time to kill, and you can answer a couple of questions, can't you? How old are you?"

Matt shrugged. "I'm twenty-two. Anyway, I can try. I get sidetracked when I'm nervous and happy."

So Matt was at least aware of his eccentricities. That was reassuring. Amanda brought up her next question. "So, is there anything unique about people who become Sentinels? Some common trait we share? Were we chosen somehow? I mean, don't you think it's weird that both Lydia and I are Sentinels?"

"The best I can figure is that we all happen to be smart. My hypothesis is that it has to do with high processing speed—how fast you're able to think. How fast your neurons are able to fire off those chemical messengers, and . . . anyway. That's my theory, but nobody really knows. Somehow, we absorb the solar flare, and it triggers an ability to generate psychic energy, which we can then expel and hit all sorts of targets."

Amanda opened her mouth to ask another question, but Matt had only taken the briefest pause. "Actually, I use the word *psychic* loosely. We don't predict the future or read people's minds. Though some of us can do a bit of mind control. I just mean that we have extrasensory abilities. Stuff we can do outside of the five senses. Uh . . . wait. Actually, nope. That's not really accurate either. It's not about sensing but more about generating. Pulse energy. I don't know how to classify that. In the past, there used to be talk of ectoplasm. Maybe that's what we produce. Am I losing you?"

Amanda dragged a hand through her hair and rubbed the back of her skull. In part, the travel fatigue was catching up with her, but Matt's overly effusive technique for delivering information was overwhelming her, too. "Let's talk about that later. Just tell us more about this Committee."

"Yes, the Committee. They're not Sentinels; they're managers, and they give us assignments. They pay us, and they get paid by the people who request our help. We're like the Mafia." At that, his mustache puffed out proudly, and it was obvious that he found this particular comparison exciting. She glanced at Lydia, who was cleaning her sunglasses. Matt rambled on.

"Some people, like other secret societies, need to have their psychic messes cleaned up. Plasmids are formed when someone uses magic. They don't dissolve on their own. So these people pay the Committee and the Committee assigns us the job. We get paid for each assignment."

Amanda was about to ask what a typical assignment might pay, but Matt, being Matt, kept talking. "If anyone tries to hurt you in any way, the Committee will rip them a new one. But don't worry! Everyone operating in the paranormal field knows this, and no one messes with us. The Committee has political connections, paid informants, and a network of assassins at their disposal. That's the protection I was talking about."

"Assassins!" Lydia jumped in her seat, abruptly turning sideways to stare him in the face. "I don't like the sound of that."

Amanda was also surprised, but at the same time, relieved. She didn't mind protection. Why would anyone mind protection? Growing up unwanted by two self-absorbed parents, and then orphaned, she had often wished for some sort of a badass brother to watch her back. This was even better. Suddenly, she was really looking forward to becoming a part of a group that gave a damn about her. *And possibly finding the man of my dreams*, she thought, but then she quickly pushed the image of James and his unassuming charm from her head.

Matt chuckled. "Don't worry about assassins, Lydia, really. Think of it as a last resort. Come on, I don't mean to scare you. There were a ton of assassinations in the Middle Ages, but it rarely happens anymore. Because now our reputation alone is enough to prevent attacks. We are totally the good guys, I promise."

"Why would somebody want to hurt us, anyway?" asked Amanda.

"Because you have very useful abilities. Can you imagine what would happen if someone kidnapped your loved ones? Wouldn't you do whatever it takes to get them back? You see where I'm going with this? The Committee ensures you're untouchable."

Amanda could see his point.

"I think I stopped listening when you said kidnapped," Lydia said. "This is scary, Matt. I don't think I like this at all."

The car drew up in front of their hotel, an older, five-story building on a quiet avenue. They parked by the main entrance, across the street from an outdoor café and a shiny art nouveau sculpture fashioned out of moving pieces of metal.

Matt spoke again, his face dead serious. It struck Amanda as a little weird, as if someone had flipped a switch in Matt's mind. "Lydia, listen, you have those powers. Whether you're alone with them or part of our group, you can't get rid of them. So choose the group. Nobody messes with us. Okay? Nobody. Ever."

He leaned over her to throw open the door. "Scooch over, babe, let's go," he urged, suddenly regaining his previous carefree manners.

Lydia gave him an icy death stare. "Don't call me babe."

Amanda promptly exited from her side. Leaving the bickering pair in the company of the driver, she walked through the hotel's front doors, pausing to take in the tastefully decorated lobby. It was small, but clean and refined, with marble floors, elegant white leather couches, and large arrangements of fresh lilies. The check-in desk sat against one wall, while a gleaming wood bar offering refreshments lined the other. She had started toward the reception desk when the front doors softly swished open behind her. A small delegation walked in: a distinguished-looking man in a polo shirt and khakis, flanked by two beefy bodyguards wearing dark wool suits, sunglasses, and earbuds.

The man appeared to be somewhere in his mid-fifties, with a mild, attentive expression and an air of calm. His hair was peppered with gray, but he looked fit for his age. He carried a sturdy black leather satchel that made Amanda think of the bags doctors used to carry decades ago—the kind of bag her father used to carry. He exuded genuine warmth. He walked right up to her and held out his hand. "Hello, Amanda. I'm Basil Blake. We spoke on the phone. I am your adviser. It's a pleasure to meet you."

"Hello." She shook his hand. "It's nice to meet you in person. I'm glad to have an adviser. I have so many questions."

"I know, my dear. We're almost there." Blake nodded to the hotel reception desk, and the two staff members vacated the post, heading to the offices in the back. "The hotel is reserved just for us tonight," he explained, then glanced at his watch. "You're the last ones in. Let's get going." He smiled. "I'm sorry, I know you're exhausted, but the induction ceremony can't wait. It won't last long, you'll hear everything you need to know, and then you can get a good rest."

He seemed exceptionally kind and paternal, but Amanda would reserve her final judgment about this whole ordeal until after she met the Committee. "Thank you, Mr. Blake," she said. "I am interested to hear what the Committee has to say."

With a wide motion of his arm, he invited her to exit the doors ahead of him. They headed out to the street, where a stretch limousine now awaited. Their original driver was lifting their luggage out of the car, and Matt and Lydia were already inside the limousine, facing each other, their arms folded across their chests. Amanda and Basil Blake climbed in, followed by the bodyguards.

The limo drove through Prague's narrow, crooked streets, sometimes taking the turns so fast that they had to brace themselves. As they rode, Basil informed them that they were heading toward Charles University, next to the famous Charles Bridge, a wide stony construction spanning the Vltava River. Amanda had read something about this ancient bridge while on their flight in, and she strained to remember what it was famous for. Probably the lifelike statues of Catholic knights lining both sides of the bridge from one end to the other.

The limousine pulled over and dropped them off near the bridge. The two bodyguards stayed in the car. As they stood on the curb, Basil whispered something to Matt, who nodded in response and rubbed his hands together enthusiastically.

"Shall we?" With a theatrical sweep of his arm, Matt directed them to a building on the other side of the road—an old university hall built of white stone. A few people clustered outside the doors, having a smoke and a chat.

"Be a little more serious, if you can, Matt," Basil reproached him with a smile before crossing the road.

Lydia rolled her eyes and hissed something under her breath. "Come on, Mandy," she said before scampering to catch up with their adviser.

But Amanda allowed herself to linger behind for a little longer, taking in the surroundings. The evening air was quiet, the city was draped in shadows, and the bridge statues stood a solemn vigil over the dark river below. Like medieval guards . . .

Like Sentinels.

Amanda hugged herself to repress a nervous shudder. God. Seriously. Was this really happening? Matt's words came back to her: *We're part of an ancient, secret society of people with special powers.* What was she getting herself into? Not yet able to wrap her mind around the enormity of the change in her life, she hurried across the road.

Chapter 4

When they drew closer to the main entrance, Amanda was surprised to find a lot of security personnel present, in the form of both uniformed security guards and local police officers. She made sure to stick right by Lydia and not lose sight of Matt or their adviser. Their group joined the crowd and the guard nodded at Basil as they passed. The guards seemed to be ensuring that everyone who entered was escorted by someone they knew. She said as much to Matt, who winked and said proudly, "We're just like the Mafia, remember?"

They drifted from the foyer to the inside of the building, into a large hall. Inside, Matt excused himself as soon as he spotted the refreshment tables. *He surely can eat,* Amanda mused as she and Lydia watched him pile a small plate with cheese, crackers, and fruit.

As if reading her mind, Lydia leaned in and said, "Why is he always so hungry?"

"I can't imagine," Amanda said as they watched him devour everything on his plate, then home in on the sweets. A waiter appeared in front of them, holding out a tray filled with flutes of prosecco. Amanda and Lydia each took a glass.

"I'll be back in a moment," Basil said, leaving her and Lydia standing alone in the crowd.

She scanned the rest of the room. Where was James? The main area appeared to contain about two hundred guests standing around bistro-style tables. Some people seemed to know each other, while many others stood awkwardly alone. At the far end of the room, a raised platform held a podium, a microphone, and a neatly aligned row of folding chairs. They must have arrived in the nick of time because a tall, dark, aquiline-faced man in an Armani suit was already taking the stage.

"Good evening, friends," he said into the mic at the podium. "I am Paolo Gioia, and as the head of the Committee, I would like to extend my warmest welcome to everyone in this room. First, let me congratulate you! You are all now part of the most prestigious, the most select, and dare I say, the most powerful secret society in the world."

"We shall begin your induction shortly. You'll come on stage one by one as we call your names, and members of the Committee will shake your hand in order to gauge your level of powers." A low murmur went through the crowd. Amanda exchanged a glance with Lydia. "No matter which level you are, each of you is exceedingly important and special. You are joining an organization with an impressive history and achievements. Ever since the Middle Ages, the Sentinels have been ridding the world of malicious psychic residue and fighting evil supernatural forces."

Despite her misgivings, Amanda felt a stirring of pride in her chest.

"Tomorrow, you'll start your training," Gioia continued. "Using your psychic pulses is quite intuitive, but you must learn to shut down your receiving functions at will. You don't want plasmids barging into your lives at inopportune moments."

He flashed a bone-white smile, and muffled conversations sounded in the room. Gioia paused to allow the chatter to run its course, then broke into his lecture again. "Incidentally, from now on, you are all under our protection. If any other society tries to get in touch with you, or tries to harm you in any way, let us know immediately. If you have any problem with the law, or even your neighbors, anything at all, let us know. We deal with such things very efficiently."

Gioia gestured to a spot in the crowd. "I would like to introduce you to my associates," he said as a dignified woman with short hair, a large nose, and a commanding presence stepped up onto the platform. "This is Nourat Halabi." Gioia motioned to two men and another woman standing next to the platform. "Please also give your attention to Fernando Rodriguez, Rudolph Wojtek, and Jalecia Navas."

The rest of the Committee now filed onto the stage and took their seats as Nourat stepped up to the podium and addressed the crowd.

"May I have your undivided attention? In your rooms, you'll find your contract of service. You may refuse, though I do not advise it. You have twenty-four hours to decide. I will point out that joining us is the only way for you to stay safe, as many organizations would like to get their hands on someone with your powers, and they would stop at nothing to make you do their bidding."

She doesn't mince words, Amanda realized with a shudder.

Nourat continued. "As official Sentinels under our protection, you are untouchable. Once you join us, you must adhere to our codes of behavior, and you are prohibited from disclosing our business to other secret societies. To speak plainly, the penalty for betrayal or disobedience is death."

At that, the room grew quiet. "Screw that!" A young woman with long black hair suddenly left her table, pushed through the crowd, and darted out of the room.

A middle-aged woman wearing a tailored suit and carrying a satchel similar to Basil Blake's called out, "Samantha!" and ducked out after her. The other inductees looked around, unsure of what to do.

Amanda turned her attention back to the front of the room to see what reaction this defection might spark. Gioia's nostrils flared. He raised his arm in a conciliatory gesture, as he craned his neck in front of Nourat to speak into the microphone. "My dear colleague always lays it on thick. She's been with us for so long that she sometimes forgets how disturbing this sounds! Trust me, in the last nine centuries, only three Sentinels have been disbarred. It is a rare event indeed. If you act honorably and professionally, you need not worry."

Nourat glared at him until he sat back down. She cast a domineering glance over the room and carried on. "What I meant is that you may not work with other societies behind our backs. Also, you may refuse an assignment for a valid reason, such as an illness or a death in the family. You may also request special permission to forgo an assignment. You can discuss this with your advisers. Only willful, gratuitous disobedience may result in your . . . termination."

The crowd broke into muffled conversation as the Committee allowed Nourat's words to sink in. The girl who had bolted came back into the room looking visibly shaken—with the woman Amanda presumed was her mentor at her side. When everything quieted down again, Nourat continued. "Harsh measures are a necessity, because what is done by one affects us all. For your continued protection, we must take action if something threatens us. Like Paolo said, this occurs rarely, and we would issue multiple warnings before taking any drastic measures."

Her face still impassive, she stepped down. Gioia flashed his brilliant smile as he once again had the floor to himself. "My dear friends! I am deeply honored to have you with us, tonight, and for the remainder of your service. We shall begin the induction in just a few minutes."

Chapter 5

As a cheerful bustle ensued throughout the crowd, Amanda turned to Lydia to discuss what they'd just heard, but before she had the chance to open her mouth, she was interrupted.

"Ladies?" She turned around, expecting Basil, but instead she found herself in front of James Graves. A slight blush crept up Amanda's cheeks at the sight of him. She darted a glance to Lydia, who was also grinning ear to ear.

Basil came out from behind him. "I know you already met James, but I wanted to take a moment to get you all acquainted. Captain James Graves, U.S. Air Force, is Purple Heart decorated, not that he'd ever mention this himself. James will also be based in Boston, so you three will be working together. Matt is temporarily based in San Francisco, for his studies. So, unfortunately, he won't be on our team this year."

"That's great!" said Lydia. "I mean, it's great that James is with us. We can use a guy who can handle himself in a tough spot."

Basil looked at the young air force captain, whose smile was slowly becoming genuine. Basil hid a small yawn behind his hand. "Very good. I think it's about time I put these old bones to bed," he said.

"Old?" Lydia challenged. "You can't be more than fifty."

He smiled brightly. "Why, thank you. You young people enjoy the party, and I'll see you tomorrow for training. After breakfast. Have a good night." With that, he was gone.

Amanda turned her attention back to James.

"So, I'm looking forward to the induction ceremony. I'm curious as to what level Sentinel I am. Aren't you?" he said, once again pulling out his tentative smile, looking alternatively between Amanda and Lydia.

Lydia was sipping prosecco and not taking initiative, so Amanda quickly settled into the conversation. "Yes. Matt thinks I'm a Sentinel 10, but we'll see. By the way, how did you earn your Purple Heart?"

He pressed his lips together, and for a second, the light in his eyes went dark. "Not really my favorite topic," he said. "Maybe another time. I mostly just love planes."

"Sure," Amanda said. She knew the Purple Heart was some kind of military award, but his unwillingness to talk about it made her wonder if he earned it under tragic circumstances. Even Lydia gave her big eyes, as if to say, "What's wrong with you?" She shifted uncomfortably, wondering what trauma he had endured, and fighting the hope that one day he'd share that secret with her.

"I was really impressed with that plane you flew us in," Lydia said, rescuing them from the awkward moment. "You're a real pro."

James nodded. He didn't seem upset. "So what do you girls do?" he asked.

"We just finished medical school, and now we are in our residency programs," Amanda said, feeling proud of her accomplishment. It finally felt real to her.

James raised an eyebrow, as if intrigued.

"Yup. I'm in psychiatry and Amanda is in anesthesiology. So she's like a pilot too!" Lydia said a little too enthusiastically. "Inducing anesthesia is like takeoff, and waking the patient is like landing."

Amanda rolled her eyes. Her attending physician made that comparison all the time, but she didn't think James would be impressed by it. What was Lydia doing?

But Lydia's smile just grew larger. "So I'll let you get acquainted. Oh, is that Matt? Hey, Matt!" she called and waved at an imaginary Matt, then walked off into the crowd, trailing a whiff of her jasmine perfume.

"Nice girl," James said, smiling. "She reminds me of an aunt of mine."

Amanda relaxed. If he was already comparing Lydia to one of his aunts, it seemed unlikely he'd be hitting on her anytime soon. Her friend was beautiful, and she didn't want to compete with her for James's attention.

The handsome pilot turned his gaze back on Amanda. His gaze felt almost too intense. She gripped her glass, trying to think of something to say.

"You really do have the most strikingly beautiful eyes," James said. "I've never seen green eyes like that. They're flawless."

"Thanks! You . . . um, so you live in Boston?"

He shook his head. "No, I'm at the Westover Air Reserve Base, about an hour's drive from the city."

Amanda desperately wanted to find out if he was single. If he wasn't, then she would nip her attraction in the bud.

"Is Lydia your roommate?" James asked, and Amanda's heart jumped for joy. He probably wanted to know if she was single, too!

"No, I live alone," she assured him. "What about you? Have you lived on the base for a long time?"

A cloud passed over his brow. He passed a hand over his hair and rubbed the back of his neck. "It's been a while," he said. "Something happened three years ago, and . . . well, it changed everything. But technically speaking, I've been on the base for a year now."

"Oh. I see," she said. In that moment, Amanda realized that James was indeed single, but perhaps not emotionally available. Clearly, he wasn't ready to talk about what happened to him, so she didn't press the issue.

Their conversation stalled after that. They took turns staring into their drinks, looking around, shifting from foot to foot. Amanda tried to think of a way to salvage the situation. James appeared to be in pain.

Suddenly she noticed that Paolo Gioia was staring directly at her from the podium. His powerful gaze sizzled across the room, locking onto her. There was something forbidding in his stare—a strange, concealed power—which caused her to shudder. When he left the stage and started making his way toward her through the crowd, she felt the need to bolt, but before she could move, he appeared in front of her, hand extended.

Not knowing what else to do, she shook his hand. Immediately, some sort of current passed between them.

"So, Matthew was right. You are our Sentinel 10," he said in a mildly pleased tone. "Welcome, Ms. Griffith."

He turned to James and offered the same courtesy. "Mr. Graves, you're a Sentinel 9. Yes, you two will make a very strong team."

Up close, the figurehead of the Committee appeared to be an elegantly mannered man around forty years of age. But it was his eyes that arrested Amanda's attention. His irises were unnaturally large and the most unusual shade she had ever seen—pale violet. Matt had said the Committee members were managers, not Sentinels, but she wondered if the strange eyes denoted some other kind of power.

"I wanted to tell you that your training at the hospital has been put on hiatus, Ms. Griffith," Gioia said while peering into her eyes, as if to carefully assess her reaction. "Our apologies for not consulting with you first, but we have a case that needs to be addressed right away. We'd like a word with you tomorrow, before your training session. This will be your very first assignment."

He sounded polite and friendly, but Amanda instinctively understood that this was not an offer she could refuse. There was something authoritative and off-putting about Gioia. Clearly, he expected complete obedience and compliance. "Okay," she managed to mumble. "I'll be there."

Seemingly satisfied, the elegant man with the violet eyes returned to the stage. Amanda watched him go. She would have to tread carefully around the Committee, she decided. She turned to James, but to her dismay, he had vanished into the crowd.

Amanda sipped her prosecco, thinking over her predicament. Gioia had already assigned her a case. She had thought everyone had twenty-four hours to decide if they wanted to join with the Committee. Apparently, that rule did not apply to a Sentinel 10—or a Sentinel 9, for that matter. Gioia seemed certain that James would be part of her team. Did anyone *really* have a choice? Even the dark-haired girl who bolted earlier had returned with her mentor. What made her come back? What did her mentor say to her? Perhaps they would soon find out. In addition, she wondered what her residency director would make of her sudden hiatus. Would they really welcome her back after she took an extended break? Was her career as a doctor in jeopardy before it had even begun?

She had no chance to reflect further, as Gioia took the mic and announced that the induction ceremony was beginning. It was simple enough: everyone lined up, and one by one, they walked across the stage, shaking the hands of each Committee member. Amanda joined the end of the line, even though she had already shaken Gioia's hand. She wanted to see the Committee close up.

As she shook their hands, she noticed that the Committee members all had the exact same pale violet eye color, which struck Amanda as bizarre. They had no other unusual characteristics. No one would have given them a second glance while passing in the street. Still, her overall impression of the Committee was negative: she just didn't like any of them, and she wasn't exactly sure why. The short, overweight man with facial hair, the one named Wojtek, held on a moment too long, his nasty little eyes boring into her. There was nothing playful or interested in his stare. He seemed to have something against her, something cold and hostile, though she couldn't imagine what that something might be. She promised herself to be very careful around this one.

Once each Sentinel had been inducted, a meet-and-greet commenced, and more delicious appetizers were passed around. Amanda finally spotted Lydia in the crowd and headed over to her.

"Did you try these cheese puffs?" Lydia asked before she had the chance to speak, stuffing one into her mouth.

"Who cares about the cheese puffs?" Amanda exclaimed. "Gioia confirmed I'm a Sentinel 10. What level are you?"

Lydia shook her head as she chewed fiercely then finally swallowed and said, "Sentinel 4. Yup."

"Oh, come on. Sentinel 4 sounds great!"

"Well, if my math is good, you're, what? Sixty-four times more powerful than I am?"

"But think of how much more powerful you are than the average person," Amanda said. She heard her voice rising; her excitement and anxiety were getting the best of her. She and Lydia had powers! The idea had finally hit her full force.

Lydia cocked an eyebrow. "You seem a little too giddy about all of this."

"This whole thing is mind-boggling, for sure. But, I don't know! I'm looking forward to learning more about it."

"Wow. Honestly, I'm not sure I'm even going to sign up. This is all crazy. It's life-changing, and potentially dangerous."

Amanda had her own fears, to be sure. But, unlike Lydia, she didn't feel she had a choice. Gioia had made it clear she had to join. Besides, the idea was growing on her. She felt special, overwhelmingly unique. And she had to admit to herself that she'd enjoyed the rush of energy coursing through her when she destroyed the plasmid in Panama. Presumably, a new life of incredible adventures was about to open up to her, and she needed Lydia by her side.

Amanda tried to keep her tone light. "Come on, you have to sign up," she said. "First of all, what else are you gonna do with energy you can shoot out of your hands? Do you really want to be all alone dealing with that?"

Lydia looked thoughtful but didn't respond.

"Plus, I'm in, so let's be in it together. We have exciting new powers and a group to belong to. A prestigious little club," she added, trying to sound confident. She took a miniature crab cake and a napkin from the tray of a passing server. "I think we can really make a difference. We can *save* people. I know we joined medicine to make a difference, but with these powers, I think we can make even *more* of a difference. Now that I've had time to think about it, I really enjoyed disintegrating that plasmid. It just . . . felt right, you know?"

Lydia did not look convinced. If anything, she looked a little annoyed. She washed a cheese puff down with the rest of her drink, and sighed. "Yeah, maybe it's great for you. You're the *extra special* one! I'm sure you'll get all sorts of perks. I'm just a low-level grunt. Anyway. I'll sleep on it. You're probably right, though. I can't handle this supernatural stuff on my own. I mean, what else am I gonna do?"

Chapter 6

Amanda was enjoying the only perk of jet lag—not being able to sleep past 6:00 AM. She had tossed in bed for a while before deciding that exploring the city in the early-morning hours—before the townspeople and tourists flooded the streets—was the ideal solution to her restlessness. So she got dressed and quietly left the hotel.

The sun was already shining over the cobblestone streets. It was a breezy and sunny Saturday morning, and it began to feel like vacation again. Amanda took a deep breath, put on her sunglasses, and headed out to explore. In spite of the life-changing events of the previous day, Amanda was determined to relax and enjoy herself. She didn't know when she'd have the chance to visit Prague again. She wanted to see the sights before she reported to Gioia. What had he said yesterday? *We'd like a word with you tomorrow, before your training session.* Who were "we," she wondered, and what was this assignment that couldn't wait? Would it happen here, in Prague? Or somewhere else entirely? Amanda knew that she'd drive herself crazy with this line of questioning, so she forcibly quieted her mind as she walked through the city.

She soon discovered why Prague was called the City of a Thousand Spires. Gothic cathedrals and baroque castles dominated the skyline, their towers and spires piercing the peaceful morning sky. Amanda began with the obligatory visit to the famous medieval astronomical clock on a plaza several streets past Old Town Square. The clock was mounted front and center on the town hall, two large circular dials in gold and blue. Still stunning by today's standards, it must have looked quite impressive in the Middle Ages. Amanda snapped a few pics along with a selfie before wandering off in the direction of the nearby square. On her way, she went into the only gift shop that was open at this hour and sampled a chocolate model of the famous clock. The chocolate was nothing special, but she enjoyed being a tourist. She felt like she had accomplished her mission.

In a decidedly relaxed mood, she circled Old Town Square and snapped a selfie under the stony arch of Powder Tower, which was all that remained of the original city gates. It was rectangular and gothic and dark, much darker than any other building in the vicinity. On the other side of it, the "new town" sported turn-of-the-century buildings, their pastel colors lining the streets, similar to many other eastern European cities. As she walked along, Amanda passed a nice mix of little boutique-lined passages and large fashionable avenues. In some ways, Prague was the epitome of old-world charm, with a distinct eastern European flavor.

When she turned the corner onto a narrower cobblestone alleyway, however, she started to feel unhinged. There was a sudden, nagging feeling in the back of her neck. Like she was being watched . . . or followed. She looked around, but she was the only one in the alleyway. Abruptly, she turned and started walking back in the direction of the hotel. As she left the alley, she whipped her head around and thought she saw a sliver of gray flash behind the corner of a building.

She narrowed her eyes. "Is anyone there?" When no one surfaced, she stomped back over to the corner, making sure to stay a safe distance from the building while still getting a good view of the main street. She saw a woman strolling on the other side, but her attention was drawn to a gray-suited man walking away from her. There he was, brushing past the woman, quickening his step.

"Hey!" she called out, fisting her hands, acting braver than she felt. The woman gave her a surprised look, but the man just kept walking at the same brisk pace. Maybe he had headphones on. She watched him for a minute, taking in his athletic gait and his short, bleached hair. He looked innocuous. She decided she was being ridiculous.

She sighed and hurried back to the hotel, her back still prickling. She thought of the black plasmid on the beach. She wondered if there was a similar invisible force hanging over her at this very moment. Supernatural beings were supposedly attracted to her energy signature, after all. At this thought, she picked up her pace.

When she at last entered the hotel's lobby, relief washed over her. If anything attacked her here, she'd have a full backup team, which was reassuring. She spotted Lydia making her way down the stairs and hurried over to her.

Lydia clicked her tongue. "There you are!" she exclaimed. "You're up early. Where've you been?"

Amanda knew that Lydia was still skittish about the idea of joining with the Committee, so she decided not to tell her of her fears—not yet anyway. "I was out exploring. The city looks beautiful in the early-morning sunlight. You know, before the hordes of tourists come out."

"We're the tourists, Amanda," Lydia reminded her. "Breakfast?"

"No, we're not tourists, we're Sentinels. Remember? And I'm not hungry, sorry. I just had some chocolate."

"You're so annoying," Lydia grumbled. "James might be down for breakfast. I'm gonna steal him from you if you don't come to the cafeteria with me."

"What? Oh, seriously, if you insist, I can grab a tea to keep you company."

In the cafeteria, Amanda watched as Lydia piled fruit onto her plate, and her thoughts went back to the alleyway. She wondered why someone would be watching her as she roamed the city. She poured her tea, and they sat at a table near the window. Even though it was nine now, only a few other people were eating breakfast. *People must sleep in late here*, Amanda mused.

"What's wrong?" Lydia asked after taking a few bites.

Amanda took a measured sip of her sencha green tea before she spoke. Her feeling of anxiety wasn't going away, and clearly, she couldn't hide anything from Lydia. Her friend knew her too well, so she decided to come clean. "When I was out exploring Old Town, I felt like someone was following me." She spoke slowly and cautiously, working to mask her own apprehension.

Lydia shot her a frightened look. "What do you mean?"

"I kind of thought I saw someone. A guy in a gray suit. But I don't know if he was the one following me. I just had this sense, of being watched."

"A man in a suit? What did he look like?"

Amanda thought back. The blond stranger had been quite far away when she finally got a good look at him. "Actually, I can't even be sure it was a suit," she admitted. "Or a man. Definitely a blond, athletic person with short hair. Heck, for all I know, he was just a normal guy, and something supernatural was watching me. But the feeling came from his direction, and I definitely felt *something*." She tried to smile.

Lydia stared, her eyes dark with worry. "I don't like the sound of this. You have to tell someone."

At the look in her eyes, Amanda felt bad that she'd said anything. Poor Lydia was worried enough. "No, it's not a big deal," she reassured her friend. "And actually, now that I think about it, maybe that guy was a bodyguard, like the guys who came in with Basil. Maybe they patrol around and make sure we stay safe or something. Yes, that makes a lot more sense. I'll ask Basil about it when I see him."

"I don't know about this . . ."

"Please, let's not worry. I don't even know why I brought it up in the first place." It was definitely time to change the subject. Amanda leaned across the table, ready for some girl talk. "Speaking of men, what do you think about James?"

She was surprised to see the color rise in Lydia's cheeks. Oh, no. Was Lydia also attracted to James?

"Uh, well, I don't know him," Lydia hedged. "Why do you ask?"

"Just curious, I guess."

The discomfort in Lydia's gaze dissolved and a sly smile formed on her face. "You like him already, don't you?" She leaned in. "What did you guys talk about, after I left?"

Amanda relaxed. Lydia always knew when she liked someone, and so far they never had to compete for a man. She wanted Lydia to move on from Hank, but if she was honest with herself, she didn't want her to move on with James. "This and that," she said. "I found out he lives near Westover Air Reserve Base. He's incredibly good-looking, don't you think?" She was relieved to see Lydia's expression remain neutral this time.

Lydia nibbled on a strawberry. "Don't worry, I don't want him. Is that what you really wanted to know? If you can get him, you can have him.

Anyway, I made up my mind. I decided I'm going back to Hank." She beamed at Amanda. "You can congratulate me later."

"No . . . Really? You sure?"

Lydia let out a sigh. "James sort of looks like Hank, you have to admit."

"He does?"

"Sure, of course you see it: tall, dark, and handsome. Anyway, seeing him reminded me of Hank. And then I just knew. If just a reminder of Hank can make my heart flutter, the relationship has to be salvageable."

James made Lydia's heart flutter? Because he looked like Hank? Puzzled, Amanda tried to figure out if her friend was lying to her.

And just then, as if their conversation had somehow summoned and manifested him, James appeared in the door of the cafeteria. He spotted them immediately and headed over. "Hi, ladies," he called.

Looking as hot as ever, Amanda noted. He was casually dressed in dark khaki pants and a nice linen shirt. But with his athletic build, he would look hot in anything. Or in nothing . . .

Amanda mumbled a hello. She felt herself blush and looked away hurriedly, pretending to rummage for something in her bag as an excuse for avoiding his gaze. She had no idea what to do about him. She rarely found anyone this attractive. Even in the modeling world, surrounded by gorgeous people, she had never felt such magnetism. His charm must come from something more than just his looks, but she couldn't pinpoint what it was about him that captivated her. She looked back up to find him staring at her.

"Is something wrong, Amanda?" he asked.

Oh, God. Why did every thought have to show on her face? She tried to change her expression from that of a smitten schoolgirl to that of a confident woman. Then, without meaning to, she blurted out, "I was followed this morning."

"Well, it wasn't me," he teased.

Lydia's lips pulled into a mischievous grin. "Yeah, it was some other guy. Amanda's very popular, you know. Just look at her."

Appalled, Amanda wanted to shoot one of her newfound electric surges into Lydia.

"Um . . . sure." James shrugged noncommittally.

Lydia gulped her espresso. "Well, I'll let you guys catch up. See you at training!" She darted away, leaving her half-eaten fruit salad on the table.

Amanda felt even more awkward now that she and James were alone. She took to sipping her tea again, trying to come up with something to say. She was getting tired of Lydia's antics every time James came around. What was her deal? Maybe she *did* like James but didn't want to be in her friend's way. That would be bad. Amanda wouldn't want to stand in the way of Lydia's happiness either. Though, on the face of it, it seemed like Lydia was just teasing her while trying to facilitate her getting together with James.

James cleared his throat to get her attention. "Gioia asked me to join you at that meeting before training. Shall we head there together?"

They walked side by side in silence to the meeting, which was in one of the hotel's conference rooms on the second floor. Amanda had to fight not to let James's aloofness sour her mood. He'd seemed interested in her the other day, but today he barely seemed to notice her. She kept discreetly glancing up at him, but he strode along next to her, oblivious. Maybe he was shy. Or maybe he just wasn't talkative. Or—hello?—maybe he had other things on his mind. Like becoming a freaking Sentinel. Maybe as they got to know each other better, he'd open up a little more. Maybe he clammed up when he was nervous, like Amanda herself. After all, she wasn't talking either.

When they got to the conference room, a dozen other people were already seated around the table—also new Sentinels, she presumed. Gioia stood at the front of the room. When he saw James and Amanda enter, he signaled them to close the door behind them.

Gioia welcomed them with open arms, literally. "My dear friends. Thank you for joining us. We have urgent business to discuss. Two psychic assassinations are currently in preparation: one in Florence and one in Nepal. Our job is to stop them." He trained his gaze on Amanda as she started toward an empty seat at the table. "No, not you two. Please come with me. The rest of you will stay here and wait for Jalecia Navas. She should be here any moment now to give you instructions. Please be patient." He moved toward the door that led to an adjoining room, motioning for James and Amanda to follow him.

The next room looked more like an office. Gioia invited them to take a seat at a small table and promptly closed the door.

"Before we begin," Amanda ventured, "I've been thinking, who was the previous Sentinel 10? Can I talk—"

"There was a small flare about three years ago," Gioia interrupted. "But no Sentinel 10 was created then. That flare was a bit of an anomaly. They rarely occur more often than every ten to eleven years."

"Oh." Amanda tried to mask the disappointment in her voice. She knew that Matt had been created during that flare, and she'd been hoping another Sentinel like her had been as well.

James leaned back in his chair and folded his arms. "What happened to the Sentinels created a decade ago? Surely, there was a Sentinel 10 then."

"I beg your pardon?" Gioia asked, suddenly uptight.

James held his pose. "What happened to the other Sentinels?"

Gioia narrowed his eyes at him. "Sentinels only serve for a decade, then they are free to live normal lives. Once they are relieved of their powers, we no longer contact them."

This statement created many more questions in Amanda's mind, but it was clear from Gioia's tone and demeanor that this topic of conversation was over. James seemed to come to the same conclusion, because he simply nodded in response. She'd have to ask Basil follow-up questions at training.

Gioia picked up a remote and pointed it at the flat-screen TV, which sprang into life. It flashed a couple of slides of Princess Diana, then some slides of a man in a Soviet military uniform, an Indian dignitary, and some other individuals unknown to Amanda.

"What unites these characters?" Gioia asked. Without waiting, he said, "Answer: They were assassinated. Each was involved in a fatal car accident. You will not find any such ruling officially, of course, but these crashes happened through a psychic attack on either the victim's driver or on the driver of the other car. Look at this."

The next slide showed a grainy security camera photograph. "The figure in the shadows over there is the psychic assassin. He needs to be in relative physical proximity to the intended victim."

The screen went dark and Gioia turned to look at them with his unsettling violet eyes.

"This is the most important case right now, which is why we need you two on it. You are untrained, but your Sentinel ratings are the highest we have. So we want to get you into service immediately. The next target is Vittorio Moro, a popular political leader on the rise in Italy. We know the most likely assassin is this man."

A picture of a Latin American man appeared on the screen. He appeared to be middle-aged, but he had unusually deep wrinkles around his eyes.

"Juan Pablo Komani, age forty-nine. We know his exact modus operandi, and we believe he will model this attempt on one of his earliest cases. Take a look at this."

On the screen, "Ukraine 1987" appeared.

He clicked his remote and footage started rolling, showing three cars driving in single file along a country road. The middle one was a luxury vehicle and the cars flanking it were clearly security. As they watched, a nondescript car appeared in the other lane, followed closely by a semitruck. The two vehicles were moving at a steady pace toward the motorcade when suddenly the car screeched to halt. The semi veered toward the center line to avoid it, its driver clearly fighting for control of the heavy vehicle as it careened toward the dignitary's convoy. The rest happened quickly. The first security car accelerated just in time to avoid a collision, but the car with the dignitary was doomed. It struck the massive vehicle head-on, bursting into flames. The third car braked just in time, narrowly avoiding the fiery mess.

"And here is a computer-generated re-creation," Gioia explained, clicking to the next screen. "As you can see, there's no clue to why the incoming car slammed on the brakes. The driver gave no explanation, nor could the driver of the truck explain why he had swerved into the middle of the road instead of onto the shoulder. He swore up and down that he never saw any oncoming traffic. Moreover, an analysis of the tire tracks of the victim's car showed very little braking. In fact, after one second of the brakes being applied, that car actually accelerated to its doom."

He paused and took a few sips of water from a glass on the table, running an indifferent purple eye over Amanda. She looked quietly back at him, quelling her discomfort at his gaze.

He put the glass down and continued. "The public immediately suspected foul play, yet there was no way to prove any wrongdoing, just bad split-second decisions. But have a look at the original video again . . . The man on the bicycle by the side of the road. Do you see him?"

Amanda and James bent toward the screen. She noticed a grainy figure on a bicycle, extending his hand toward the road as the car and semitruck were coming into view.

"There he is. Juan Pablo Komani. His powers of mind control are quite advanced. Oddly enough, Juan is otherwise a rather placid man; he believes himself to be an artist and a pacifist. Right now, his paintings are on display in a gallery in Corsica, and his employers go through the pretense of buying his art to cover up their payments for his hits. Nobody questions the artistic value of a painting, as we all know."

Amanda was struggling to take all of this in. "Can we be affected by his mind control?" she asked, worried about what that might mean for them out in the field.

"Yes, Sentinel, you can. However, the more powerful you are, the less he can affect you. We only send out Sentinels 8 or higher to deal with powers at Komani's level. As a Sentinel 10, you have the advantage. He has nothing to protect himself against your energy pulses. Nothing whatsoever."

"Does he know we're coming after him?"

"He might. We try our best to hide our plans, but he may well be aware. If he is, there is little we can do." He shut off the screen and looked at his watch. "Good. Now that you know who you are up against, it's time to rejoin the rest of your group for training."

"Will the training protect us from the mind control?" James asked as they exited the room into the hallway.

"No. The power you have is what you have, no more, no less. This training is more of a harnessing of that power. An understanding."

"I *don't* understand," Amanda said.

"Just know that using your energies is as much a part of you as any other bodily function," Gioia explained. "It's not gymnastics. It's more like opening your eyes."

Chapter 7

A group of new Sentinels were gathered in the center of a large conference room, with the tables pushed against the walls. Mr. Blake had already explained that he was the adviser for the northeast region of the United States. There were nine Sentinels in attendance: three men (including James) and six women (including Amanda, Lydia, and Samantha, the young woman who had tried to make a break for it during the induction). Amanda was puzzled by her presence until Basil cleared his throat and answered her unasked question.

"Welcome, Sentinels. Samantha has been reassigned to our group. The Committee felt I'd be a better fit than her former mentor." He turned to Samantha. "I think you'll enjoy relocating to Rhode Island. I think you'll fit right in."

Amanda glanced at Samantha. Based on how she was dressed, she wasn't sure Samantha would fit in anywhere but New York City maybe. She was wearing jeans and a gothic-looking black top with winged sleeves. Her black hair was pulled back in a messy bun, and up close, Amanda noticed that she had hoops running up the outside of both her ears and a bone through the bottom of her nose. This girl didn't look like anything could scare her, or even faze her. And yet, she'd been terrified. This thought was not exactly comforting.

Amanda also couldn't help but notice that the women outnumbered the men and wondered if this was because women were smarter? Wasn't that Matt's theory, that Sentinels were always the smartest ones?

"For our first exercise, I'd like everyone to close your eyes." Basil Blake paused and waited for everyone to follow his instructions. "Once your eyes are closed, take in the room with the rest of your senses."

A thin girl with dark-blond hair who was standing close to Amanda uttered a noise that sounded like scoffing. She glanced at Amanda and mouthed the word *boring*, rolling her eyes for good measure. But Amanda did not think any of this was boring. She frowned at the girl and closed her eyes, determined to take the training program seriously. All she could think about was how terrifying it had been to encounter that plasmid in Panama and how equally empowering it had been to destroy it. She never wanted to feel as helpless as she was in that moment, before Matt showed up and helped her take control of the situation.

With her eyes closed, she focused on the darkness. Soon her other senses kicked in. She perceived the rustling of clothes, the distant noises of the city outside, the smell of perfume, the slight musk of James . . .

Soon she felt a presence. Like a darker circle, taking shape at the periphery of the darkness, to her left.

"Do you sense anything?" Blake asked. "Do not open your eyes, but please nod when you do. I will wait for everyone to sense something before we carry on."

Amanda nodded. She obeyed his instruction to keep her eyes shut, although she wanted so badly to open them to see how the others were doing.

The presence remained. It did not enlarge or change in focus. It just stayed at the periphery, flat and immobile.

"Very good. We're all on the same page," said their adviser. "Stay like this, my friends. Now I want you to imagine that you're closing something. You must find the mental image that works for you. In the past, some Sentinels have told me that they use the image of closing a lid or shutting a door. Others picture a butterfly flying away and disappearing into the sky. Try a few different mental images and tell me when you no longer sense the presence."

Amanda tried to imagine a door closing first. A huge wooden door, like in a castle.

Slam.

Nope. The darker-than-dark presence was still sitting to her left.

All right, a smaller door. Her apartment door. And once she closed the door, she made sure to turn the key in the lock, for good measure.

Damn. Nothing, still nothing. The door wasn't doing it for her.

What next?

She shook her head in frustration. *Focus*, she reminded herself. But she was having trouble keeping her eyes shut. She wanted to see how everyone else was doing.

"I did it!" someone announced.

"Me too, wow!" someone else called. She didn't recognize either voice, and she was happy at least that James and Lydia hadn't beaten her to it. Though with two others already ahead of her, her competitive sense had definitely been awakened. She was Sentinel 10, damn it. She was supposed to be the best!

"Me too!" called a voice she recognized as Samantha's.

"I've got it," announced James.

Now she was embarrassed. Her powers were supposedly much greater than everyone else's in this room, including James's. Her powers were like a river. Like an ocean . . . Like . . .

A waterfall.

She focused on the image of a waterfall, as tall as one of the cathedrals she'd seen this morning in her walk of the city. Immensely powerful, raw and unstoppable, toppling over the edge of an invisible cliff, roaring down in heaps of water, tumbling to infinity.

She kept the waterfall roaring down, falling and falling into the abyss . . . the dark abyss in front of her eyes. And then she made the abyss swallow the waterfall, so it flowed no more. The abyss then shrank to the size of a dot before disappearing entirely.

And the presence disappeared with it.

"Yes!" cried out Amanda, a little louder than intended.

"Me too!" said Lydia. "No, wait, never mind. Oh yes, I have it!"

Amanda finally opened her eyes. Only a couple more people were struggling to find their way at this point, but they soon found it. She turned her eyes on Basil Blake. He was holding an open box. She craned her neck and saw that it was empty.

"Well done, everyone," he congratulated them. "You've just turned off your receiving functions. Now, you can't be detected by any paranormal element. Okay, shut your eyes again, and try *opening* your receiving functions. Just use the reverse image."

Amanda did so, and the mystical waterfall roared back to life.

"Open your eyes, everyone," Basil instructed.

As soon as she opened her eyes, Amanda was startled to see a large gray plasmid floating above the box. It had gathered in a thick canopy above Basil, covering a good portion of the ceiling. Despite its size, it seemed inert; something was wrong with it.

"With your receiving functions open, you can see all paranormal elements, which is important on assignments. Obviously, you need to see what you are destroying." Basil put the box on the table in front of him, and the gray canopy slowly followed, spreading over the ceiling in layers, like a rolling thundercloud.

"I use this plasmid as a teaching tool," he explained. "It has been partially drained, and the box acts as a cage. It can't break free, it can't feed, and it can't coalesce with other plasmids. Use it to practice your receiving functions. It should take you about two hours to really master it. At the end of this exercise, turning on or off your receiving functions shouldn't take longer than a second, with your eyes open. It should become second nature to you. If you're unable to achieve this goal within two hours, you need to continue trying. It is absolutely crucial. Otherwise the plasmids will sense your energy, and trust me, they will come find you."

Murmurs filtered among the students. Lydia and Amanda nodded in unison.

"Can you tell us more about what these things are?" asked some guy in a red shirt.

Basil nodded. "Of course. A plasmid is a collection of used-up psychic energy. Magical and other paranormal activity around the world leaves psychic garbage in its wake. In time, similar types of leftovers assemble into plasmids. They are hungry and mobile, looking to feed on psychic energy to sustain themselves. They have no intelligence and no other desires. In a sense, plasmids are exactly like slime molds, which are individual cells that can fuse, unfuse, and assemble by the hundreds into a moving structure called a slug. You can extrapolate that knowledge to understand our plasmids. For the next ten years, plasmid cleanups will be your bread and butter."

"What happens after ten years?" the blonde next to Amanda asked. Amanda leaned forward, eager for the answer.

"Nobody told you yet? At the end of each solar cycle, there is a large solar flare. This happens every ten years or so. So, after ten years, the new cohort comes into place, and you are relieved of your powers by the Committee."

Amanda knew that much. "But why?" she asked. "Why don't any Sentinels keep their powers and serve longer terms?"

"If you stayed beyond ten years, you could die from brain cancer," their adviser explained. "Ten years is the longest tried and true, safe, time range. The body can only sustain this kind of energy load for so long. We don't know exactly *how* long, but ten years is absolutely safe."

A murmur arose in the room, and Basil raised a hand to quiet them. "I know you all have many questions, and I will do my best to answer them throughout this training program. But we really need to get started. Now, I know that most of you have already vanquished plasmids. That's how we found you. What's one thing you remember about your experience? Anyone?" He looked around the room. The Sentinels-in-training all stared at each other.

"It was . . . intuitive?" Samantha said.

Basil beamed. "That's right! Intuitive. Meaning, essentially, that you did it on your own. Controlling your receiving functions is one thing. But destroying plasmids, it's like learning to walk. One day, it just clicks. For Sentinels, it just clicks." A din of affirmations took over the space in the room as the group of new Sentinels began describing to each other the instant they first destroyed the plasmids that had found them.

Lydia cleared her throat. "Um, I've never destroyed one," she said, sheepishly. Amanda's heart squeezed for her friend. This wasn't going to be easy for Lydia, who was used to being at the top of the class.

"Well then, let's do it now, my dear," Basil Blake said warmly, and he gestured for Lydia to come forward.

She joined him in the front of the room. Lydia did not enjoy the spotlight, especially when it was on her for some perceived failure.

"It's okay," Basil Blake said reassuringly as he opened the box. The plasmid, as if instinctually understanding its freedom, began to rise to the top of the box. It hovered for a moment before drifting toward Lydia. Amanda could almost feel her friend's sense of panic. Basil Blake said, quietly and calmly, "Don't panic, child. Just let it come to you." Lydia did what she was told, and Basil continued to instruct her. "Now lift—"

But she was already there. Her hands were raised, fingers pointed. It was clear from her body language that Lydia was feeling the power coursing within her, and then out of her. Within seconds, the plasmid had disintegrated.

"See? Intuitive," Basil said. He motioned for Lydia to rejoin the group.

After another two hours, the team had mastered destroying plasmids quickly and efficiently.

Basil, who had been moving from student to student, evaluating their progress and helping them individually, went back to the front of the room. "Let us now turn to the different types of residue, so you can familiarize yourself," he said. "Remember, psychic residue is what remains after any paranormal activity. It consists of fractured remnants of energy. Now, don't be fooled. Residue can be dangerous even before it coalesces with others to form a plasmid. If you would kindly turn your attention to the row of tables on your left."

The students did as instructed. Each table had a box on it. "Please turn on your receiving functions." Basil opened one of the boxes.

Amanda watched as a residue appeared above the box. The residue was thin, vaporous, and almost without substance. She was surprised she could see it at all.

"Now," Basil instructed, "come forward."

When the trainees approached, the residue began to take shape. "It looks like a snake," James commented.

To Amanda, the residue looked like a vaporous tiger, its tail whipping its sides, snarling at her.

"It kind of looks like a nun," said another trainee. "A woman with a long veil on her head."

"How are you getting a veil?" James asked. "It's, like, folding. Undulating. Like a cobra about to strike."

"No, that's wrong," Lydia said. "It's a thin man with very long arms."

"Actually, none of you is wrong," Blake explained. "Each Sentinel will see a different image and experience a different sensation from the residue as it tries to cling to them." As he approached the table, the residue began to take a new shape and circle around him.

"Whatever you're seeing, no doubt it is unsettling," he said. "These are the dark arts, after all." He looked around to size up his students. "This is a strong group here, I can tell. This dark residue has the power to drive weaker minds to madness with the images and sensations it generates. You've all done well." He began closing the lid and the residue disappeared back into its box.

After that, Blake took them through each box. Each one held a different type of residue. Some were formed from spells and curses, some from voodoo magic, some from evil intentions, and the rest from other dark sources.

Amanda whizzed through the boxes without difficulty—until she reached the last one. Before the box was even opened, she could feel a small fissure forming in her psyche.

"Now, this is a nasty one. Sometimes childhood trauma can trigger an intense reaction to the residue. Be careful." Basil opened the box.

Immediately the fissure inside Amanda widened, as if tearing through the fabric of her mind, the pain quickly spreading into the rest of her body. A blackness was taking over her; a void.

"Try not to think of things that have caused you pain in your life, or even better, try to put a psychic wall or barrier around your traumatic memories." It was the last thing Amanda heard before the void overtook her completely.

It started to wail deep inside her, drowning out all other sounds: high-pitched, writhing wails. Like a hurricane desperate to be set free, building up momentum, spinning and screaming, threatening to overtake her. She cried out, shattering the wailing, but she couldn't stay in the room. She had to get out of there. She turned and hurried to the door before breaking into a sprint.

"Amanda!" she heard Lydia call after her, but she kept moving, determined not to stop until she was out of the building and onto the street. She had to put as much distance as possible between her and the residue.

She barged through the lobby, past the startled desk clerk, and found herself outside on the street.

Once the sun hit her, Amanda started to feel herself returning to normal. She hugged herself around the shoulders, breathing in and out. *You're fine*, she told herself over and over. She spotted a café across the road and darted toward it, taking an empty table beneath an umbrella that would shade her from the intense July sun. She ran her eyes over the menu over and over, focusing on calming down. Things were normal here. She ordered a glass of chardonnay and tried to relax. Life was good, and she was sane. What she had experienced was only in her mind, and she would learn how to conquer it. This was day one. She had time.

Childhood trauma can trigger an intense reaction to the residue. Basil Blake's words resonated in her memory. Why had she thought about her parents' disappearance? About her being an orphan? She remembered the emotional storm it triggered. So there was indeed a hole inside her, which even after all these years felt impossible to close. She sighed and looked around. A familiar older man was crossing the road, coming toward her. Basil Blake, of course. He greeted her politely and, without asking, sat down at her table. Amanda kept a neutral face, but inside, she felt embarrassed about running out on him.

Blake smiled. "It's okay, Amanda. The residue, it can have a big effect on untrained Sentinels. But I promise you, you are strong. You just needed to escape and regroup. That was the right thing to do. But you will conquer this darkness from your past. This grief. This emptiness."

Amanda raised her eyebrows. "Are you a mind reader?"

"No, just exceptionally empathic. All the advisers are natural empaths. I can intuitively tell . . . a lot, about a person, because I sense exactly how people feel. It's my superpower, if you will. I don't know how I know—I just know."

She tilted her head to the side. "Wow. So, what else can you tell about me?" she asked, trying to affect confidence even though her foot was shaking uncontrollably under the table.

For a moment, Basil Blake looked her in the eyes. "You're sad, Amanda. You're sad and a little angry, and being very strong about it. You've been this way for as long as you can remember. Yet you also have what I would call a *purity of spirit*, a willpower that carries you through difficult times. I don't know if I can define it better. Like the blade of a sword that ultimately cuts through the darkness and steadies you. You might be a bit of an empath yourself, at least with those close to you. I could feel it in you when Lydia had to approach that plasmid on her own. I could feel how deeply you worried for her, and how much you wanted to help her. That's probably the biggest reason you decided to become a doctor, to help others."

Amanda didn't know what to say. She liked the purity of spirit part, but she didn't consider herself sad, or angry, in any way. Not anymore. She was fine.

"I'm not angry or sad; I don't know why you'd say that," she replied. "I'm fine, really. Maybe it's best to switch topics. Like, what am I missing right now, in training?"

He smiled. "Nothing of importance. They are learning about the secret societies around the world—there's a great deal to learn, with flow charts and diagrams, but I can give you all that information whenever you need it. The real training starts on the job. Now, tell me, do you realize your importance, Amanda?"

She blinked. "Sure. Of course. I'm sixty-four times more powerful than my friend, for instance. So I'm really powerful."

Mr. Blake smiled. He had a kind way of smiling, a bit wistful, a bit condescending, but still very nice. "I miss being young," he said. "It's part of the reason I am devoted to my job as your adviser. The Sentinels are always young. I feel like a father to them. I see them grow within their functions and within themselves and within the rest of their lives. It's an absolute privilege."

He leaned forward. "But a Sentinel 10 is not like the others. Your kind are always very special, strong people who have faced a painful challenge early on, one way or another. There isn't a Sentinel 10 that ever existed who did not carry a significant wound, a painful burden. I don't know why that is. Also, you're not exactly twice as powerful as a Sentinel 9. Approximately so, but not exactly. The exact conversion factor is variable, more dependent on the Sentinel 10 in question, and your powers will evolve over time. Theirs never will. Ten years from now, James will remain at the exact same Sentinel 9 level. But a Sentinel 10 could grow stronger, and many discover adjunctive powers along the way. However, because of your extreme strength as a Sentinel 10, you are also in danger from that power."

"What do you mean, Mr. Blake? Brain cancer?"

"Please call me Basil. And no, I don't mean brain cancer. Don't worry about brain cancer. Nobody gets that. No, what I mean by danger is that sometimes the power can go to people's heads, and they lose themselves in it. I really don't think you need to worry, though. This purity you have will protect you."

"I don't understand. Do you mean I could become arrogant in some way, or open a plasmid-hunting business of my own? Put you all out of business?"

Basil chuckled softly. "No, not quite. I'll explain in more depth later." He looked at her closely. "Ah, the green-eyed wonder. Amanda Griffith. You remind me of my daughter. She was a green-eyed wonder, too."

Amanda warmed at that comparison. She wanted to ask about his daughter but held back. He'd said "she *was* a green-eyed wonder." Maybe his daughter had died. The waiter came to take their orders. Basil declined; it looked like he wasn't planning to stay. Amanda ordered ice cream and sparkling water. She would have lunch with Lydia in a bit.

"There's one more thing I should tell you," her adviser said, and Amanda's warmth gave way to a chill of dread. *What more could there be?*

"Don't worry, it's a good thing. It's mind control," he said. "You are one of the Sentinels with this gift. I can sense the ability in you."

"Mind control? Like the mind control the psychic assassins use?" She wasn't sure she liked the idea of having that power.

"Yes and no. It's not that extensive. You can make people see certain things. You can induce them to take minor actions, such as leaving a room. You can compel people to tell the truth. But you can't manipulate their feelings. And you can't force them to do things they strongly object to."

She tried to make sure she understood what he meant. "Wait, so I could, like, make you order pasta from this menu, as long as you didn't have a strong hatred of pasta? But if you were dead set on ordering a sandwich, I couldn't force you to change your mind?"

Basil chuckled. "That's the general idea, yes, but we will work on honing your ability. All in good time. There's too much to learn right here, right now." He stood up from the table. "I'll talk to you soon, okay? Training's almost over for the day, so enjoy your afternoon."

She watched him walk across the road, calm and dignified.

What a nice but weird, weird man. Was he trying to warn me or comfort me?

Twirling her glass by the stem, she started puzzling over Basil's words, trying to discern his intentions. She must have gotten lost in her thoughts for quite some time. She was jarred back to reality when she felt a small itch in her hand. Slowly, she turned it over, palm up. She darted a quick glance around her, then focused. A marble-size globe of energy immediately took shape within the curve of her palm. It was transparent and without substance, almost invisible. But at the same time, it was elastic and electric, vibrating like a tiny, raging storm. The globe appeared to be constantly collapsing and remaking itself, as if it were fighting against the physical reality around it. She didn't know how she had manifested it.

For the next several minutes, Amanda sat there, gazing at it, wondering what she was getting herself into. Who, or *what*, had she become?

Chapter 8

As the final day of training was winding down, Basil gathered all his new Sentinels in the conference room, telling them he'd always be available to them, whenever they needed him.

"The Committee has arranged for you to remain in Prague the rest of the week, if you so choose," he told everyone. "With all your expenses covered. However, if you'd prefer just to return home, we understand. This has been a lot to absorb in very little time."

"Oh, I'm totally staying here," Sam said. "This city is *sick*!" Her face was so animated with excitement that everyone had to laugh. She seemed to have settled in to the idea of being a Sentinel.

"Stay as long as you like, dear," he said. "We'll cover your expenses whether you stay here or return home. Remember, everyone, I'm just a call or text or even a Skype away if you need it." Basil then proceeded down the line and shook everyone's hands, congratulating each new Sentinel individually on successfully completing their training. The look of pride he wore with each greeting was unmistakable.

When he got to Amanda, he took both her hands in his. "How are you feeling, dear? Ready for your first assignment?"

Amanda took in the warmth of his hands and the kindness in his eyes. She could already feel his support without him saying one word.

"I think so," she said. Over the last few days, she had obsessively practiced zapping residues and plasmids, projecting her psychic shield, and trying out her low-grade mind control. She'd also looked over the files on the psychic assassin, Juan Pablo Komani, studying his previous hits. In her free time, she'd even perused photos of his artwork to see if they would give her any insight into his mind. She *thought* she felt ready, and Basil's confidence gave her the extra boost she needed.

She looked at James, standing next to her, and it was easy to see that Basil had a similar effect on him. Calming. Reassuring. The two men shook hands, and Basil gave James a quick, affectionate clap on the shoulder. "I would tell you to look after her, but . . ."

James chuckled. "Yeah, she's twice as powerful. I get it." He raised an eyebrow at Amanda. "So, you'll look after me?"

"If you're nice to me," she shot back playfully. His smile vanished temporarily, then came back in a flash, somewhat forced. It probably wasn't the easiest thing for a brawny, decorated military man like himself to need the protection of the slip of a blonde that she was, but he was just going to have to deal with it.

Basil looked down at his watch. "The car should be here shortly to take you two to the airport." He turned to the rest of the group. "Let's all head out to see them off?"

The Sentinels nodded and followed. "I feel like I forgot everything already," said Sam as they walked to the hotel entrance. "What if we need, you know, a refresher?"

Basil smiled warmly. "In your package, you will find a sheet with helpful information, including a list of links and access codes for online webinars. However, you can use each access code only once, so use them selectively. This safety measure is in place so that our information isn't spread to unsavory parties."

"So, we can only view each webinar one time? What happens if we forget the material again?" Lydia asked, her voice laced with concern.

Basil went right back into reassuring mode. "Then you call me. Anytime. That goes for all of you," he said with a sweeping hand gesture. "You're not alone."

They stepped out onto the sidewalk. The scorching sun was mercifully masked behind a cluster of clouds.

"I'll miss you," Lydia said, pulling Amanda into a hug. "Try not to get into too much trouble."

"Try not to get back together with Hank," Amanda jabbed. Lydia would be flying back to Boston the next day.

Lydia rolled her eyes.

"At least wait till I get back? Give yourself a few more days to decide?" Amanda asked, affectionately brushing an errant strand of Lydia's hair away from her eyes.

"I'll see what I can do," Lydia said. "No promises."

Now it was Amanda's turn to roll her eyes. "Fine," she said, in a mock-stern tone.

As if on cue, a white Mercedes pulled up to the curb. The driver got out and opened the back door for Amanda and James.

Amanda slipped into the backseat while the driver placed their bags in the trunk and James made his way to the other side of the car.

Basil poked his head in on Amanda's side. "Remember, you're not alone."

Amanda couldn't help but grin. For the first time in her life, she truly felt like she was a part of something. Basil beamed back at her, his eyes kind. The super-empath must have picked up on her feelings. She wondered if it was possible to hide anything from Basil Blake.

Their adviser closed the door and James took his seat, immediately clicking his seat belt around him. Amanda followed suit.

"I'm excited to see Florence again," she told him, with a hair flip and more giddiness in her voice than she meant to show.

"Hmm." He turned his focus to the window and kept it there for pretty much the entire ride to the airport.

Deflated, Amanda hoped they wouldn't be seated together on the plane. If a short car ride could be this awkward, how excruciating was a flight going to be?

She had been to Florence once, during her modeling days. While she hadn't had time to take in the sights, she could well remember that it was a beautiful city, full of history, cobblestone streets, ancient cathedrals, and museums filled with famous masterpieces. On top of that, it had a general air of relaxation. No one hurried anywhere. A perfect atmosphere for vacation. Unfortunately, she imagined that this Sentinel business was probably going to be at least as hectic as modeling had been.

She and James checked in separately at the airport and weren't seated together on their first flight. During their layover in Barcelona, James suddenly offered to buy her a cup of coffee. She happily agreed, working out conversation topics in her head, but after bringing her the coffee, he said, "I'm going to stretch my legs," and wandered off on his own. *Damn that guy*, she thought. Could he make it more obvious that he didn't like her? In Florence they went through customs separately, claimed their bags, and finally met outside the airport to wait for their ride.

James smiled politely. "Good flight?" The effort at conversation seemed to pain him. How was she going to work closely with this person, who struggled to say even two sentences to her? He had seemed almost flirtatious in the beginning, when they'd first met. What could have changed him so much over the last week? Was it something she said?

Well, fine. Whatever it was, let him figure it out on his own. She just wouldn't speak to him, if that's how he felt. She raised her eyebrows and nodded, then folded her arms across her chest and looked away.

The car ride to the hotel was spent in the same awkward silence. Sitting beside James, she could feel the heat of his body against her leg, and she fought the desire to look at him as they drove through the rolling hills and the quiet green landscape on the way to their hotel. But it seemed uncouth to show interest in a man when the man didn't show any interest in her, so she continued to ignore him. Not that he noticed.

His lack of concern further soured her mood. She was sure she'd felt something between them in Panama. An attraction. A spark. Was the spark just the Sentinel currents that were now apparently a part of her? No, it had to be more. Because, seriously, how dare he not be interested in her?

The car pulled up in front of the Grand Gala Hotel and Spa, just down the street from the Museo Leonardo da Vinci. The spa called to her. She wasn't here on a vacation—she well knew—but she couldn't help but think how good a massage and a soak would feel after so much traveling. But of course, that would have to wait. After the assassination was thwarted, well, maybe she'd get a reward.

After the chauffeur lifted their bags from the trunk and placed them on separate luggage carts, he handed the car keys to the valet and turned to James and Amanda. "Mr. Blake has advised that this car be left for your use for the remainder of your stay. Good luck with your mission."

At his words, Amanda started to feel the full gravity of the situation. She couldn't help but be afraid now, knowing what she and James were up against and why they were in this beautiful city together. She was keenly aware of the power and influence of the Committee. She knew she was the Sentinel 10; she was the powerful one. Despite that understanding, she found herself feeling vulnerable. Only a few days of training, and now they were up against an assassin who'd mastered mind control?

"What's wrong?" asked James, as if suddenly noticing her.

She hesitated, still upset with him. What was she going to tell Mr. Strong Air Force Guy? Then she softened. If they were ever going to open up to each other and form a real bond, now was the time. "It's about tomorrow." She glanced down, biting her lip. "Tomorrow we have an assassination to stop. Think about it." She turned toward him. "It seems sort of crazy, right? Unreal, somehow?"

He gave her a vague smile and shrugged. "Sure. It all is." His tone was matter-of-fact.

If this man feels any emotion, you'd never know it. Maybe if she showed him what she was feeling—maybe, just maybe—he'd open up to her.

"I'm worried," she told him. "Actually, I'm afraid. How about that? I'm afraid."

Kindness came into his eyes. "Amanda, if you're afraid, think of how it is for me. I mean, you're twice as powerful as I am. I could fall victim to his mind control, but you are too strong for that." Unexpectedly, he laughed. "I guess that wasn't helpful. Okay, listen, I'll be right there with you. We're a team." At that, he took her hand and gave it a gentle squeeze. His hand felt rough in spots but smooth in others, and his touch set a slight shudder through her. What was she going to do about this one?

He kept her hand in his as he began to lead her inside the hotel. But just then, something caught her eye. A sliver of gray. "Wait," she said, frowning, craning her neck around. But there was nothing. "Never mind," she began, but when she turned back to the hotel's front entrance she saw it again, reflected in the glass doors. The sliver of gray was behind them, across the street. It was a man wearing a suit, and he was watching them. She turned around again and glared directly at him. This time he didn't slip into the shadows. He stared at them boldly, the same man in a gray suit, with bleached-blond hair. Amanda locked eyes with him for only a moment and felt a surge of something—she didn't know what. Then he turned and began walking away at a brisk pace.

Oh, there was no doubt about it this time. He was spying on her. On them.

"Hey!" she yelled. Letting go of James's hand, she took off after the man, as fast as she could run in her stiletto heels. She continued to call after him, but he paid no attention to her, his straight back in the gray suit getting farther away, then disappearing around a street corner. By the time she got to the same corner, the man was nowhere to be seen.

James ran up behind her. "You lost him?"

She turned to him, panting. "You saw him too, right? It's that same guy! The same guy who was following me the other day!"

His gaze searched the street, then he looked down at her, his face grim. "I saw him, all right. He was staring right at you. I bet he ducked into one of those shops, but which one?"

"Maybe he's Komani's accomplice. Or am I just being paranoid?"

James's gray eyes were serious. He reflected for a few seconds then replied, "We'll find out soon enough. If we catch him watching us again, we won't let him get away. Come on. Let's go check in."

They walked back to the hotel, their senses on high alert. Amanda's feet were pinched in shoes absolutely not made for running. She was surprised she hadn't snapped off a pencil-thin heel in her pursuit of the spy, or whatever he was.

She thought about James's reaction. If he had chased after her to protect her, he must care for her, right? And when he held her hand, she'd felt that he was really there, right with her, present and interested in her company. As they entered the hotel, past a delightful-looking restaurant, she decided to find out how far his caring extended. "After I put my things away and wash up, I think I'll come back down to the restaurant here and grab some dinner. Any interest?" She didn't look at him, trying to sound nonchalant.

"Thanks, but I'm beat," James replied. "I think I'll just order dinner up to my room and hit the hay. Big day tomorrow."

Disappointment caught in her throat, but she pushed her words through it. "Sure, get some rest. See you in the morning."

She went directly to the reception desk and checked in, making sure not to spare James a single glance. Even as the elevator doors were sliding shut, and he was still at the front desk, well within view, she refused to look. She was tired of not understanding this man.

Once on the fourth floor, she dragged her suitcase down the corridor behind her and told herself that James did not exist. Period.

She was relieved at the sight of her spacious room. From the double bed to the partially drawn curtains, all of the décor was color-coordinated in shades of lavender and white, which complemented the pale pink wallpaper that was peppered with tiny red roses. The room breathed cozy romanticism. A tray of strawberries had been set on her bedside table, along with a small bottle of pinot noir. She'd love a glass of wine right now. But first, she kicked off her shoes and walked over to the window, happy to see that she had a balcony and a view. She eagerly pushed open the doors and stepped outside. Most buildings in Florence were less than six stories high and from here on the fourth floor, she could see many of the city's distinctive red tile roofs. In the distance stood the Duomo, the iconic cathedral with its large, terracotta-tiled dome. She hoped to visit once she was done with this mission. She pressed her palms over the back of her tired neck and tipped her head back with a little moan. She remembered reading that she'd have to climb a thousand steps to get to the Duomo's very top. Then she'd be rewarded with a sprawling view of the city.

Amanda brushed her locks to the side and leaned on the balcony's railing, letting her hair float in the gentle evening breeze as her thoughts roamed. Things would be okay, she told herself. *Don't think about tomorrow. Don't think about anything. Just relax.*

Looking down on the people walking in the street below, she also thought of her stalker: the mysterious blond man who she was sure had followed them from Prague.

What was his business with her? Did he know she was a Sentinel? Did he know why she and James were there? Was he hoping to thwart their mission? His presence gave her a feeling of foreboding, but also, oddly, of wonder. Stranger yet, she did not feel afraid of him. Only curious.

With a suppressed sigh, Amanda walked back into her room and closed the blinds. She decided she'd follow James's lead and stay in, having her dinner sent up. She had a big day in front of her. She didn't want any distractions. She now considered it a good thing that James had turned down her offer to have dinner together. He certainly would have been a big distraction.

Amanda called the front desk and ordered up an authentic *risotto funghi porcini e zucchine*. She then took a long, hot shower while she waited for her food to arrive. Yes, tomorrow was going to be a big day, and she was going to be ready for it.

Chapter 9

Stopping an assassination. What does one wear to that sort of thing?

Amanda rummaged through her suitcase, full of the light clothing she'd packed for the Panama vacation that seemed like a lifetime ago. Her flower-print bikini was cute, but definitely not appropriate for the occasion. Chunky-heeled sandals were not suited for quick getaways, should she need to make a run for it. She pulled out one item after another, dismissing each, finally settling on her coral jumpsuit. Not exactly great camouflage, but compared to her short skirts and sundresses, it was a clear winner. She strapped on a pair of flat gladiator sandals after donning the jumpsuit, and headed down to breakfast.

Downstairs, she spotted James sitting at a table in the hotel's small café restaurant. She couldn't help but notice how his black T-shirt subtly wrapped his sculpted, muscular form. He was looking down at his menu when she approached, a cup of coffee in front of him.

He looked up. "There you are!" he said, now oddly friendly again. When he stood to greet her, her gaze dropped to his perfectly fitting olive-green pants, which showed off his lower assets quite nicely. He pulled out a chair for her.

"Good morning." She sat down and placed her supple brown leather sling purse on the table in front of her. She was moving slowly, deliberately, giving herself time to think.

"I came down to join you last night," he said. "I waited a while, but you never showed."

"Oh?" He'd come down and waited for her? But why? He'd been pretty dismissive of her invitation.

He nodded. "As soon as I got to my room, I realized it might be good for us to talk a little, you know, about this evening. So I took a quick shower and headed back down."

"I went to bed."

He chuckled. "I thought maybe you'd run off with the blond guy in the gray suit." He shot her a playful smirk. *As if.* As she was opening her mouth to say what she thought about his insensitive joke, the server came to take their orders.

"Did you give some thought to our mission?" she asked instead. "I still feel like I have no idea what to expect, despite their video and all. I think we should start planning."

He shook his head. "We'll play it by ear. I spoke to Basil last night, and he said we're so powerful that ninety percent of the job is just to show up."

Amanda hiccupped from the surprise. Her hand flew to her chest and she swallowed. "Seriously?"

"That's what he said. He reminded me our powers are intuitive. Told me to trust our instincts. Besides, they don't really know how Komani will operate. They're just hypothesizing that he'll use the same method as his previous hits, but nobody knows for sure. There's no guarantee he'll even be there tonight, if the Committee is wrong about the exact location of the hit."

Amanda could not exactly disagree. It reminded her of something they'd been told as med students: most of the time, half the job is to show up. It didn't help her anxiety, but in a crazy way it made sense.

While waiting for their food, Amanda told James how she and Lydia had first met when they were seven, then lost touch because her parents moved away, and how they'd reconnected in their first year of medical school. She learned that James had moved around a few times as well. He was originally from Georgia, but his family had moved to Ohio when he started high school, and he had since lost his accent. "That's when I met my fiancée," he said.

That caught Amanda off-guard. "Oh, I didn't realize—"

"No. She's not my fiancée now," he said, his voice cracking. "You know, I'd really rather not talk about this. I'm sorry I brought it up." He got misty-eyed.

Amanda was confused. It seemed strange that anyone would have broken up with James—she'd taken him to be more the heartbreaker type. "Sure." She was about to change the subject when he rose abruptly and motioned for the check. The server hurried over, and James asked to have his breakfast taken to his room, scribbling his signature on the bill without looking at it. He barely glanced at her while explaining that he'd forgotten about things he needed to do before they headed out later, and he was gone before she could respond.

She finished her breakfast alone. His behavior no longer offended her. Clearly, James was not boyfriend material; he was prone to mood swings and was downright impossible to read. As for tonight, let the chips fall where they may, she thought, sipping her tea. She'd just have to trust that it was going to be okay.

After breakfast, she went to the front desk to get a map of the city. Since she and James clearly weren't going to spend any more time planning, she had hours to kill before the start of the mission. The best thing to distract her from the evening ahead would be to check out some of the sights.

As she walked the ancient streets, she couldn't believe she was here again, in this beautiful city she'd hardly had time to see the first time around. She'd done a shoot with a prominent photographer named Pamel and a male model whose name escaped her. She remembered very clearly, however, the only real sightseeing she'd done—climbing to the top of the ancient portico in six-inch heels. What a workout for her calves that had been. The ad was supposed to illustrate that wearing a certain designer cologne would create an intensely romantic moment between male and female in vaporous clothes—but her most vivid recollection was the insane attraction between Pamel and the male model. She might as well have been invisible!

As Amanda joined the crowds passing the massive, carved stone façade of St. Vitus Cathedral, she thought about what a strange time that had been in her life. And how bizarre it felt to be back in this romantic city with a man who couldn't show less romantic attraction to her. Well, at least his broken heart made that easier to understand.

Her modeling days had been odd, but this new job was even odder. As she wandered about, peeking into various shops, she kept thinking about the huge task ahead of them. Less than a week ago, she'd been a promising medical resident; now she was the most powerful of an ancient force of Sentinels, about to thwart an assassination. Yep. Life was odd.

Thinking she should keep her strength up, Amanda stopped at an outdoor trattoria and ordered a light lunch. The atmosphere was pleasant enough and the pasta dish looked and smelled heavenly. But she couldn't eat much. With a deep sigh, she fished her phone out of her bag, toying with the idea of calling Paolo Gioia. Perhaps they'd found out something more, since their debriefing in Prague. He'd given them his number, but despite his suave manners, she didn't find him approachable. Instead she dialed Basil. He was their adviser, and she needed to hear him say that they'd be just fine.

"Yes, my dear. How are you holding up?" he asked.

"I'm managing." She smiled. "Did my nervous voice give me away?"

"Oh, I am a super-empath, after all," he reminded her with a chuckle.

"I see. Mr. Blake, why did you tell James that we don't need to prepare for this mission? That seems counterintuitive to me. We are stopping an *assassin*, after all."

"Actually, my dear, you already have all the tools you need. And call me Basil. It might seem like a daunting task right now, but this mission is not even a real challenge. It is hardly a challenge for a Sentinel 9, never mind for a 10."

"But I'm brand new at this! I don't—"

"Amanda," he interrupted her. "My dear girl, the only thing you need to fear is your lack of confidence. New or not, your powers are within you already. In fact, I'll tell you something right now that I have not told James."

She waited, as he seemed to be searching for the right words.

"Your powers are within you, but they have not been entirely awoken. They've been primed, so to speak, but the full activation needs a challenge. Something that creates an adrenaline rush."

"Oh, wow!" she scoffed. "Trust me, I had my rush when the plasmid found us in Panama."

Basil paused. "That may have been enough, but it may not have been. It depends on the Sentinel in question, and your level has nothing to do with it. The sooner you get a complete awakening, the better. So I encourage you to trust the danger, so to speak. It is good for you."

"What the hell. Seriously, did you just say to *trust* the danger? To go for the adrenaline rush?" Her heart thudded.

"My dear Sentinel 10, you will do just fine. I think this is what you wanted to hear when you called me, anyway. Am I right?"

She sighed. Great. *Show off your empath powers, Gramps.* She'd never call him that aloud, of course, no matter how annoyed she was. She respected her elders. "Sure. It's too bad that it is not *your* powers that need awakening, I'd love to see how you handle anxiety."

"I handle it fine. And so do you, my dear girl. You are the best. The absolute best, you just don't know it yet. But after tonight, you will. Take care of James, okay?"

She blushed a little. What if Basil knew how James turned her on? He probably knew! Oh, that was embarrassing. "Sure. Okay, thank you. You'll be the first to know how it goes. Talk soon!"

She went back to the hotel and tried resting, but couldn't sit still. Finally, she went to the lobby—it was still too early, but she'd rather wait down there than be pacing her room. She took a comfortable armchair and texted James that she was ready to go anytime.

In spite of Basil's assurances, her stomach was in knots. Watching the people enter and leave the hotel lobby, she was envious of how carefree everyone looked—relaxed and in vacation mode. No one else had an assassination to stop. Where was James? What was taking him so long? Basil or no Basil, they should have met to think things through. She was starting to panic.

James finally appeared, striding toward her from the elevators. Several female travelers watched him cross the lobby toward her. "Ready?" he asked, friendly again.

"I'll ask them to bring the car around." She stood up and smoothed her jumpsuit over her hips.

"Already took care of it." He motioned toward the front of the hotel, where she saw that the car was waiting.

"Let's go, then."

Outside, Amanda reached the valet first, took the key, and went over to the driver's side.

"You're driving?" he asked. He seemed surprised. "Are you sure? It's Italy, you know. They're all crazy here."

She laughed. "I've driven here before, thank you. And besides, I thought you were a pilot! I'll be the driver." She adjusted the seat and mirror to her comfort. "And if anyone messes with us, I'll just blast them away with my energy pulses."

He smiled. "Yeah. Never mess with a Sentinel. You won't know what hit you. Road rage, paranormal style," he joked, strapping on his seat belt.

Amanda laughed again and punched their destination coordinates into the GPS mounted on the dashboard. She confidently pulled into traffic and accelerated.

Save a few random remarks, they drove the rest of the way to the fields in silence. James didn't seem to want to talk, and Amanda didn't feel like forcing it. She tried not to think about him while she focused on the road ahead, enjoying the luxurious car. One day, when she became a successful anesthesiologist, she would drive a car just like this one. Maybe she'd have a couple of them. One for her and one for her husband. She glanced at James, who was gazing out his window, his chin pressed into his palm. He seemed lost in thought.

The GPS told them that they were approaching the tunnel. As soon as they passed through it, she switched the hazard lights on and pulled off the road onto the shoulder, pausing just outside the tunnel's dark mouth. She looked over at the line of trees in the distance, about three hundred yards from the road. That's where they could hide, but it seemed awfully far away from where the action would be.

"Okay, let's recap," James said. "Here's what we know. There are three cars in the official procession—two security, and the politician in the middle car." He looked around. "If he uses the same approach as last time, Komani will arrive on a bicycle and wait by the roadside, like an innocent guy taking a break."

"This sucks," she said. "I looked this tunnel up on Google Maps. But now that I see the terrain, those trees are way off. See, I thought we could hide there, and we can't. But we can't stay in the car, either."

James twisted his head around to examine the entire area. "Agreed. We can't stay here."

"What do you suggest?" She tried not to sound as tense as she felt.

"Let's drive the car into the field behind those trees. Then you and I can find opposing ditches to hide in. When the assassin appears, we ambush him. I'll go first, and if things get dicey, you can surprise him from the other side."

Amanda was not thrilled. Just the thought of lying in a ditch made her feel vulnerable and exposed. But there was also another problem with the plan. "The ditches aren't that deep. I'll stick out like a sore thumb and we'll lose our element of surprise." She looked down at her coral jumpsuit. Given the circumstances, maybe the bikini would have been a better choice after all.

James looked her up and down. "You're right. Okay, new plan. You drive to the tree line and stay in the car, that's even better. Keep an eye out for me. If we lose the daylight, I'll text you when things start happening, so you can come rescue me."

At least he hadn't suggested that she be the bait so he could swoop in and save the day. "Sounds good. And don't worry, I'll hit him with everything I've got." She looked into his eyes. "You'll be safe."

James cracked a grin. "I know. We'll be fine, partner."

Time moved as slowly as molasses while Amanda sat alone in the car with the doors locked and the lights off. She didn't quite reach the tree line, as the grass got significantly wilder and taller, and the light was going. As dusk fell over the fields, she could barely see James lying in the ditch beside the road, the tall grass slowly moving around him in the lazy evening breeze. He was wearing the right colors, that was for sure. He probably didn't even own brightly colored clothes. Regardless, the sun was going to set, and she was going to lose sight of him. The roads weren't lit at all. Once the sun went down, it would all go black.

"Oh I hate this," she whispered, craning her neck to make sure James was still out there. She couldn't help but feel the worry forcing its way back into her chest; she worked hard to will it out.

You are a Sentinel 10. You are the most powerful Sentinel on earth. You can do this.

But the pep talk wasn't working. "Crap," she muttered. "Shit, shit, shit. What if I can't do this?"

I hate this. James is in the military; this makes sense for him. But me . . .

Just then, her phone buzzed. She stared down at James's message on the lit screen: *now.* The moment of truth had come.

James stood up just as a man emerged from the tunnel. She recognized him from Gioia's video. The assassin had come on foot, from *inside the tunnel!* And Moro's convoy would be along any moment. There was not a second to lose. Amanda scrambled out of the car and ran across the field toward James in the gathering darkness. Her heart pumped furiously as she stopped near the ditch, across the road from her target. Not far from her, James and the assassin were facing each other, immobile, staring. Despite their immobility, she could tell that James was already engaged in a psychic struggle to retain control of his mind. She prepared to hit Komani with everything she had.

At this precise moment, a malevolent energy invaded her limbs. Something was messing with her mind—or rather, her motor control. A gnawing sensation tore at her muscles, its malignant control intensifying, gripping her in a strange, numbing vise. She let out a loud, terrified gasp. James turned to her, his face filled with fear. And then she saw them.

Both of them.

There were two figures now, one on each side of the tunnel. Two assassins, not one! The other must have remained hiding inside, just as James had been lying in wait in the ditch.

The malignant control that had seized her limbs clenched her more firmly, and Amanda felt herself walking toward the middle of the road. A vehicle was coming from the other direction. She could see it grow from a dot of light into the headlights of a speeding vehicle. One of the assassins was making her walk toward it . . .

No. She fought against it. That's when something opened in her mind, as if she'd suddenly woke up in some way. She realized she could simply shake off the malevolent energy. The experience was like walking through a sticky spiderweb that clung to her face—it was horrifying, but all she needed to do was wipe it away. Amazed at how easy it was to get rid of the malignant force, Amanda stood there, wondering how it had even been possible for such puny power to control her at all. She had nothing to fear! Her powers were immense.

James suddenly broke free of the assassin's hold and made a belated rescue effort. Although she had already backed away from the road, he grabbed her in a bear hug and pulled her toward him. They narrowly avoided falling into the ditch. Standing tall, James held her against him, their hearts beating, their faces inches away from each other. For a moment, she was unaware of the two assassins only yards away, as she stared into his eyes.

If she had felt a malignant force before, what she felt in that moment between herself and James was anything but. The electric currents that always ran between them shifted and magnified when their bodies pressed against each other. She wanted more than ever to kiss him.

"I'm okay," she whispered, gazing up at him, finding herself falling more deeply into the moment.

He gently set her back down, his gray eyes still locked onto hers. But she knew that they did not have a second to spare. The assassins were still sending malevolent energy, and flashing lights bounced off the walls deep within the tunnel to their right, which meant that the procession was almost here.

"James, I'm fine. We need to move!"

The trailer truck was much closer now and rapidly bearing down on them. While James had been "saving" her, things were quickly escalating. Flashing lights grew brighter in the tunnel, and now the procession was emerging. But instead of a security car, two motorcycles led the convoy, followed by Moro's vehicle, with another car bringing up the rear. Amanda heard a rumbling noise and turned to see the semitruck racing from the other direction, its metal mass fully in view. The assassins had redirected their efforts away from the Sentinels, presumably because this was their only chance to get their targets.

She stepped back, energy surging through her arms, a feeling already familiar to her.

"That one!" she directed James. "Get that one, the one on the left!"

James sent the assassin on the left side of the tunnel a major hit. His psychic energy sizzled through the air; the assassin was thrown against the side of the tunnel and was out immediately. For her part, Amanda targeted Komani with a large power surge, sending him flying upward. He hit the roof of the tunnel and was already unconscious when he hit the ground.

You little bastard, she thought, lifting her chin. *A bonus concussion for you.*

But it was too soon to gloat. The semi had already started to skid sideways down the middle of the road, setting up a clear collision course with the motorcycles. Eerily, the events in the video were happening again, just as Gioia had predicted. The assassins must have seized control of the truck driver's mind before she and James eliminated them, and the events were inescapably set in motion.

She had to act fast. The motorcycles parted around the semitruck as it barreled sideways toward the tunnel while Amanda focused on the car with the dignitary. Arms extended, she felt her pulse energy surging out, deep and powerful, acting on the hunk of metal. James joined her in the effort, and the car's wheels spun as their combined strength held back its forward trajectory. Through the windscreen she could see the driver's hunched figure over the wheel, still accelerating, obeying the psychic assassin's earlier command. She watched in fear as the heavily reinforced car finally stopped just a foot away from the truck, now sprawling across the road. Unable to stop, the security car rammed into them from behind and she could see Moro and his bodyguards knocked unconscious by the impact. Amanda quickly disabled that driver too.

The security guards on the motorcycles returned and began to circle the Sentinels, shouting in Italian, their weapons drawn. Amanda and James knocked them unconscious with mild pulses, and they fell where they rode, their bikes toppling, one landing closer to the tunnel and the other one in the grass just off the ditch. Moro's driver must have come to his senses because he wove around the truck and sped off to safety. The truck driver stayed put, cowering behind the wheel.

In the silence of the evening, Amanda sauntered toward James, hands in her pockets, happy and confident, and perhaps even a little smug. "Woo-hoo! We nailed our first assignment! I can't believe how insanely powerful we are."

"I can't believe how insanely powerful *you* are," he hedged, wiping his brow with the back of his hand.

Amanda wasn't sure he meant this as a compliment, but she didn't care. She was strong and free and dauntless. The rush was exhilarating!

"Wait!" James said. "Look! There's someone else."

She followed the direction of his gaze. A man's shadow moved in the tunnel. At first he froze, then darted out and immediately mounted one of the abandoned motorcycles.

James reacted nearly as fast. "It must be that guy in the gray suit, from the hotel!" He rushed over to the grass and heaved the other motorcycle upright. "Jump on!"

Chapter 10

"What?" A hot panic seized her. "I don't go on these things." Even her newfound powers didn't give her the confidence she needed to ride a motorcycle, and certainly not without a helmet.

James narrowed his eyes at her. "You were right about that guy: he's stalking us, and we have to find out why. Just climb on the front, partner, and hang onto me. I won't let you fall off." As the mystery man screeched away from them, he shouted, "Now!"

"Fine!" she snapped, getting on as instructed, onto his lap but facing him, gripping his waist with her legs. James was right. If they were in for a long, high-speed chase, she wasn't sure she'd have the physical stamina to hold onto him from behind. She wrapped her arms tightly around his neck and buried her face in his chest.

She would never forget that ride. The steady whir of the engine as the evening air whipped against her back, sending wild strands of hair into her face. Fields flashing by as they revved up the road. The warmth of his body against hers. But the sensuality of the moment would dawn on Amanda later, in the comfort of her hotel room. Right now she barely registered any of it. All she could feel was terror as she tried to figure out whether an energy surge could be used as a cushion when falling off a moving vehicle.

When the country roads started curving and winding, James kicked the bike into an even higher gear. Though Amanda couldn't see the man in the gray suit from her vantage point, she could tell they were losing ground. James was grunting from the effort. On one curve, they leaned so far to the left she could feel gravel spitting up onto her flats. She held on even more tightly, which probably wasn't helpful. She had to be severely limiting James's maneuvering ability. After a particularly crazy lane switch, which made Amanda gasp in terror and bury her face in James's chest, he slowed down and pulled over. "We lost him," he announced.

"Thank God that's over!" Amanda cried, hopping off the bike. She swatted her hair out of her face and tried to slow her breathing.

"Yeah. Well, we had to try. There was no way we could match his speed—not with two of us on the bike."

"You should have taken off on your own, James." She nervously smoothed her jumpsuit over her hips.

"No, I couldn't leave you out there alone. What if this was another trap?"

She rolled her eyes. "Come on. Didn't you say I'm the heavyweight champion here?"

James leaned over the handlebars, angling his head at her. "Your stalker dude was getting away, so I had no time to think it through."

He looked like a billboard picture: a rugged guy on a black bike, with the dark fields surrounding him. The last thin line of a purple sunset created the perfect backdrop for him. She broke eye contact. He was so damn attractive, she didn't want him to know how it had felt to ride on top of him.

"Besides," he added, surprising her with a mischievous smirk, "maybe I wanted you with me for my own protection."

"Ha. I tell you this, if I ever see that guy again, I will pulse him so hard he won't even remember his name."

"You and me both. If there is a next time." James sighed.

She wasn't sure how to respond. She knew her moment of hesitation had made it impossible to catch him. Still flushed with mixed emotions, she ran her hands through her tangled hair, smoothing it out. "So . . . should we head back and get the car?"

He grinned, as if he knew something she didn't. "I don't think the Committee cares about that car."

"Oh, they better not! I was thinking of my comfort, I don't want to be riding this beast again." She eyed the motorcycle warily. "But fine, fine, I can manage. Oh, and I'm sure there's all sorts of commotion happening there right now, what with the bodyguards and the truck blocking the road." She stopped as James's grin grew larger. "Oh. You thought of that already, didn't you? Fine. Let's ride back to the hotel, very slowly this time."

"Sure. You chicken," he teased.

She rolled her eyes at him. "Chicken? I just took out a world-famous assassin."

"And I took out his less-famous accomplice. Get on. Let's have the Committee buy us an excellent dinner and a nice bottle of wine."

She stretched, stalling the moment where she'd have to get back on the bike. "That sounds nice." She imagined what it would be like to finally share a romantic dinner with James. Now that this first mission was behind them, they could both relax. Basil was right. Had she understood just how powerful she was, she would have been relaxed in the first place. She started to climb on the bike the way she had before, but then she stopped and corrected herself, clambering onto the bike behind him.

James shook his head and chuckled.

"What?" she asked. "Are you laughing at me again?"

"Not at all. We're a weird team, Amanda, but I'd still fly with you anytime."

"Uh-huh, great. Just no more flying on this thing anymore today, okay?"

Resting her head on his back, her arms around his stomach, she enjoyed this second ride quite a bit more than the first one. As they wove through the evening traffic in the city, she had ample opportunity to feel the contours of his muscles as the bike leaned left and right. He definitely has a six-pack, she thought. Wow.

She caught herself. No way should she be groping this guy just because she had to hold onto him. And it's not like he'd done anything to reciprocate her attraction. Except for what she'd felt between them in the field when he thought he'd saved her from the truck. Was it she the only one who'd felt that? It was so powerful. So intense.

Surely he must have felt something too?

When they got back to their neighborhood, they left the bike in a narrow, cobblestone alley that reeked of trash, and hurried the few blocks to their hotel. Once in the lobby, they slowed down and headed to the restaurant entrance to their left. There were two couples ahead of them, waiting to be shown in. Suddenly, Amanda was hit with the realization that they might be going on an actual date! Her mind raced as the silence became strained.

"Hey, I read something on *MSN News* today," James said, saving the moment. "Naples is drowning in their garbage. Their streets stink so bad, the European Union asked tourists to avoid it. But that's not even the worst part."

Amanda wasn't sure where James with going with this conversation. "Oh? Because that sounds as bad as it can get."

He looked down at her, cracking a grin. "See, the problem started because the city couldn't be bothered to put out enough dumpsters. And when the official dumpsters were full, people started getting really desperate. They're now paying for illegal dumpsters managed by the *camorra*, the Neapolitan mafia. Business is booming."

Clearly, James was going for levity. Amanda lightly tapped his arm in merriment. "You must tell Matt; he'll run down there in the hopes of becoming the next garbage mafioso!"

They both laughed. It took them a few moments to settle again.

Amanda had a different question on her mind, and she felt braver. "You know, maybe garbage isn't the best topic before dinner. That smelly alley was bad enough." She took a deep breath. "Let's talk about something else. Like, this morning, you told me about your former fiancée . . . How long were you guys together?"

James turned to her. Something akin to despair filled his eyes, and he stared at her a moment before saying, "We were together for a long time."

The conversation died right there. They both stared ahead, Amanda thinking desperately of how she could salvage the situation once they got to dinner.

Then James said, "I'm so sorry, Amanda. I just remembered something—I promised to call my parents. They don't know I'm a Sentinel; they think I'm out here helping a friend, and because I won't tell them what's up, they're worried. I'm going to need to take a rain check on dinner. I'm really sorry."

Disappointment squeezed Amanda's heart. She hoped it didn't register on her face.

He added, "And that whole assassination thing. It took a lot out of me. What about you?"

"I feel fine," she said flatly.

"Great. I'll take care of reporting to the Committee when I get upstairs," he hedged, edging away from her. "Good night, Amanda. See you soon." He gave her a quick smile before rushing away.

Standing alone in front of the restaurant, Amanda watched him go. She wanted to be annoyed with him for ditching her like that, but she just felt sad for him. She wasn't going to get anywhere with a guy who was so clearly pining for a lost love. That was okay. It meant he had a heart, and he needed time. James wasn't the only guy in the world. She was done thinking about him romantically. She'd stay upbeat, reveling in her first victory. Besides, things were better this way. She and James were slated to work together for the next ten years, after all, and she knew romantic drama could make things messy and dangerous. Yes, she was done pining after James. He could take all the time he liked.

Instead of heading in to the restaurant, she strolled across the floor to the café. She treated herself to a large, fluffy chocolate pastry and cup of steaming tea to celebrate her first assignment. She was much too awake to retire for the night so she people-watched. A man in a crumpled suit was draining a cup of coffee. A couple was making out in a corner booth. As she stirred the tea bag inside her cup, Amanda inevitably glanced at the stairs James had just taken. She rolled her eyes and told herself to stop thinking about him.

The high she had felt over taking down the assassins was starting to level out. There was almost a sense of routine about it already—kind of like when she had run track and field as a teenager. As soon as she left each obstacle behind, she was ready to focus on the next one.

Was that how James felt about their mission? About her? This was probably as routine to him as his work. Mission accomplished, time to go to sleep. He probably saw no need to celebrate because this moment wasn't as special for him as—

Stop making excuses for his lack of interest in you, she reprimanded herself. And suddenly, she understood. James turned down the invite because he realized she was into him, and he didn't want to give her the wrong impression or lead her on. That was a more plausible explanation. James was not having mood swings; he became friendly again only when he thought Amanda had gotten the message. But she kept bringing up his fiancée. *This has been going on all along, and I was too self-absorbed to see it. Well. I see it now. Took me long enough . . . Whatever. It's fine.*

She frowned and finished her tea. Afterward, she crumpled her napkin, then headed upstairs to get some much-needed rest. Tomorrow she'd go exploring, alone. She would climb the thousand steps to the roof of Duomo, and tower over this historical marvel of a city, like the powerful Sentinel 10 that she was.

Chapter 11

Back home in Boston a couple of days later, Amanda woke up in an excellent mood. It was seven in the morning, and normally she'd be on rounds at this hour. *No more rounds for a month,* she thought to herself. Then she remembered it was a Saturday anyway.

With her cheek comfortably resting on her pillow, she gazed out her floor-to-ceiling bedroom window as sunlight poured in. Now on the twelfth floor, the bustle of the city below didn't penetrate. She no longer had to deal with the student ghetto and her noisy, cannabis-stinking neighbors. In fact, if she had neighbors at all, she couldn't hear them. The soundproofing was state-of-the-art. After Florence, the Committee had put her up in this luxurious two-bedroom condo in downtown Boston. They'd also arranged to have it furnished, and all her things from her old apartment were moved in by the time she came back. The Committee certainly seemed efficient and resourceful, if a bit cavalier when it came to asking for consent. To put it mildly.

She had also been given a $75,000 recruitment bonus, which she immediately spent on the car of her dreams. In so many ways it was like winning the jackpot, and she was looking forward to more victories. When she got the hang of being a Sentinel, she could return to her life as an anesthesiology resident—just with more wealth and more confidence. And a kick-ass weekend hobby of hunting plasmids and psychic assassins.

She smiled and stretched with a little groan, then turned over to her stomach and caressed her pillow absentmindedly. There was only one thing missing, she thought. Someone to share her luck and her future with.

She thought about James. Was there still a chance there? Those brooding gray eyes. His shy smile. Oh, and the motorcycle chase . . . His body was pure muscle, so comfortably strong. Before getting up, she allowed herself to fantasize about what could have been. She pictured him stopping in those fields, on their way back, and confessing his irresistible attraction to her. That particular fantasy ended with him stripping off her jumpsuit and letting her ride him in quite a different way.

Amanda sighed and chased the images away. She had to get up and get going. She was supposed to meet Lydia and James in an hour, for their first local assignment. So she threw back the covers and got ready, spending extra time on her hair and makeup, keeping it summer-light and daytime appropriate. Satisfied with her looks, she adjusted her white summer dress, made sure her bra straps were covered, and stepped out of the condo into her new life.

After a quick stop to pick up fresh bagels, she jumped back into her new car and drove to Cargolan Storage, the Sentinels' local headquarters for the next ten years. It was on the outskirts of town, and for a sizable portion of the trip, she drove alongside a riverside promenade. It curved around a lake, which was as serene and as blue as the Arctic Sea. On the lakeshore, couples sat on the grass, families played Frisbee, and friends barbecued. Amanda opened the window and let in the warm summer breeze. It was amazing how much things had changed in a matter of weeks. Life was so good!

Once parked outside the storage building, she stood beside her brand new black Jaguar and took in the surroundings. Everything was quiet and deserted. The storage facility itself stood next to a stout, off-white office building with a couple of windows and concrete steps leading to a front door. Amanda lingered in the sun for a moment, breathing in the sweet, fresh morning air. Then she grabbed the bagels and headed inside.

She entered a conference room with a plain couch, a table, and five chairs. Lydia was there, sitting on the couch in a denim miniskirt and red flip-flops, reading *Psychiatric Times*.

After greetings and hugs, Amanda took out her laptop and switched on Skype so they could speak with Basil when the time came.

Lydia began chatting excitedly about the fender bender she had been in recently. "So Hank had to drop me off," she explained. "He essentially volunteered to drive me around today while my car gets repaired."

"He brought you *here*?" Amanda asked, knowing full well how odd it was to come to a place like this on a Saturday morning.

Lydia laughed. "I know, right? It wasn't easy to justify coming here, but I pulled it off!"

"What did you tell him?"

"Remember when I was really into ketamine research? Well, now people are using it in psychiatry. So I told him that you, James, and I are working on a research project together to see how ketamine could treat PTSD in soldiers. James is providing the military connection, of course."

Just then they heard the muffled noise of a motorcycle pulling into the parking lot, and minutes later, James Graves entered the conference room. In washed-out jeans and a white polo shirt stretching over his shoulders, he looked as casually hot as ever. He had takeout coffee for everyone.

"Ooh, thanks!" Lydia greedily reached for one of the cups and downed about half of it right away. She'd been a coffee fanatic ever since they started med school.

Amanda took a cup to wash down her bagel.

"How's everyone doing?" James asked.

Amanda hoped she didn't have a dopey look on her face. "Great," she said noncommittally.

"No Matt?" He pulled up a chair and sat down beside her. "I know he's based in San Francisco now, but I thought he was supposed to drop in on our first day."

"No, he got the best assignment ever," Lydia said with a sigh. "He was sent to the Dominican Republic to deal with some kind of a voodoo baron, with some other Sentinels. Oh, I miss the beach. We never got to finish our Panama vacation, Amanda. It's not fair." She sighed again, and joined them at the table.

"I bet once we hear about our assignment, we won't be envious," said Amanda.

Lydia gave her a look. "Doubtful."

Soon Skype came alive with its familiar jingle, and Basil appeared on-screen. He seemed in an excellent mood. "A very lovely Saturday morning to you, dear friends. Thank you for coming."

"Hi, Mr. Blake," Amanda said.

"Basil, dear. Just call me Basil."

"Right," she agreed, but it still didn't feel right to her. After all, the man was over fifty years old.

"What's shakin', bacon?" Lydia asked, and Amanda wondered how she could be so openly irreverent. She shot a glance at James, who, from the look on his face, seemed to be thinking the same thing.

"Well, we have an unprecedented and urgent situation developing. There's been a string of suicides in your area."

"Suicides?" James asked. "How does this affect us?"

"Yes, glad you asked. It seems the victims have all worked for the Committee in one way or another. All three victims went skydiving at separate times. They didn't open their parachutes."

"Victims?" Amanda asked, thinking that was an odd term for a suicide.

"Aha!" Lydia interjected with sudden enthusiasm. "I've just been reading up on the latest news about early suicide prevention. It's right here on page four." She picked up the magazine she'd been reading and showed it to Basil.

Her comment was so out of place that it made James laugh. Amanda just shook her head. She was used to Lydia's fascination with her studies.

Lydia shrugged. "What? He said suicide."

"These were not actual suicides," said Blake.

"What do you mean?" Amanda asked.

"I believe they were staged as suicides to cover up a darker truth. Two of the victims left suicide notes. One called his wife just before jumping. To normal investigators, that would leave no doubt that these deaths were intentional suicides. However . . ."

"These sound like copycat suicides," Lydia said confidently. "If these things get publicized—"

"No," Basil interrupted. "No, they weren't copycat suicides. It's murder, nothing less. But the method is entirely unprecedented. I'm leaning toward hypnosis and mind control, but I'm not ruling out witchcraft. It will be up to you three to figure this out."

Lydia arched a perfect eyebrow, but stayed quiet this time.

"How are we supposed to figure out who did it?" asked James. "I mean, we're not detectives. I'm a pilot; Amanda and Lydia are doctors."

"My dear friends, you are Sentinels now," he reminded them. "From time to time, you will be assigned a more challenging task, such as this one. You are perfectly capable of handling it. As your adviser, I shall be with you every step of the way. I have all the knowledge you need. I will guide you."

No further objections were voiced, so he held a photo up to the screen. "The first victim was Tom Mulberry, one of our top tax lawyers. The second, Martin Campbell." He held up a new photo. "He was an accountant we occasionally employed on special projects. Nothing remarkable about him, although his spouse, whom we also employed as an accountant, is absolutely devastated. He is currently hospitalized in a psychiatric unit."

They all looked at Lydia, sure she would make a remark, but she contained herself. Basil held up a new photograph. "The third victim, Brian Stafford, was on the police force and the Committee payroll. He's the one who phoned his wife minutes before getting into the plane. He told her he wasn't going to open his parachute, and he was going to a wonderful place. He said he wished she could join him, then he hung up. Mrs. Stafford frantically called the skydiving company. When they didn't answer, she drove over there herself. But it was too late. Open your files. There's an article in there."

Amanda picked one of the folders off the table and read out loud: "Stafford jumped from a plane Tuesday morning at about 10:00 AM, just seconds before the crew received a message from dispatchers on the ground, urging them to stop him. According to a revised police report . . . yup . . . On Tuesday, Antonina Stafford, 25, ran in to the skydiving company's building, begging employee Tanya Rivette to stop her husband from jumping. She had just received a call from him, saying he was 'not going to pull the cord and was going someplace wonderful,' police said. Rivette immediately radioed the plane, but Stafford, age 27, had already jumped. Rivette told police that she had seen Stafford before the flight, and that he had seemed normal. She could not be reached for comment."

"That's heartbreaking," Lydia said, and they all had to agree. "I mean, they'd just gotten married and everything."

Amanda placed a caring arm around her friend as Basil made his closing remarks. "So there you have it, my dear Sentinels. I am going to suggest that you speak to the wives only. Let's leave Mr. Campbell's husband out of it for now. I'm told he has a psychotic depression. He doesn't make much sense when he talks."

"Ooh, psychosis! Can I talk to him?" Lydia said, sounding almost giddy at the proposition.

James smiled at her. "I'm not bringing coffee next time, Lydia," he warned her. "I think it makes you a little hyper."

"Come on, I was kidding. Lighten up, everyone, it's the weekend, and our first real assignment together. And it touches on psychiatry. YAY!"

"I'm glad you're so enthusiastic," Basil said. "Before speaking to the families, see what you can find at the crash site. Any vibrations or plasmids or residues. Anything. If there are no residuals, then my first hypothesis is correct and we'll direct our efforts to interviewing potential suspects versed in hypnosis. Fewer than five people in the world are capable of mind control that can force the suicide of an otherwise happy and stable adult. I know going to the crash site might be boring for some of you . . ." he paused, as if searching for the right word.

"I'm happy to do anything, to keep learning," Amanda chipped in.

James nodded in agreement. "Yes, me too. I'll go with you."

"Good, very good. At this stage, no matter your level, you need experience. This is the real training: you learn on the job. For a Sentinel 9 or 10, waiting for an appropriate assignment may take months."

"We're happy to do what we can," Amanda reiterated. Then they said goodbye to Basil, and he ended the call.

Lydia rolled up her clinical journal and stuck it inside her straw tote. Then she brushed her gorgeous hair to one side. "Okay, guys," she announced. "I know we have work to do, but Hank wants us to talk over breakfast. He's coming to pick me up. I'm sorry, but it's so important. We're trying to figure things out between us. Oh, and can both of you stick around to say hi? Please? Otherwise, he'll think I'm having an affair."

Chapter 12

After obliging Lydia and helping with her cover story, Amanda and James drove together to investigate the site of the most recently crashed skydiver, in a field not far from a park outside the city. Beeping her car locked, Amanda walked across the parking lot to join James at the edge of the grass.

"Hey." She smiled at him, getting a smile and a nod in return. They began walking to the tree line some way ahead. James was being his usual quiet self. "I bet you've jumped out of a plane before," she said, trying to engage him.

He smiled warmly at her. "I may have jumped out of a plane or two in my life, sure."

"Was it scary?" She almost immediately regretted asking this question. Of course he wasn't going to admit if he'd been scared. Like she wasn't going to admit that his thrill-seeking daredevil side was kind of sexy.

He winced. "I don't think that's the word I'd use. More like exhilarating. Life-affirming. It's like a free fall. Except, then you open your parachute."

Amanda shuddered. "It must have been terrifying, falling out into nothing like that. The ground getting closer. I can't even imagine it."

He shook his head. "Not me, either. But my guess is that the victims weren't fully aware. You know, with the dark force still clouding their thoughts."

"Let's hope so," she said, thinking how incredibly odd everything in her life had become that she would be thankful for the presence of a dark force.

As they approached the place where the skydiver had fatally crashed, Amanda could definitely feel something. A residual she hadn't encountered before. A dark one.

"Do you feel that?" James asked her.

"It's like one of the residuals we trained with," she said, relieved that he felt it too.

"But not even close," he replied.

"You're right," she agreed. "This is very diffuse, yet sticky. It's hovering all over the site. Basil was wrong. This wasn't mind control; the residual is indicative of some sort of dark magic."

"It's giving off a weird vibe."

"Yes. It feels like sickness and morbidity. Almost like rotting flesh. Not enough of it to form a plasmid, though."

James zapped it as easily as snapping his fingers, and they were about to walk away when the residual suddenly gathered all around him again. She could see it moving, a clinging fog. James stopped in his tracks and gasped a little. Seeing his eyes glaze over, Amanda grabbed his hand. He didn't react. Instead he stared straight ahead with a strange, almost unnatural expression. As much as she didn't want to make him feel like he couldn't handle himself, this could only go so far! She prepared to zap the residue for him.

"I'm all right, Amanda, I'm handling it . . . It's interesting . . ." It was his normal voice, but he was still staring straight ahead, as if paralyzed. In the next moment, he came back to life, snapping out of the trance. His arm movements became precise and controlled. The energy pulse leaving his fingertips was devastating with the full force of a Sentinel 9, and the residue instantly disappeared, this time for good.

"Did you see it?" he asked, turning toward her.

"Oh yes, disgusting little fog, very clingy. Definitely psychic residue, powerful and atypical. What did you see?"

"I saw some faces in it. Weird ones. And there was some time distortion. It was all very vague. I think it's more attracted to men. I really can't say more."

"Me neither. Actually, I got no images at all. I just felt there was this gooey, sick quality to it. Like cancer or gangrene."

"Just like a doctor," he said with a smile. Oh, that smile. She could get lost in that smile for days. But she knew he wasn't smiling for her; James just had a naturally charming personality. When he wasn't busy running away. He reached for his phone. "Let's report it to Basil." But halfway to his pocket, his hand froze midair as he stared to their left. He grabbed her elbow. "Look! It's that guy from Florence."

She whipped her head around and followed the direction of his pointing hand. "Huh." The man in the gray suit with the bleached blond hair was standing at the edge of the parking lot, about eighty yards to their left. He had followed them here. Again! But how? And why did he keep showing himself? It almost seemed like this was a game to him. But to what end?

Apparently, it was absolutely no game to James. As determined as ever to catch him, he immediately took off running. Showing surprising agility, the unknown stalker raced away from him across the parking lot.

"Hey! Hey man, why are you following us?" James shouted.

Completely ignoring him, the mystery man jumped into a gray Mercedes and drove away. James slowed down and was repeating the license plate when Amanda reached him.

"He's pretty fast," she observed, trying to de-dramatize the situation. With the kind of power she felt in herself after their run-in with the assassins in Florence, she was finding it hard to be concerned or afraid. But she could see the frustration on James's face.

James finished typing the plate number into his phone. "Yeah. I run every morning, but this guy is faster. I like a challenge, but I really don't like him." He crossed his arms. "Back in Florence, I thought maybe he was there to assist us in some way. But a good guy doesn't creep around after people without answering questions. And the Committee didn't know anything about him. I asked when I filed our report."

Amanda patted him on the shoulder. "We'll catch him next time. He's playing with the Sentinels, and soon he'll learn that's like playing with fire."

Touching his shoulder made her remember their motorcycle ride, and she wished they could do it again. Like, now. Or go to brunch first. But James seemed concerned only with reporting back to Basil.

For some reason, Basil didn't seem worried about their stalker. When they went back into the car and called him on James's cell phone, he said dismissively, "We'll deal with that later." On the other hand, he showed a keen interest in James's experience with the residue.

"Black magic would be my guess," he said, after listening to James's description of the distorted faces closing in all around him. "Very atypical. I know of no instance where black magic was used to push to suicide in such a precise way. Yet the quality of the residue seems fairly conclusive. I will make some inquiries. Good job."

After James hung up, he immediately called another number.

"Who are you calling now?" Amanda asked.

"An army friend. He's a police officer now." He waved Amanda quiet. "Hey man," he said into the phone, then gave his friend the plate information from their stalker's car. He nodded, then said, "Alain Proctor. Yes, copy on the address. Suite three-twenty. Got it."

Alain Proctor. The name wasn't familiar, but the sound of it lingered, like Proctor's presence had in the shadows of Prague. It intrigued her. And despite the fact he'd clearly been following them around the world, she remained curious. Not afraid.

She watched James plug the address into his Maps app. "Wait, we can't go now," she remembered. "I have to meet Lydia soon, so we can interrogate the widows."

James raised an eyebrow. "That's okay. You can just drop me off, and I can look into this without you. Not everything is paranormal and needs the powers of a Sentinel 10. Some things are just, well, abnormal. Like this guy following us around. Seems abnormal."

"I can handle abnormal."

"But I could handle this without you. I'm military, remember? Purple Heart?"

"No. Absolutely not," Amanda insisted. "That guy is after us, and I want to know why."

"I can find out and tell you why."

She paused. Why did it matter to her so much that she be there when this Alain Proctor was confronted? She wasn't totally sure except . . . "I don't want you to scare him off."

A tense moment passed between them as they stared sternly at one another. A Sentinel standoff.

James finally relented. "Fine. We'll go together," he said with a sigh. "When you're done with all your interviews."

"Sounds like a plan." Amanda looked down at her watch. "Wow, I really have to hurry. We're supposed to meet with Mrs. Stafford in forty minutes."

"The widow," he said with a surprisingly deep sigh.

She considered asking him about what his sigh meant, but she realized now was not the time. She was going to be late, and she hated being late. "I'll drop you off back at Cargolan Storage before I go pick up Lydia."

They drove back in their usual silence until, a few blocks from the facility, James tapped on the dashboard. "You know what? You can just drop me here, if you don't mind."

Amanda was confused. There was nothing around them except a cemetery. She pulled over. "Are you sure? I mean—"

He waved her off as he jumped out of the car. "I need to get some exercise and clear my head a little. I'll meet up with my cop friend for lunch, see if I can find out more about this Alain Proctor. See you later," he said, then slammed the car door shut and darted away.

"Okay, see you later?" she said to the empty air.

She drummed her fingers on the steering wheel as she watched James disappear down the path leading into the cemetery. Something about his behavior was nagging away at her. She waited another minute. Then she turned off the engine, got out, and followed him, maintaining a safe distance. For added stealth she projected a transparent, electric shield around herself, as they'd been taught in training, so that her footfalls would be muffled.

After a few minutes of walking she spotted him hunched over a gravestone about twenty feet away. She ducked behind a mausoleum and watched him. Then slowly, moving from one tombstone to the other, she came closer.

He stroked the top of the headstone. "It doesn't seem to be getting much easier for me, Charlene. They say time heals all wounds, but . . ."

Amanda held her breath, straining to hear.

"Why wasn't I there to save you, Charlene? I would have lost my career, but I would have saved you."

His face folded into a painful grimace. Clearly, this moment was a very private one. Amanda wondered if she should reveal her presence, but before she could decide, James swiped at his eyes with his sleeve and walked away.

When James was out of sight, Amanda walked over to the stone. A heart-shaped gold frame at the top showed the face of a stunning brunette woman. A girl, really. She could not have been more than twenty years old. Glancing down at the dates on the marker, Amanda confirmed that the girl, Charlene Brennan, had died three years ago, just days after her twenty-first birthday.

It stabbed at Amanda's heart that someone so young and so happy and so full of life could be taken so soon. She shuddered as she came to a horrifying realization: Charlene must have been James's fiancée.

Chapter 13

Apparently, not all Sentinels were treated equally. While Lydia and Amanda each made two thousand dollars per weekend task, Lydia's recruitment bonus was only twenty thousand dollars, and she hadn't been moved to a luxurious condo. Instead, she still lived in the one-bedroom apartment she'd shared with Hank before the trouble between them ensued. They had one of three apartments in a brick, bungalow-style house. Hank was staying with a friend until things worked out between them. Or at least, Amanda hoped he was still living away. She was happier to see Lydia when he wasn't around.

As Amanda drove through various neighborhoods on her way to Lydia's, her thoughts turned back to James and Charlene. She understood his distance now, his hesitancy to get into a relationship. He was not emotionally available. She wondered how Charlene had died, and she wished more than anything that she could discuss her revelation with Lydia. But she knew they needed to focus. Talking with widows was a delicate task.

Lydia was waiting on the porch when Amanda pulled into her driveway, still wearing the miniskirt with flip-flops.

"You didn't change? Do you really think that's the right outfit to wear right now, all things considered?" she asked when Lydia climbed in.

Lydia shrugged. "You're gonna use mind control anyway, right? Basil said that you're powerful enough to make them see whatever they think a reporter should look like. I mean, I could be wearing a tutu over a bikini and she'd still see a woman in a pantsuit with a microphone, if that's how she thinks of reporters." She flipped down her visor to look in the mirror and applied cherry-red lip gloss. Seeming satisfied with her effort, she tucked the visor back up and looked at Amanda. "I can't imagine how I'd feel if something this awful happened to Hank. I mean, just months after getting married— What?"

Amanda realized she'd been giving her friend a sharp look and tried to soften her expression. After Hank cheated on Lydia, she could have easily imagined the rat jumping to his death without a parachute. Then Lydia could find a man worthy of her. But she checked herself; she didn't really wish Hank dead, just gone. "I just can't imagine you marrying Hank," she admitted. "After what he did."

"Well, maybe one day you'll fall madly in love, and you'll finally understand how I feel."

Amanda rolled her eyes at the old argument. She opened her mouth to reply, then decided against it. This was like one of those arguments that came up again and again between people who have been married forever. An argument that persists but never gets resolved. Really, what was the use?

Instead of responding, she pulled away from the curb and turned her attention to the road. She would use this time to think about what the best questions to ask Mrs. Stafford might be, and how to ask them. She was training to be an anesthesiologist, not a detective. Most of the time her patients were asleep. What did she know about subtle interrogation techniques?

Of course, none of that mattered. She could use mind control, ask whatever questions she wanted, and she and Lydia would get all the answers they needed. A small thrill surged through her. Today would be her first chance to test out this ability in the field. She concentrated on accessing that part of her mind as she turned down another road.

Unlike Amanda's new digs in bustling downtown Boston, the Stafford home was in a quiet, tree-lined neighborhood not unlike Lydia's. Amanda could tell by the look in Lydia's eyes that she was ruminating over how devastated she'd be if something bad happened to Hank. She must really love him, she admitted to herself. At least for the time being, she'd stop encouraging Lydia to leave him.

The Stafford residence was a small, white-shingled house with black shutters. It looked like a modern storybook cottage. A place where a couple had planned to start a family and live happily ever after. The thought of that pulled at Amanda's heart. One day your life is normal and everything is ahead of you. The next, your husband loses control of his mind, and it's all gone. She pulled into the driveway and turned off the car.

"Ready?"

Lydia nodded.

They walked up a charming flagstone path that led to a red front door, the click of Amanda's stylish heels at odds with the thwack of Lydia's flip-flops.

A petite brunette wearing an oversize button-down shirt and leggings answered the door. Amanda recognized Mrs. Stafford's face from the photos in the file.

"Hello," Amanda said. "My name is Rona Ellerson, and this is Jane Petrowski, my associate. We're reporters with the *Boston Globe*. We were hoping we could speak to you for a few minutes? Ask you a few questions about . . ."

She trailed off. While her powers of mind control would ensure that Mrs. Stafford wouldn't see through her ruse and wouldn't be thrown off by Lydia's attire, she felt terrible standing in front of this gutted woman, lying to her. But what was she supposed to do? Tell her, *My friend and I are part of an ancient force of paranormal cleaners, and we're here to get to the source of what took over your husband's mind and propelled him out of that plane*—uh, no.

Instead, she coated the widow's mind with her own, encouraging her to believe what she'd just heard. The widow would perceive them however she expected two professional reporters to look and behave. This process of blocking her perceptions required a degree of focus. It wasn't easy. Compared to sending out energy pulses, it was sweat-breaking work. Amanda felt like she had a pendulum on her outstretched hand that she had to constantly watch and keep in perfect balance. She glanced at Lydia. She'd rather her friend took the lead on this discussion.

"We are so sorry for your loss," Lydia chimed in. "We just want our readers to know the truth of what happened to your husband. I know you don't really believe he wanted to die. It's so hard to believe such a thing."

Mrs. Stafford gave them a weak smile. "You read the police report, didn't you? Yeah. That's what I told them. We were so happy . . . Won't you come in?" She looked lost, her reddened eyes eloquently expressing the extent of her grief. Amanda nodded gratefully, and they followed her inside.

"Have a seat," she said, gesturing to the living room. "Can I get you anything?"

"No, thank you," Amanda said. They took a seat on the sofa and Mrs. Stafford took a chair opposite.

"So, Mrs. Stafford," Lydia began.

"Call me Antonina." The woman looked clenched, fighting hard to hold back tears. She held the sleeve of the shirt to her face, breathing in the cuff. "Sorry. This is all so . . ." She buried her face in the sleeve again and this seemed to calm her. She looked back at them, tears in her eyes. "This was his. It still smells like him. Just a little."

"Of course," Amanda replied, nodding sympathetically.

"Take all the time you need," Lydia added. "We just want to know if anything unusual happened around the time of his . . . passing. Like, in the days leading up to the incident."

Antonina took a shuddering breath. "Well, I'm not sure where to start. They said he must have been depressed. He'd lost some weight lately. Had headaches and trouble sleeping." She pulled at a loose thread at the end of her sleeve. "We also started getting weird phone calls. Here at the house. I suspected he was having an affair, even though it seemed pretty brazen for a lover to call him at home, you know?"

Amanda nodded. Lydia looked away.

"Anyway, I picked up the other line, one time, to listen in. But there wasn't a woman's voice on the other end. I only heard a shrill, screeching sound. Like a fax."

"That must have been scary," Lydia suggested.

Amanda was impressed with the kindness and understanding Lydia showed in her tone and body language. She could see Antonina begin to relax into the questioning.

"I just thought it strange at the time. Now, thinking back . . . You can't imagine," the young widow whispered, a faraway look in her eyes. "I keep thinking I should have known something was wrong. That I should have done something," she added in a hoarse, low whisper.

"It's a horrible tragedy," Lydia said, leaning forward. "But we need to know those details, to try and understand how this happened. Maybe someone was trying to scare him? When did the phone calls start?"

"About two weeks ago." She tugged harder on the stray thread until it broke off. "But that's not all."

"Oh? What else?" Amanda asked, getting better at the balancing act. Maintaining her control over Antonina's mind was like trying to keep a pendulum as still as possible.

"Well, about the time of the first phone call, a black dog started coming around here. I know it's weird to notice that, but it wasn't a normal dog. One time it was howling under our windows at night. I saw it looking into our house, right through this window," she said, pointing at the window behind them. "I was waiting for Brian to come home, and it came right up to the glass. I say it came over, but it kind of just . . . appeared. It had the most terrifying eyes. They looked human. With white around the irises, you know? It didn't make any noise, it was just staring at me. Then last weekend, I heard Brian calling for me from the yard," she said, and started to break up. "Excuse me."

Lydia jumped up from her seat, grabbed a box of Kleenex off the coffee table, and handed one to the sobbing woman. "Whenever you're ready," she said. "Can I get you a drink of water or something?"

The woman shook her head then blew her nose. Her eyes downcast, she took a few steadying breaths. "He was calling for me from the yard, so I went to look for him. But he wasn't there. It wasn't him. I heard his voice, but it wasn't him. It was late. I went outside to see what was up, and he appeared to be standing by the fence. He kept repeating, 'Come over!' in the same exact tone. It was so strange. Eerie. Like he was stuck on repeat."

"That must have been so scary," Lydia said.

Antonina nodded. "Yeah. I asked him if he was hurt, but he just jerked his arm, like he was trying to wave, and repeated, 'Come over!' I moved a bit, but I was scared to get close."

"Oh." Amanda wondered whose mind control the man had been under.

"You have a question?" The widow asked.

"No, please continue."

"I kind of inched closer, so I could see his face more clearly. But that face . . . it looked like my husband's face, in a way, but it was more like a picture of him. One-dimensional. It was just . . . wrong. That thing in front of me, it wasn't Brian."

Amanda listened with raptured attention. The lady took a shaky sip of water. "Then it crouched on the ground, on all fours, like an animal. I was shaking and crying. I bent down to his level, asking him what was wrong. And that's when . . ." She trailed off.

Amanda and Lydia exchanged glances, not knowing what to say.

Antonina stared at them, as if her widened eyes could convey the horror she'd been through. "What was there . . . What was there instead . . ." She struggled to speak.

"What?" Amanda asked, gently using mind control to draw the information out of the poor broken woman and feeling terrible for every ounce of pain she was causing.

Antonina swallowed hard and shook her head. "It wasn't him. It was this huge black dog, with those strange, unnatural eyes. Human eyes. But that's not the worst of it."

"What?" Amanda and Lydia asked in unison.

"I ran back into the house, and I found Brian in the basement. He'd fallen asleep watching TV." The widow shook her head. "And yes, I know what you're thinking. That maybe drugs were involved here. But I don't do drugs."

Amanda shuddered. This was quite unsettling. Of course, she had no reason to be afraid. All things supernatural now ran in fear of her. Not the other way around. She needed to remember that. She cleared her throat. "I see. Can I ask you, how was your husband acting on the morning of . . . on that Tuesday morning?"

"He seemed fine. He was smiling at me. He was absolutely fine. Maybe a little distracted, but nothing unusual. He ate breakfast with me and then headed out. He never mentioned any parachute jumping. Ever. Absolutely never. I don't know how I missed the signs . . ."

Amanda could tell that Antonina was becoming fatigued. Her shoulders slumped. Even the dark circles under her eyes seemed to grow darker.

"It's not your fault," Lydia said quietly.

Antonia's voice thinned. "I'm sorry, I haven't slept for days. I can't think of anything else to add. That's all I remember."

"Of course. I think we have what we need." Amanda glanced at Lydia, and they hurried to the door. Amanda felt terrible. It was frustrating that despite her great powers, she was powerless to truly help this woman.

"Thank you for your time, Antonina," Amanda said as they turned to say goodbye.

"Once again, we are so sorry for your loss. Let us know if there's anything we can do," Lydia added.

"Thank you. So when will the story run?"

"Story?" Lydia asked. Her eyes widened, but she quickly caught herself. "Oh yes, of course. Soon. That's up to our editor."

"We'll be sure to keep you posted." On impulse, Amanda did her best to block the dark unrest from Antonina's mind. The widow smiled softly at them, and Amanda felt hopeful that maybe she had managed to give the woman a tiny measure of relief from her inner torment.

"Strange phone calls and shape-shifting black dogs." Lydia sighed as they headed back to the car. "It's so weird. Basil thinks it's black magic?"

"Yup," Amanda replied.

"So sad, her wearing his shirt," Lydia said.

Amanda nodded. Suddenly she was confronted with a memory of herself as a young girl after her parents were killed. Wrapped in her father's shirt, her head on her mother's pillow, breathing in what scent of them still remained in the fabric. Always trying to feel close to them, and never getting there.

She got a whiff of something unpleasant, something dark. A residue. She wrinkled her nose. "Do you feel it? It's still here. It's like a gooey, sickening fog, all over the house."

"Sort of," said Lydia. "For me, I just have an uncomfortable feeling in my gut."

"Let me take care of it." She brought her energy through her, zapping the residue and distress away, hoping to give Antonina Stafford her first night of peaceful sleep since her husband's death.

"That black dog terrifies me," said Lydia. "I'm afraid of dogs as it is, but a powerful supernatural one? I'm going to ask Basil to take me off this case."

"Really?" Amanda shot Lydia a look of concern, remembering their training and the Committee's intense warning about asking to be removed for emergencies only. She was just about to say something when Lydia seemed to read her mind.

"Hey, I'm only a Sentinel 4. It's different for us. I asked Basil about refusing cases, and he said it would be fine under circumstances like these. You don't mind, do you, Mandy?" Her lips curled into a sly smile. "That will give you more alone time with James."

Amanda smirked. "Or give you more alone time with Hank?"

"Yeah, that too," Lydia sighed, looking off into the distance. "Things are still not quite there between us. I think we're both working at it, but I don't know. It's just not the same."

Amanda understood. "It might not ever be the same. But who knows, it might get better," she ventured. It was hard to know what to say.

Chapter 14

Back at home, Amanda Skyped Basil to report what they had learned.

"So we still have no idea who the perpetrator is," she told him. "Is there any way to follow the residue somehow? We've zapped it away, of course. But is there another path?"

"No, unfortunately it doesn't work that way."

Amanda thought a little. "I guess we'll just have to talk to the other widow and see where that leads us," she surmised.

"That won't be possible." Basil shook his head. "She and her daughter left for England for a month. We just found out. It was a last-minute arrangement. Her daughter is quite depressed, so Mrs. Mulberry is trying to do what she can."

"Then we should interview the last survivor." Amanda straightened in her chair. "Whether Mr. Khananian is making sense or not, we should talk to him. I'm sure all the loved ones had scary experiences leading up to their losses, but he's the only one who ended up in the psych ward."

Basil paused in thought before he spoke. "Okay, I'll allow it," he said. "But just you this time. Not Lydia or James."

"Oh. I know that Lydia said she didn't want to work this case anymore, but why not James?"

"I spoke with James. I'm reassigning them both tomorrow. There's a small but important cleaning at a warehouse tomorrow, and I asked him to take Lydia to that. I don't know if you've noticed, but she's feeling left out. She can't compete with either you or James, and she's losing interest in being a Sentinel. We have to be more supportive." Basil's gaze refocused on Amanda. "Also, you're a doctor, and Mr. Khananian is in a hospital. You'll fit right in. He speaks to a lot of doctors."

Amanda waited until evening before dressing in her scrubs and heading to the hospital to visit Mr. Khananian, the partner of the second victim,

Martin Campbell. She rationalized that by going late, there'd be less chance of running into someone she knew. She made it to the elevator and was relieved when the doors slid closed. "One step down," she murmured. How many left to go?

The doors opened onto the sixth floor and she walked down to the unit, which had restricted access and required a special pass. "But nothing's off-limits to a Sentinel 10," Amanda told herself, forcing a confidence she barely felt. She felt like such an imposter. She had to remind herself that although she might not have much Sentinel experience, at least she was an actual anesthesiology resident. She summoned her courage and pushed the buzzer to alert the nursing station to her presence. She was buzzed in immediately.

"Hi! I'm an anesthesiology resident, here to do an ECT consult on Davit Khananian," she said with a smile, her confidence returning. "Can I see his chart?"

The attendant nodded and thumbed through some files in a Lucite holder attached to the wall over his desk. He handed her a clipboard without asking any questions.

She thanked him and read through the notes as she went to find Mr. Khananian's room. She learned he'd been admitted the day after his partner's suicide, brought in by the police, who had found him cowering behind a bus stop near his house. He had apparently been rambling about a black dog that was after him. According to the notes, it appeared he had not stopped talking about the dog since. She paused in the hallway to read the recent entries more closely.

The patient hallucinated again last night. Same black dog with human eyes. Persecutory delusions about lawyers. Believes the dog killed his partner. Has delusional guilt. No SI, no HI. Eats very little. His sleep is frequently interrupted by the hallucinations.

No response to Ola. Keeping venlafaxine. Patient was reported to be crouching on the floor, howling at the window last night. Instances of bizarre and disorganized behavior were also noted during the day, e.g. walking on tiptoes in the hallway around something invisible, then running down the hall, screaming.

Impression and Plan: Major depression with psychotic features, including delusions of guilt, persecutory delusions, and prominent visual and auditory hallucinations. Failed two trials of antipsychotics. Differential diagnosis includes onset of schizophrenia.

Yup, Amanda thought. *He's not doing well at all.*

She walked down the hall, passing by the TV lounge. It looked fairly normal, almost cozy, without the offensive smells found on the other medical floors. Unoriginal poster prints hung on the walls. One was of a fish leaping out of the water. Another depicted a posy of flowers. *Must be therapeutic in some way.* Khananian's room was at the end of the hallway, the door ajar. Almost unconsciously, her steps slowed.

The patient was sitting on his bed, looking out the window. He turned around when she knocked.

"Mr. Khananian? I'm here to do an evaluation for your next treatment. I need to ask you a few questions."

"Anesthesia?" he asked, eyeing her badge as she approached. "Yes. Please put me out. Just put me out. I can't take this anymore." Normally he might have been a handsome man, dark-haired with large brown eyes, but his face was drawn and his eyes were glassy with fear.

Amanda remembered to switch gears. She wasn't actually here to do a consult. "What happened, Mr. Khananian? Why are you here?"

"They killed him," he said, his expression flat. "Now they won't leave me alone. It will come again tonight. It comes for me every night. I don't know why they killed him. Martin never hurt anyone."

"Who killed him?"

"It had to be the lawyers. They came over the day before the dog showed up. The young man gave him a card. I walked in on them, and—"

He was rambling. She tried to refocus him. "Okay, hold on, what were these lawyers doing?"

"Who?" He stood up, and she realized he was a short, stocky man.

"The lawyers, Mr. Khananian, the lawyers."

He stared at her blankly, no thought registering in his features. She gave him time to respond, but he merely changed the direction of his gaze, looking down at his shoes. After another few seconds, she asked, "What was on the card?"

He lifted his eyes to her again, blinked, and sighed, then began moving toward her slowly, tears in his eyes. "There was something black on it," he whispered. "And when Martin touched it, it stung him. There was a little streak of black, like a greasy spot, on the card. I picked it up afterwards. It was hard to wash it off my hands."

Great, they were getting somewhere. Finally!

"Did they give you their names, Mr. Khananian?" When he shook his head, she said, "No? What did they look like?"

"The guy looked Italian. He was so young. Early twenties. He was tall and slim. He was with a girl, a blonde." He looked up at Amanda. "But she didn't look like you. She looked like him. They could have been twins."

"And what else do you remember about the card?"

"There was a W and C, in gold letters on the back." He paused, his eyes narrowing. "Why do you ask?"

"I'm just trying to understand what happened." Seeing that he'd gotten suspicious, she plunged ahead with the pretense of the consult. "Okay, Mr. Khananian. Let's have you sit back down on the bed so I can examine your neck."

"My neck," he muttered. "Why?"

"Because your next treatment requires general anesthesia. We put you to sleep, like for a surgery. I have to make sure we know what your airways are like."

His eyes glazed over. "Yes," he said. "I need anesthesia. That's what they do to dogs. It's the right thing to do." He looked placid and indifferent again. She didn't argue. He came back to sit on his bed, his hands dangling over his knees. Amanda was about to ask him to open his mouth, so she could see the back of his throat and assign him a Mallampati score. She'd make a realistic entry into the medical portion of the psychiatric chart, as if this were a real consult, with an unrecognizable signature. But just as she bent down to look, he thrust his neck forward and lunged at her hand, his jaws wide open to bite. On pure reflex, Amanda jerked back and used an energy surge to block his face. Her control was still developing and the surge pushed him head over heels across the bed. He landed on all fours near the wall, under the window.

Amanda stared at him. That was a close call!

Khananian was getting up, seemingly unharmed, so she hurried out of the room in a fast walk. One glance over her shoulder told her that the deranged man was coming after her. He began screaming, "Put me down! The dog wants you to put me down!"

Amanda took off running toward the nursing station. The nurses were already out, alerted by the commotion.

"He just tried to bite me!" she explained.

The closest nurse, a woman in her sixties, with graying hair and blue eyes behind little glasses, clicked her tongue in dismay. "Dear me, he's never been violent before," she said, almost apologetically, as she began dialing the phone. "Dr. Owoeye? Sorry to disturb you, this is Kimmy. I'm calling because Davit Khananian just tried to bite someone. Yes, she's okay, but . . ."

Amanda didn't want to stick around in case the resident on call started to ask questions. Walking away, she imagined the next chart entry: "Patient attempted to bite the anesthesia resident. Resident unable to finish ECT consult." All in all, just a normal day on inpatient psychiatry. Nothing to it.

Once outside, Amanda got out her phone to call Basil, but she stopped in her tracks at the incoming text. It was from James. Her heart fluttered a little at seeing his name.

We can say hi to Gray Suit on Thursday, after the cleanup. See you then.

Disappointment flashed through her. Why couldn't he have texted something like, "Hey, what are you doing tonight? Let's grab a coffee together"? Why did it always have to be business?

Amanda sighed and tilted her head back, looking at the sky. James wasn't interested in her. He was still in love with Charlene. She could not compete with a dead woman, no matter how hard she tried.

She headed home. She couldn't face calling Basil to rehash the disturbing events in the psych ward. She'd see him tomorrow anyway. Instead, she made herself an extra-large vanilla matcha tea, which she sipped while aimlessly flipping through TV channels. With her feet up on the coffee table, she put Khananian's disturbing behavior out of her mind and mulled over her baffling lack of success with men—just like she had done on so many other nights.

She was almost dozing off when the Skype tone sounded, startling her. She accepted the call and found an uncharacteristically unsettled Basil on the other end.

"Is anyone else with you?" he asked, after they'd said their hellos.

"No, I'm alone." Judging by the pillows behind him, he was in bed. She checked the time. It was only 10:00 PM in Boston. "Where are you?" she asked him.

"That's not important. Listen," he said.

She waited. When he didn't speak, she said, "Basil, what's going on?"

"I had a horrible dream," he finally said. "You were calling me for help. But it wasn't you."

"Huh? Me? Not me? *What*? Basil, what are you talking about?"

"I don't really want to get into it because it's my worst nightmare. Just promise me you'll be careful, okay? I don't want to speak in front of the others, and I don't want to worry you, but I just can't . . . I can't lose another one."

"Can't lose another one? What does that mean? Basil?" she called, but the screen had already gone dark.

Amanda nervously scratched at her cheek. Was Basil drunk or something? What was she supposed to think? *Jesus.* All the men in her life were insufferable. She gave up on guessing and worrying, and went to bed.

Chapter 15

The following morning, Amanda arrived at the storage facility a full fifteen minutes before the designated meeting time of eleven. She'd woken up unnerved, with Mr. Khananian on her mind. So, she'd treated herself to a hot stone massage to alleviate some of the stress of the previous day, but she still felt unbalanced. Davit's behavior had unhinged her. For a moment he really seemed to believe that he was the dog. The worst part of his delusion, though, was that it might not be a delusion at all. In this new reality, almost anything was possible. Basil Blake seemed to understand this truth as well. Otherwise, he wouldn't have bothered calling her about his nightmares. She needed to ask him what the hell he meant by his warning.

As she was getting settled into her seat at the conference table, she heard a rustling at the entrance and what sounded like giggling. She looked up to find James and Lydia coming in, grinning like idiots. The hair rose on the back of her neck. There was something different between them. She'd never seen them so, well, friendly with each other.

When they saw her, they both started talking a mile a minute about the plasmid cleaning they'd just come from.

"You were so late," James taunted Lydia playfully.

She punched his arm. "What? Me? No, I'm never late." They broke out laughing.

Amanda felt like she was in an alternate universe. James was actually acting human.

"You know, I'm so glad I've met you girls," James said, gazing into Lydia's eyes. "The last three years have been rough on me."

A shadow passed over Lydia's face, then she flashed him a smile. "Really? I'm so glad! And I think it's possible you were depressed, you know what I mean?"

Amanda felt like her face was on fire. She was the third wheel here, no question about it. She composed herself enough to say, "Wow, I see you guys totally bonded. That's nice!"

The brown-haired pair turned to her.

"Hi, Amanda," James said. "You're included in that, of course. I think we're an awesome team. The three of us."

Lydia walked over and gave her a hug, with a quick whisper to her ear, "Wait till I tell you what I found out."

Mildly curious now, though still irritated, Amanda busied herself with pretending to look for something in her hobo bag. "Anyway," she mumbled, "I'm glad you two had such a good time. But we have some pretty serious business we still need to look into."

"With the suicides? Did you find out something?" James reverted back to his usual serious self.

"Yes, and there seems to be a new twist. Let me get Basil on Skype." They all gathered around the monitor.

When Basil joined them on the screen Amanda told everyone what Khananian had said about the visit from the two so-called lawyers who'd given Martin Campbell the strange card with gold lettering.

Basil nodded. "We're lucky Mr. Khananian saw that card. It tells us a lot."

"Like what?" James asked.

Basil leaned back in his chair, as if preparing for a long explanation. "The card is a *token*, an object that contains a type of black magic passed on to the target by touch. The black smear on the card was probably the conjurer's blood, mixed with other ingredients. The mixture clearly has a mind-control component to it that works something like a computer program. When Martin touched it, that program was essentially uploaded to his brain. Khananian's information tells us that this particular program—the skydiving suicides—also involves an activator. In this case, the activator was a *familiar*—the black dog. When the subject is haunted by the familiar, the program is immediately set into motion. Like a trigger, if you will. Suffice it to say, this was a very, very complicated piece of black magic. Writing a spell like this one is very much like writing a symphony."

"What do the W and C mean?" Amanda asked.

Basil sighed. "Initials for the Whip and Compass, a secret society dating back to the Renaissance." He hesitated, choosing his words carefully. "So now we've identified the culprits."

"From the Renaissance? But I thought he said they were in their early twenties," Lydia said.

"Yes, that is true. I suspect that these lawyers, as they called themselves, are in fact the niece and nephew of the Whip and Compass leader, Antonio Santoli. They match the description. They're twins."

"I hope you're not saying they'll get away with it," James said.

Basil's expression remained unchanged, but his voice hardened. "No, James, they are most definitely not getting away with it."

"Good."

"Is there anything we can do for Mr. Khananian?" asked Lydia. "I mean, if all this is true, he's not crazy. He doesn't belong in the psych ward."

"Unfortunately, no. You see, Lydia, the way these spells work is that the haunting stops within days of the termination of the primary target. In other words, once Campbell jumped, the program ended, leaving only the residue. Which means, Mr. Khananian actually *is* insane. There's no black dog anymore, only hallucinations."

"That is so sad. But I suppose it makes sense. Stress can trigger mental illness," Lydia said. Amanda noticed that Lydia's eyes momentarily flickered toward James.

"Okay, so what about the niece and nephew?" Amanda asked. "What are we going to do about them?"

"The Committee will take it from here," Basil said.

"Oh? And what will they do?" Amanda was genuinely curious.

But Basil had clammed up. "We have our ways." He smiled. "Don't worry about it."

Amanda and James exchanged glances. She thought she read frustration in his eyes, or maybe she was just projecting. Personally, she was getting a little tired of having things only partially explained.

Their adviser shifted closer to the screen. "That's one of the reasons we're called the *Sentinels*," he explained. "Somebody must hold these people accountable. No law can touch them. They have murdered innocent people. But this is beyond my scope. The Committee will decide how best to proceed, and at this point, I don't exactly know what will happen. One way to deal with this situation would be to capture the twins and erase their memories. In fact, erase all their knowledge of black magic, so they can't do this again. Complete amnesia, and a fresh start."

He leaned back, adding, "But try not to preoccupy yourselves with them. You've successfully completed this assignment—that is all you need to know."

It was obvious that Basil was not going to tell them more, not even if they insisted. She was beginning to know Basil. He was kind and diplomatic, but he was also secretive.

As if sensing her thoughts, he added, "The Committee will ensure they will not be causing any more trouble. You'll have to learn to make peace with that."

The meeting was over. Everyone got up to leave, saying their goodbyes. As Amanda walked to her car, she remembered Basil's strange call from the previous night. She had been distracted first by James's and Lydia's giddiness and second by the news of another secret society that was targeting theirs. Oh well. She'd just have to ask him about it later. She knew that if she were in real danger, he'd get in touch with her himself.

Basil had probably lost a Sentinel, to whatever misfortune. Maybe he'd just been having a nightmare with her in it. Maybe, in the light of day, he was embarrassed about it. In any case, it was best not to probe him for answers related to painful memories. She had tried to probe James, and all it accomplished was to push him away, making him confide in Lydia instead. Lydia wasn't even single, damn it!

Amanda threw her bag in her passenger seat, heaved a frustrated sigh, and started the powerful engine. It all sucked. Part of the reason she'd been so enthusiastic about joining the Sentinels was to meet young people like herself, to finally belong. Instead, she was stuck working with James, who treated her with complete indifference. And this first local assignment, the suicides, had left an unsatisfactory aftertaste. She would definitely be asking Basil for an update. For a moment, she wished that Matt had not been reassigned to San Francisco. Matt was not her type, but at least he'd bring a little levity to the situation. She needed a laugh. It was the end of August now. She had just turned twenty-five a couple of weeks ago. When would she finally get a real boyfriend?

As she drove back to downtown Boston, Amanda stewed. She liked being powerful, but she had mixed feelings about the organization itself. It seemed both benevolent and uncaring—they showered their Sentinels with money and luxury, but they provided mediocre training, poor briefings, and sporadic and inadequate guidance from mentors who were rarely even in the same state. Most of the time, she was left to fend for herself. As she sped through the streets in her dream car, she'd never felt more alone.

Chapter 16

Amanda woke up with surprisingly little apprehension about it being Thursday. She made herself a nice smoothie and texted James: *Are we still investigating Alain Proctor this afternoon?*

Radio silence.

She didn't have much else to do, so she pulled out her iPad and browsed some online shopping sites. In the end, she didn't feel like buying anything.

James finally texted mid-morning, and they agreed to meet in the parking lot of Alain Proctor's apartment building. Amanda's GPS led her to a luxury condominium building in downtown Boston, not unlike her own. She and James arrived almost simultaneously. She appreciated that *he* was never late, unlike Lydia.

Thanks to her mind control, the concierge let them pass to the elevator bank, and they rode to the third floor in silence. At unit 320, James lifted his hand, preparing to open the door with a power surge, but she stopped him. "Wait. It seems wrong to break down his door and just burst in on him like that."

James stared at her. "Yeah, normally it would be wrong, but he's run away twice already. We don't want him to escape again, do we? This time, the surprise is on him."

Amanda caught her breath, still unsure.

James sighed. "The next time he runs, you go after him by yourself, okay? I'm done chasing this guy."

"Okay, okay," she agreed. "You're right, go for it."

His power surge blew back the heavy door. "This is custom made, heavily reinforced," he said.

She simply nodded. The blast was sure to have alerted Alain of their presence. She opened her receiving functions, and they stepped into a sparsely decorated yet chic space. Before they had a chance to look around, the young man with bleached hair and a longish face stepped into the room, impeccably dressed in a well-fitting charcoal suit and a dark red shirt.

Up close he was attractive, though his looks couldn't hold a candle to James's. But there was something devious about his features. He emanated a sort of hidden, sensual depravity. His hooded eyes were the most remarkable thing about him: intense, yet dead at the same time. Pale and empty, like a well-dressed storefront with nothing but bare shelves inside.

"Hello," he said. "I'm Alain Proctor." His voice was pleasant enough, with husky undertones. He was obviously expecting them.

He first looked at James, as if sizing him up, then turned his gaze to Amanda, locking onto her. Something twitched in his features. He gasped and abruptly moved forward.

"Hey, man, stop right there." James demanded, stepping forward to block Proctor from getting too close to Amanda. He was taller and much bulkier than the gray-suited stranger.

He keeps forgetting I'm twice as powerful, thought Amanda. Nevertheless, she was quite pleased about his instinct to protect her.

Proctor stopped, his gaze still locked on Amanda's. His expression showed a curious mixture of awe and confused wonder. James stood his ground, frowning.

Suddenly something sparked in Proctor's eyes, and to her considerable amazement, Amanda saw that they were, in fact, blue. She could have sworn they were pale gray, almost colorless. They had looked so empty just a minute ago.

At the same moment, something unusual started happening to her, too. She felt like her consciousness was splitting. Time itself seemed to stall, slowly spreading and ebbing around her. She looked up at James, and he responded with a tiny reassuring smile, appearing unaffected by whatever was making her feel this way. It was as if her consciousness was slowly detaching from her body and floating upward like a balloon. Hovering near the ceiling, she was looking down on them now, zooming in on the man in the gray suit.

"*Amanda . . .*" She heard Alain's voice as if he were right by her side. A ghostly whisper, soft and strangely pleasant.

She forced herself to think of her physical form, her fingers, her arms, her legs. She zoomed back into her own body, then out again for a split second, then back in for good. After chasing the sensation away, she looked at James, still in the same position. And she realized that this uncanny, surreal standoff must have lasted only a few seconds.

Proctor stepped back, still staring at her.

Still dizzy, Amanda touched James's sleeve, then leaned on his arm to help ground herself.

"Are you okay?" James asked, supporting her weight with ease.

Warmed by his concern, Amanda nodded that she was fine. "Just a little dizzy," she whispered. She didn't want to tell him what she'd just experienced. Especially not in front of the other guy.

James wrapped a protective arm around her shoulders and pulled her against him. She breathed him in, feeling stronger under the pressure of his warm, muscular arm.

James looked sternly at Alain Proctor. "Okay, man," he demanded. "Tell us why you keep following us."

"I'm following *you?*" the man repeated slowly, mocking him. "Aren't you the ones who just broke into *my* apartment?"

James made no reply. Amanda followed the direction of his gaze and noticed that it was trained on the desk by the wall. His face twitched, and his fingers tightened around her shoulder. She moved in front of him to get a better look.

Displayed across the desk were pictures of people who had been shot to death. She gasped in horror and whipped around to face the stranger. "What are *those?*"

Smirking, he unabashedly looked her over. She crossed her arms. First Prague, then Florence, now here. She'd had just about enough of the way he looked at her, especially now that she'd seen those photos. What kind of a monster was he?

"What are these horrible photos?" she insisted. "Why do you have them?"

He slid his hands into his pockets, shrugged, and averted his gaze. "Proof for my clients. Proof of a job done."

"Oh my God," she gasped. A killer for hire. *Following them!*

Worse, he wasn't shy about it. In fact, he seemed to have known they were coming, and if that were true, he must have left the photos out for them to find. This was borne out by the way he seemed to enjoy their shock and revulsion.

"I see." James stepped in front of Amanda again. "You're coming with us." He grabbed Proctor's arm to escort him to the door, and predictably, the man resisted. Amanda rolled her eyes. James was a Sentinel 9, so what macho nonsense was this? Pushing and shoving—completely pointless.

She decided to knock Proctor out with an energy pulse and wrap things up quickly. To her astonishment, the pulse had an unexpected effect on the man. His body tensed up, and he began gasping and moaning, but not in agony. In fact, he seemed to be enjoying it.

She hit him again, even stronger. Alarmingly, he seemed to derive an intensely sensual pleasure from her hits. There was no mistaking it. Sweat beaded on his forehead, and he tossed his head up, panting and biting his lip.

"Hit me up, I love it," he said, looking at her, leaning against the wall and opening his body up to the sensation.

James and Amanda exchanged dismayed glances, and James obliged— this time with his fist. Proctor sagged to the floor.

"What is *wrong* with you?" James demanded.

"I absorb your energy," Proctor explained, catching his breath. "Feel free . . . such power . . . it's wonderful." He licked his lips again, catching his breath, looking directly at Amanda now. "Give me more. Hit me hard, my pretty. You're so strong, maybe I'll die, but I don't care. I want more of you. I love what it does to me."

"Pervert," she said, looking down at her shoes.

"He's a tricky little prick," James added, then addressed Proctor directly. "Now get up, or I *will* hit you again. But not how you like it."

"Okay, Purple Heart."

James was startled. "How do you know us?"

Sitting on the floor, the blond man ignored the question. In fact, he mostly ignored James altogether. He seemed to have eyes only for Amanda.

She was fresh out of patience with his lecherous looks.

"Okay, that's enough," she said. "Now that we know what you are, tell us, what do you want? Why are you following us? Did someone hire you to kill us?"

"Don't worry, beautiful. I'm not going to hurt you. To me, you're like a beautiful little rose. So pretty. So deliciously pretty. You want me to come with you? Sure. That's fine. I need to make one phone call first."

James clenched his fists. "Are you kidding me?"

"No, I am not kidding you, Purple Heart." He chuckled again. "Where do you propose to take me, anyway? Basil Blake? The Committee? Ha ha. My dear Sentinels, I have them on speed dial."

James and Amanda just stared at him. He narrowed his eyes. "Go ahead. Call Basil. Ask him about Alain Proctor. Ask him what you should do with me."

"Oh, I'm about to," muttered Amanda. Her heart pounding, she dialed Basil's number. To her relief, he answered on the first ring. "It's Amanda. James is here too. Listen, Alain Proctor is with us. We're in his apartment." To her surprise, there was only silence on the other end. "Hello? Are you there?"

"Go on," Basil said.

"We have him right here. He's been following us, and we just learned he's a killer for hire. What should we do?"

She began to think the call had been dropped, but Basil finally spoke, his voice grave and compelling. "Let him go. Try not to engage. He can be dangerous."

Let him go? She must have misheard him. "Too late!" she said. "And by the way, he was immune to our energy pulses. Now, where do you want us to bring him?"

"I know he's immune. Let him go, Amanda. He's an informant. We have an agreement: we won't touch him, and he won't hurt any of us."

She couldn't believe her ears. "He's not going to hurt *us*? Do you know that he kills people? He's a hired assassin!" Proctor's invulnerability to their energy pulses was troubling enough. She hadn't even known such a thing was possible. But Basil had barely reacted.

"We know everything about Alain," her adviser said. "Let him be. The people he kills . . . They aren't nice—for the most part."

"You can't be serious!"

"I'm sorry."

"No, I don't accept that," she snapped. She bit her lip as the man in the suit got to his feet, an *I told you so* smirk on his face. James had taken the opportunity to take a quick walk around the living room, as if trying to glean all the information he could about this dangerous individual.

There must be some explanation for Basil's behavior. She turned away and lowered her voice. "Tell me, Basil. Who is this man? Why are you on his speed dial?"

"I'm sorry, Amanda. Pass the phone to James," Basil ordered. When she didn't move he added, "Right now, please."

She handed the phone to James, who listened for a while then hung up. Without looking at Proctor, he handed the phone back to Amanda and said, "Come on. We're leaving."

Proctor was leaning against the wall, a lazy smile on his face.

"You can't be serious!" Amanda burst out. "Wait, what did he say?"

James took her by the elbow and directed her gently but firmly out into the hallway, shutting the door behind them. As they walked to the elevator, he said, "I'm a military man, and I was given a direct order." He pushed the button for the lobby. "And I trust Basil. Don't you?'

Amanda had never been the kind of person to blindly obey orders. She glared at James and pressed redial on her phone as the elevator descended. It went to voice mail. So, Basil was ignoring her! No, she would not accept that. Not when her insides were churning with anxiety. "Give me your phone, James."

"Give it a rest, will you?"

"No."

He darted her an amused glance, but she stubbornly held out her hand.

"Fine. But it won't do you any good."

She growled under her breath as he dialed their adviser and handed her the phone. It was ringing.

"We need to meet immediately," she said to Basil as he picked up.

His voice was cautious. "All right, Amanda. You're terribly stubborn. Meet me at my house in Vermont next week. I do have an important matter to discuss with you. I haven't forgotten about my call the other day. It's about something you need to be aware of as a Sentinel 10. And then Alain will make more sense to you, I promise."

"I don't want to wait a week," she complained. "I need to see you now."

"I'm sorry for the delay, but it can't be helped. I am out of the country on official business."

She glanced at James and lowered her voice. "God, what's going on, Basil?"

"Nothing for you to worry about. At least, not for now. I will explain all when I see you."

He was freaking her out. "Does this have to do with the dream you told me about?"

His tone turned decidedly stern. "What's important is for you to stay away from Alain Proctor. Under no circumstances are you to interact with him. Do you understand?"

As if she was about to stalk a hit man immune to her powers. "Sure, Basil. But what do I do when he's following *me*?"

"Just stay away from him." Basil hung up.

They were out of the elevator, and she handed the phone back to James as they exited the building.

"I'm exhausted," she said flatly. "I've no idea what's going on. See if you can find out something more about this guy? See you later, James."

She didn't have the energy to say anything else. They parted and walked to their cars.

As she unlocked her driver's side door, she glanced up at the building and saw Alain standing at his front window. He pressed his forehead into the glass. Even from this distance, she could see that his eyes were pale and empty once again. She thought she saw him mouth these words: "My diamond rose."

She shuddered, locked herself into the car, and sped away.

Chapter 17

For the next several days, Amanda obeyed Basil and stayed away from Alain Proctor, but her questions about him grew unchecked, like a cancer. She wanted to know about the pull she felt toward him—a man she'd never met; a man who murdered other men. An assassin. A killer. Why wasn't she terrified of him?

Her mind kept returning to the confrontation in his condo. His demeanor, so unaffected. Her own out-of-body experience, if that's what it was. Something had occurred between them, something undefinable. *Supernatural.* She remembered his eyes, and how the shade of them changed. His lonely form at the window when she drove away.

My diamond rose. Whatever did that mean?

Amanda arranged to meet Lydia for dinner that evening to talk the situation over and clear her head. As she exited her apartment building, distant flashes of lightning punctuated the sky. It was going to rain. She thrust her hands into the pockets of her black velvet jacket and quickened her pace, carefully stepping around puddles, her pumps clattering sharply on the wet pavement.

As she approached her Jaguar, her train of thoughts was abruptly interrupted. A flower was clipped under the windshield wiper. *What on earth?* She immediately cast a look around, but saw no one.

She got closer and saw that the object was a large lavender rose. She lifted it gently, its delicate petals stirring in the wind. A note had been clipped to it. She unfolded the paper and read: *Hello, beautiful. I know this is strange, but can we talk? I need you. Only you can save me.*

She dropped the note and it fell into a puddle, the water obscuring the message. Seriously concerned, she raised her eyes again. There, in the gray of the twilight, she spotted him only ten feet away: Alain Proctor. Light-gray suit, blond hair, standing completely still. She couldn't make out his expression, but she could almost physically feel the weight of his gaze. How long had he been there? And why?

The thought that he was trying to trap her crossed her mind, yet she felt no panic. Instead, she felt angry.

"No, we can't talk," she snapped, then beeped her car fob and opened the door. "You make me sick! Keep away from me!" She jumped into the driver's seat, threw the rose in his direction, and slammed the door.

He didn't move. He didn't speak. He just stood there. Silent. Still. He had the most intense way of standing still. Her heart pounding, her cheeks pink with excitement, she started the car and began to drive away.

What a creep. No, not a creep. A disgusting murderer! Leaving me a rose and a note? This is all insane.

She glanced into her rearview mirror as she slowed down. The psychopath was still standing there. He knew where she lived. How long had he known? How long had he been stalking her? Was Florence the first time he'd followed her, or simply the first time he had shown himself? It would be sane to feel afraid. Yet she didn't.

She watched him step over the crushed rose and move into the shadow of the building.

She couldn't shake the image of the rose from her mind. Frowning, she used the voice activation technology in her car, "Hey Siri, what is the significance of a lavender rose?"

"Parker Posey is an American actress . . ."

"Gah! No!" she shouted at the dashboard. She couldn't wait. As she drove, she dug into her purse to retrieve her cell phone, opened her Google app, and tapped in "meaning of lavender rose." Recklessly darting quick glances between the road and her phone, she read, "The lavender rose is often a sign of enchantment and love at first sight. Those who have been enraptured by feelings of love and adoration have used lavender roses to express their feelings and intentions."

"Love and adoration?" She rolled her eyes and made a gagging noise.

When she and Lydia met, she said nothing about the incident. Lydia would freak. But before the evening was over, her flustered annoyance had turned to deep concern. After all, this was a man who killed people for a living. He might still be at her apartment when she went home. Why wasn't she more afraid?

It would be several days before she could speak to Basil. Why was he avoiding her like this, just when she needed him most?

After she left, the man in the alley stood still for a few minutes. The effect of her presence lingered for a little longer this time, but he knew it was about to dissipate again, leaving only his psychopathic self standing there, indifferent and devoid of emotion, except for his longing for her. This desire for her was one of the few things he had in common with his shadow self.

"I need you, my little diamond," he whispered, a dreamy look in his eyes. "Only you can save me. Pull me out. I've been drowning for so long now. So close to the bottom."

In the gathering darkness, his eyes soon paled again. Turning around, he walked by the rose in a dirty puddle, and disappeared behind a corner.

Chapter 18

The night before she was supposed to meet Basil, Amanda packed a small bag and turned in early, just as she had nearly every night since Alain Proctor had stood outside her home. She was trying to lie low. She declined an invitation to join Lydia and Hank for dinner, which was easy enough. Amanda still didn't like being in Hank's presence. Plus, Lydia would have a heart attack if she knew what was going on—and possibly diagnose Amanda with something. But when James texted her to meet for coffee, Amanda found saying no more difficult. Yet not impossible. Not like before. She no longer wanted James the way she used to. She couldn't explain it. Whatever the reason, something in her feelings toward him had definitely changed. Perhaps she was simply done chasing him.

The next morning, Amanda got up early and began the two-hour drive to Basil's large countryside estate in Vermont. He'd told her that he also had residences in other places, including a large apartment in San Francisco and a farm in Iowa, where he planned eventually to retire. But he spent most of his time in Vermont, where he could be in close proximity to his group of Sentinel mentees, who all lived in the northeastern United States.

After a two-hour drive, she pulled up at the large iron gate to Basil's estate and rolled down the window. She hit the buzzer and waved at the camera that monitored visitors' comings and goings. When the gates swung open, she drove another half mile over a winding tree-lined drive. It was still summer and the leaves created a lovely canopy, casting dappled shade over the road. She passed a small lake with a rowboat docked to the side. She imagined Basil out there, rowing around in circles to relax. Did men like Basil need a way to relax? He certainly didn't have the intensity of the other men with whom she had recently become acquainted. *What does Alain Proctor do to relax?* Immediately, all she could see were those horrible photographs of his victims lined up on his desk, like trophies. She shuddered and pushed the thought away.

The house came into view. As sprawling as it was, the thatched roof and ivy that climbed the stucco walls made it seem more like a woodland cottage than a grand country house. Amanda parked her car and approached the inviting entrance, where a kindly-looking housekeeper was already standing in front of the open door. She greeted Amanda by name and showed her to Basil's study.

Basil was sitting at his desk. When she entered, he rose and gave her a friendly smile. "Please have a seat, my dear. How are you?"

Amanda complied, but she was seething, and his usually calming demeanor was doing nothing to defuse her emotions. "Mr. Blake, for shit's sake." She threw up her hands in frustration. "Why did I have to wait so long to see you?"

"I told you, my dear. I was out of town. Business. Quite serious Committee business." His eyes seemed to go dark for a moment.

She wasn't about to relent. "Basil, there is a disgusting murderer out there killing people, and now he's stalking *me*. You know about it, and you don't seem to care. Wait. Did you hire him to spy on me? For who? For you? The Committee? This man is a monster. We have to get rid of him!"

Basil seemed dismayed at her anger. "Careful, Amanda. I hope you don't mean what I think you mean. We cannot just destroy what we fear. This is how it starts, feeling righteous and ready for destruction, and then . . . something goes very wrong. It never ends well." He pulled a chair over and sat near her, his palms on his knees, looking keenly into her face.

She glared at him, her foot tapping agitatedly. "This is how *what* starts? I wasn't suggesting you kill him—for God's sake—just get him to stop following me."

He sighed. "I should not tell you this, but I will. Listen. He isn't a spy, and he isn't an informant. I lied to you, I'm sorry."

Basil had lied? She thrust her shock aside. He probably had a good reason. He'd better tell the truth now. "Then what the hell is he? He was at my apartment building the other night, waiting for me. He left me a note saying he needed me." She stared into Basil's kind brown eyes, willing him to say something reassuring.

After a long, painful pause he said, "Alain Proctor was a Sentinel."

A Sentinel? As crazy as this answer seemed, it also made sense. Proctor had said he had Basil on speed dial—just like they all did. But how could he be a Sentinel? He was so . . . evil. And so vacant, with his pale stare. "What happened to him?" she asked, sharpness edging her words. "How did he become a killer?"

Basil sighed. "He had barely been with us for five months when he was faced with a situation that made him go into Overload. It was quite tragic, really."

"Overload? What is that? I don't remember that from training."

He shook his head. "We don't teach that in training."

The mantel clock ticked loudly as she gazed at him, waiting for more. When he remained silent, she prodded. "I don't understand."

He looked regretful, as though he was about to give her bad news. "An Overload is not something most Sentinels will face, so it's not relevant to general training. We made a decision long ago to discuss it only on an as-needs basis."

"So we need to discuss it now?"

"I'm afraid so."

He was silent for a moment, as if weighing his words carefully. "Sometimes, when faced with a life-threatening situation, a Sentinel's instinctual drive takes over and blows the psychic energies out of proportion. Like an explosion of psychic energy. Everything you know, every awareness, it all expands. It gives you clairvoyance. Knowledge of things you never knew before."

She leaned back. "That doesn't sound like a bad thing."

Basil shook his head emphatically. "It's a very bad thing. Don't fool yourself. There are only a handful of cases of Overload; most are obscure descriptions from the Middle Ages. The most recent one before Alain occurred around the Great Depression."

"So what happened to Alain?"

"He was powerful, and I'm sure that he was targeted."

"Targeted? By whom?"

"I don't really know. It doesn't really matter. What matters is what actually becomes of a Sentinel who goes into Overload. What *could* happen . . ." A faraway look clouded his eyes.

Amanda needed to know. She was not going to let him off the hook. Not that easily. "Tell me. Please."

Basil sighed. "An Overload will make a Sentinel kill. The body is flooded with raw power that has to be expunged—and Overload victims usually unleash it on the enemies in front of them. It's like a reflex, a defense mechanism, like pulling your hand out of a fire. It's not something you can help at the time. The kill reflex is only temporary. Or has been in all reported cases. Until Alain. For some reason, Alain continued to kill."

"But why? Those people in the photographs—did he kill them for the group that targeted him? Or is he killing on his own?"

"On his own," Basil said. "He sells his services. Alain wasn't exactly kindhearted to begin with—and the Overload corrupted him further. He was killing street thugs for a while, until he turned himself in to the Committee. He wanted help."

"You couldn't help him?"

His eyes filled with regret again. "We didn't know how. We still don't, in fact. Generally, when a Sentinel goes into Overload, it—well, it tends to kill the Sentinel. They all die after a short while. We've had no experience dealing with a Sentinel who survived it. But we tried to bind his energies."

"What does that mean? Bind them to what?"

Basil avoided her question. "Throughout our history, since the creation of the Committee in 1322, we have routinely bound the energies of Sentinels after ten years. It's a well-rehearsed procedure, so we thought we had a reasonable chance of success with him. By then he was willing. But, unfortunately, by even trying, we . . . *we* . . ."

"You what?"

He ran his fingers through his peppered hair. "We made him worse. The procedure permanently changed the makeup of his brain. He became a real psychopath, unable to feel any empathy at all."

Amanda was trying to absorb what Basil was telling her when a thought sprang into her mind. "Wait! The solar flare from three years ago." She remembered being told that the flare hadn't produced a Sentinel 10. Or had it? "Was Alain made a Sentinel 10 then?"

"Indeed. You're very smart. Very observant."

His flattery did nothing to assuage her outrage. She jumped up and began pacing. Something felt very wrong about this situation. "Since joining the Sentinels, I've had a great deal of respect for this institution. I haven't always understood why the training was so short, or why you give us so little information. But I never thought that . . ." She stopped at the bay window and looked out at the rolling green hills that lined the lake. The serenity of her surroundings was completely at odds with this dark revelation. How could the Committee condone a murderer? "Now I find that we are harboring and *enabling* monsters." She set her jaw and turned to Basil.

He stared up at her like a rabbit in a snare. "Enabling . . . ?"

"Of course! I'm not talking about the failed binding procedure; that's nobody's fault. We are enabling him by doing nothing to stop him. It's incomprehensible. He's not even human! Empathy is the essence of humanity. I say there are no excuses. The Overload was the reason for his behavior, but it can't continue to be an excuse. So what if he didn't ask for it? Do you think his victims care about that?"

Basil Blake nodded. "I agree with you. But it's not his fault. And don't you think that it would be immoral for us, after botching the procedure meant to cure him, to, well, remove him?"

"*Not his fault?*" she repeated. "Do you really believe that, Basil? Do you?"

Basil blinked a few times, as if thinking things over. He shook his head. "I've been an adviser for a long time now. At this point, I'm just looking forward to my retirement. Please don't misunderstand me: I care about all of you very much, I truly do. I took what happened to Alain to heart, and I pray it won't ever happen again."

She looked him in the eye. "Uh-huh. Don't try to avoid the question. Do you really believe you have no obligation to the rest of society to protect them from a murderer you essentially created? Like Dr. Frankenstein! Don't you have a high-security Sentinel prison or something?"

Basil looked down. "No, unfortunately, we don't have the means to hold him. And like I said, I don't condone killing him. Do you? Is there darkness in you, after all?"

That didn't faze her. "No, and yes, of course there is darkness inside all of us, but not all darkness is equally dark. There are degrees." Her anger spent, she sank back onto her chair. She hadn't hurt anyone in her life. "Basil, you know I would never condone murder. I would be a hypocrite if I suggested that. But something needs to be done. He has to stop killing. And he has to stop following me. Why don't you have any reaction to him stalking me? You know he's dangerous."

Basil reached out and gave her wrist a reassuring squeeze. "He's not going to hurt you."

She wrenched her arm out of his grasp. "How can you say that? He's a killer, he's disgusting, and he's completely fixated on me!" *And I think I'm starting to like his attention . . . What's wrong with me?* Was that why she was so angry? She had some sort of strange connection with a murderer.

She rubbed her hands together nervously, avoiding Basil's gaze. "When James and I went to his place, there was something else. Proctor's eyes changed. I can't explain it. It was like . . . I can't really explain it."

Basil leaned forward, his eyes bright with interest. "His eyes changed? Tell me more. What did you feel?"

"Me? I felt nothing," she said defensively. "No, that's not exactly true. I sort of had an out-of-body experience. Like I was looking down on the situation. But it only lasted a moment. I felt nauseated and dizzy afterward. But he definitely felt something too, just before his eyes changed color. It was like something surprised and awed him, like he couldn't believe what was happening."

Blake stood. "I need to contact him. He must answer some questions."

She stared at him. Basil was supposed to be her mentor. He was supposed to care. She had been so sure she could trust him, yet he was clearly keeping information from her. If she couldn't trust *him* to care about her, then whom could she trust?

"Why is he following me?" she challenged. "Do you know? Tell me if you know!"

Basil looked at her, his eyes kind and understanding, yet also alight with something akin to wistful amusement. As if she were a child. Hurt, she felt her eyes begin to fill, and his expression shifted. He began to look like he was fighting the urge to hug her, as if he suddenly understood her feelings. And then she remembered that he actually could. That this was a super empath who could feel her feelings as clearly as if he were reading her thoughts.

"I know this is very difficult for you, Amanda," he said. "I am sorry. I wish I could tell you more, but I need to do some research first. And there is much you don't know about the organization."

"Does Proctor have something to do with your urgent Committee business?"

He shook his head. "Let's talk about that another time."

She sighed and leaned back in her chair. "Fine. Just make sure you tell him to stay away from me. That's all I want. Make him go away."

"I know. I'll work on a resolution to this . . . situation. I'll call you as soon as I have something definite."

She made a final, halfhearted attempt to get more from him. "Can you at least tell me why he's immune to our energy pulses?"

Basil sat back down, clearly hesitating about what to withhold and what to reveal. She opened her eyes and jutted her chin forward a little, as if saying, "What?"

"The green-eyed wonder," he said, smiling at her. "You are so much like my long-gone daughter."

Seriously? Did he think she would fall for this, and lose her train of thought? He was trying to distract her, but she wouldn't be distracted. "No offense, Basil, but I don't have time for any of this sentimental nonsense. I want answers, and I want them now!"

"Just as pretty and just as feisty," Basil mused.

"Unbelievable," Amanda said with an eye roll.

Basil smiled again. "Fine. I will tell you. He absorbs the energy, but he can't keep it in. It goes right through him. That is one difference between Alain and the rest of you. But, in a way, he's still a Sentinel."

"It goes right through him? Like psychic diarrhea?" She folded her arms over her chest. "Wow. Nothing can surprise me anymore." Then something occurred to her, and she leaned forward again. "Wait. You just said, like *us*. Meaning *we* absorb energy too? But I thought we generated energy?"

He tented his fingers and touched them to his lips. "A Sentinel is an energy accumulator. The process starts with absorbing the solar flare, and then you continue to attract, devour, and transform energy."

"So, what you're saying is that we actually have no personal power?"

"Well, you have the power to use and mold psychic energy to your will. But no, I'm afraid you have don't have the power to *create* energy out of nothing. But we don't want you guys to think this way. We want you to feel confident in your powers. Listen to me, Amanda." He leaned forward. "You have the power to use and mold psychic energy to your will. That is some incredible power."

Despite herself, she felt comforted by the warmth of his touch and the kindness in his eyes. She hadn't gotten many answers, but she understood better why Proctor had been allowed to live and to . . . operate. The organization felt responsible for his condition—that was a good sign, wasn't it? They were probably still looking for a solution. And Basil would be speaking to Proctor about leaving her alone. She would have to keep trusting in Basil and the Committee, she decided. She would have to be patient and let them to do their work. The problem was, she was never very good at being patient.

Chapter 19

On Labor Day weekend, Amanda was finishing yet another solo job—a warehouse at the edge of the city needed to be cleaned of a single plasmid, and not a very strong one. That was it. The drive to the warehouse had taken longer than the assignment. Walking from where she'd parked her car in a nearby alley had taken longer than the assignment. Turning the doorknob to enter the warehouse had literally taken more time. The weak little thing had practically greeted her at the front door when she entered. In a snap, it was gone. Like it had almost been waiting for her to come and put it out of its misery.

She wondered why Lydia or another lesser Sentinel hadn't been sent to do the work. Then she immediately hated herself for looking down on Lydia and others like her. She vowed to be better. They were all extremely intelligent and talented individuals. Plus, they were still balancing day jobs. She was not. Of course she would be the one going on the most assignments—she was available. Still, she couldn't help but wonder why she had been assigned such a menial task. Was Basil trying to distract her? Keep her busy so she wouldn't have so many questions about Alain Proctor?

Alain Proctor. That man and his mysterious eyes. She hadn't seen him since that encounter at her car, but there was something about him that never left her. And now that she understood that he had once been not only a Sentinel, but a Sentinel 10, she couldn't stop thinking about him.

The events of the past week were definitely starting to wear on her. Time for some retail therapy.

She left the warehouse and drove to the nearest mall, parking in the less-crowded rooftop lot. She chose a spot quite far from the door so she could stretch her legs and get some fresh air on her way inside.

She strolled lazily through the mall, checking out some of her favorite shops, but nothing struck her as tempting. She found it funny that now that she had money and could afford to buy whatever she wanted, she seemed to want things less.

Just as she was leaving the shoe store, something felt amiss. She couldn't shake the feeling she was being followed. *Not again!*

She looked around but didn't spot a gray suit. Rather, she became aware of several suspicious-looking figures lurking in shop doorways and behind pillars. Was she being paranoid? She turned on her receiving functions, just in case, and hurried toward the elevator to the rooftop parking lot.

When the doors opened onto the lot, she started to feel more at ease. The day was sunny, light gleaming off the few cars in the sparsely populated lot. Up here, the sense that she was being followed was gone. Her receiving functions weren't picking up any paranormal activity. All she saw was a young woman heading toward her, carrying a large shopping bag. Nothing unusual about that—she was probably rushing to make a return before the stores closed. Otherwise everything looked quiet. Amanda breathed a little easier and turned off her receiving functions.

But as she headed toward her car, she noticed something odd: despite the lot being practically empty, a small car was parked right next to hers, just one spot over on the driver's side. She frowned and began hurrying toward her vehicle. She didn't like this one bit. She fumbled for her key fob and beeped open the doors from a distance, her hand outstretched.

It happened so fast. Out of nowhere, the young woman she'd seen earlier brushed past her with a casual whisper of an excuse, then slapped something on her bare wrist. Amanda felt it tighten, pinching her skin. She lifted her hand and saw that it was a metallic cuff bracelet.

"Hey!" she said. Her voice fell flat. The woman just kept walking, not looking back. Confused, Amanda raised her hand, stupidly staring at it. She tried to make out what was on the bracelet. It appeared to be of hieroglyphics. Before she could try to figure out the strange message, she was overcome with a heavy sense of weakness. Her knees gave out and she sagged to the ground. Her purse slid off her shoulder and she could not muster the strength—the will—to do anything about it. She swayed woozily on her hands and knees, staring at the concrete. Soon she could barely move. Soon she could barely think. It was as if a heavy force was pressing her into the concrete.

But then a deeper-seated instinct kicked in and told her she needed to act, and fast. She had to call on her powers and send out a surge, try to hit whatever it was that was trying to harm her. She tried to lift her hand again, but could not. She tried to turn on her receiving functions, but nothing happened.

If she couldn't fight it, she needed to protect herself. She struggled with everything in her to brace herself against the force pushing down, but it seemed no use. Her mind felt separate from her body—sluggish, apathetic. Disconnected. Some deeper part of her was desperate to reconnect them, but she just couldn't do it. Her enormous powers were intact, clawing at her from somewhere deep within her soul, but it was as if she had lost the motivation—the will—to do anything.

The bracelet.

Her brain was foggy, but this much was clear: some power inherent in the bracelet was crippling her. But what power? And how?

Head still down, staring at her hands on the concrete, she squinted again at the hieroglyphics. Just as she thought she recognized some of the symbols, something hit her from behind, hard and fast. Pain exploded in her skull and she hit the ground facedown. Her sight dimmed.

As she lay there, trying to move, trying to speak, trying to process what was happening, she heard voices. Dazed, she struggled to lift her head, the asphalt scratching her face.

Mustering every ounce of strength, she managed to bring herself up onto her elbows and raise her head. That's when she saw it: the emblem. A black smudge with a gold W and C emblazoned on it. The symbol of the Whip and Compass, purveyors of black magic dating back to the Renaissance.

The emblem was on the back of a phone being held a foot from her face. A man was filming her. She forced open her mouth, straining to speak, when a blow struck her in the ribs. Someone was kicking her. More than one person. Blows hit her from both sides, crunching into her ribs. The video captured her face as the beating intensified.

Blood trickled in the back of her throat. Despite the pain, she couldn't even open her mouth to scream. But deep down, she could still feel her essence bottled up inside—her determination to survive, to fight to the very end. She had to force it out, allow it to the surface, so it would wash over the apathy.

She would not let them win. She had to get the bracelet off, now, before the power it held led to her death. She wouldn't have long before they ruptured an organ or caused a traumatic brain swelling. It was now or never.

Fighting to focus, she forced her mind to use her muscles and drew her arms together. In a short reprieve between blows, she slid her fingers between the skin of her wrist and the bracelet. Then, summoning every bit of strength she had left in her, she yanked it off.

Just as she did, an overpowering, violent surge of rage and fear took control of her mind. The determination, the will to fight and destroy and live, took hold of every fiber of her being. Her skin came to life with the sense that she was all-powerful. Invincible. Liberated. Free from all constraints and moral considerations, values and doubts. Free to bend this world to her will.

Overload.

The word vibrated in her mind as energy coursed through her. She rose without effort and faced her would-be assassins, feeling their shock and fear. One man held the phone slackly at his side. The other two stood staring, as paralyzed by fear as she had been by the bracelet's magic. She had become a being of pure power, and their end was near. They knew it and she knew it.

While the sense of absolute raw power exhilarated her, a memory flashed in her mind's eye: Basil, warning her about Overload. Perhaps he had somehow known she would soon face it. Perhaps his dream had been about this very moment—the dream that had frightened him. But she was unfazed. The Overload's usual outcome wouldn't apply to her. She, Amanda Griffith, the new Sentinel 10, the One and Only, was invincible.

Part of her wanted to take control of this Overload. To stop it from corrupting her. From changing her. But another part of her, a part that was proving stronger in this moment, wanted to fully experience it and come out of it more powerful than any Sentinel had ever been; so powerful, she could bend reality to her will.

Slowly, she levitated a few feet off the ground. All three men jumped back in fear.

Blood seeped from the corners of her mouth and from a gash on her head as her platinum hair slowly blew in the wind, undulating in long strands around her face. Silent and deadly, she dealt such a blow that their bodies flew back a couple dozen feet, as if hit by a truck. Death was instantaneous. She alighted on the bloody pavement next to her car and looked around. The woman who'd brushed past her was long gone. Nobody else was in sight. A glimpse of her reflection in the car's tinted window showed her that she was hardly recognizable—her expression wild with rage and triumph, her pupils so dilated that her eyes looked almost black.

She willed the phone marked with the Whip and Compass to come to her, and it flew into her hand. She glanced down at the screen and scrolled through the most recent contacts, unsurprised to see "Mr. Santoli" listed among them. She'd known it, somehow. In this exciting new state, she only had to focus on a question and the answer came.

Next she turned to the piece of metal with hieroglyphs that was sitting by the traces of her blood on the ground, and pulverized it.

Quietly raging, she picked up her purse and got into her car. She cared for nothing. She was afraid of nothing. She would rip to pieces everyone and everything that had hurt her. Judging from the serious beating she'd just sustained, she must have internal bleeding. Yet she felt no pain, and she knew that she would be fine. The Overload promoted healing with fantastic efficiency. She knew all that, somehow.

Still, at some level she felt trapped inside her mind. Her real, inner essence was caught at the bottom of a spinning cluster of emotions, unable to break through. Oh, she'd show them. She'd show them all! She was the One and Only: magnificent, fearless, ferociously real. The most powerful being on the planet. How dare they attack her! How dare they . . .

She snarled like a mad leopard and started the engine. She felt compelled to act. Not only for self-preservation, but for revenge.

Chapter 20

Antonio Santoli, the head of the Whip and Compass society, had ordered the hit on her himself. Amanda knew this fact and fixated on it. Because the Overload expanded her psychic powers in every possible way, she was now clairvoyant. The Overload had made her omniscient. She only had to turn her thoughts to a question and she immediately knew the answer.

Basil had lied. When he was being evasive about what would happen to the twins who pushed the three men to suicide, Basil was shielding his Sentinels from the truth: there was no magical way to deal with supernatural criminals. Legally they had done nothing wrong, and the Committee did not keep jails. The nice fairy tale about erasing their memories and thus removing all knowledge of black magic was just that, a fairy tale. Basil knew full well that no such thing was possible. The only way to prevent future transgressions and murders was to execute the criminals.

Clairvoyance allowed her to gain instant knowledge of this truth, and of the events that transpired just before her Overload. The twins were promptly found and brought before the Committee, which had jurisdiction over all cases in which their associates were the victims. They listened to Santoli Senior plead for their lives. They watched him go on his knees before them. And they impartially decreed that his feelings notwithstanding, the evil within the twins was unmanageable. His niece and nephew had freely admitted they came up with the parachute-suicide scheme out of boredom. They were murderous thrill-seekers, and they would do it again. They were but twenty years old. They had decades of thrill killings to look forward to, with no one to stop them. They smiled and promised to be more careful. They gave their assurances they would never involve anyone associated with the Committee. They'd make sure that only regular people were murdered, with no ties to any society, no protection behind them. Having said so, the young psychopaths were greatly surprised to hear an order for their execution. They'd had every confidence that their uncle would get them off, as he had covered up every one of their transgressions up until then.

After the twins were executed by a gunshot to the head in the very next room, the boss of the Whip and Compass swore to make the Committee regret it. He invoked the ancient oath of his family, going back to the glory days of the Borgias, to whom his ancestors were servants, and swore on the Borgias' sword not to rest until his family was avenged. Yes, she now knew all. The information poured into her while she sped past Boston's suburbs, navigating the toll-free highways.

She was astonished that *anyone* would retaliate against the Committee by attacking a Sentinel 10, knowing full well what the consequences of such a transgression would be: to bring the power of the Committee down on his organization. Santoli was not right in his head. Given her status of great importance to the Committee, he ordered her assassination in retaliation for the lives of his precious niece and nephew. An eye for an eye.

Thanks to her new clairvoyance, she also knew where he lived. In fact, she knew where all the big bosses lived, including the leaders of the Rosicrucians, Whip and Compass, Skull and Bones, Freemasons, and Solar Lodge. Anyone she cared to turn her thoughts to.

Under the setting sun, she sped toward Santoli's Lake George estate. She didn't dwell on what she was about to do. She was no longer a thinking person who could reason out solutions or question her emotions. She was a feral creature who had been terribly wronged, and was about to right that wrong with a might that had never been felt before. She'd show them.

Four hours later, she arrived at the sprawling, medieval-looking estate that housed the secret society and its corrupt ruler. It was close to 10:30 PM. Despite all the time behind the wheel, she felt no fatigue; she felt nothing but her purpose.

"Whip and Comp-*ass*, I'm about to whip your ass." She bared her teeth and spat some blood out the window, then ran her tongue over her teeth. Those bastards in the parking lot had better not have broken any. She growled a little.

Her mood was now shifting into an even stranger, more excited state. With one energy surge, the iron gates flew open in front of her. She rolled full speed into the estate, to the mansion's doors, raising clouds of gravel dust as she skidded to a halt. Security guards ran toward her, guns drawn, but her next psychic surge knocked them back, strewing their bodies across the lawn and terrace. All had broken bones, some were dying—she knew it without even looking, but she didn't care. Given that shooting at her was of no help, the remaining guards fled before her approach, and Amanda walked right into the house.

Like everything in Overload, her projected psychic shield was incredibly strong, stronger than she'd ever experienced. The force field could now deflect machine gun bullets, and she employed it to protect herself. Not that it mattered, because hardly anyone could sustain physical proximity to a Sentinel 10 in active Overload. The force field alone emitted maximum-strength infrasonic oscillations; anyone within a radius of a hundred feet was overwhelmed with terror and pain.

She paused in the large posh hallway, seeing herself in an ornate mirror on a wall—a statuesque figure in dark-green velvet pants, brown hunting boots, and a leather jacket, her arms extended to the sides, as if feeling the air.

"Hey!" she roared. "Santoli? I will root you out, pig!"

She quickly located him by reading his mind; he was hiding in his state-of-the-art panic room. Her lips twisted into a cruel smile. There was no defense against her. A panic room couldn't keep her out if she wanted in. But she didn't have to go to that kind of trouble. Instead, she applied mind control and within seconds, the man stumbled out of the room and into the hallway.

The once-powerful head of the Whip and Compass cowered before her. He didn't need to speak. She could read his thoughts as they raced through his head. His fear, his futile rationalizations for sparing him. The moments of his life as they flashed before him. His current state. His battle with terminal illness. His fears that his legacy would not survive. She didn't care. She couldn't care. The Overload stifled all empathy. Focusing intently, she made his brain herniate, squashing it against his brainstem, squeezing it through the opening that connects the brain to the spinal cord. In seconds, he was no more.

No excuses, no forgiveness, no escape.

Next she used her clairvoyance to find the estate's security cameras and blew them to smithereens. Then she wiped the digital recordings. She did not need to see them in order to do so: she only had to will it for it to be done.

"Anyone else want a piece of me?" bellowed the Sentinel 10 as Santoli slumped on the floor in front of her. "I dare you. I'll blow your heads off. You're all shit! Every single last one of you."

She psychically connected to all the other secret societies' leaders, and spoke directly into their minds, all at once. She made sure they could see, feel, and *know* what she was doing.

"I am the Sentinel 10. I am power like you have never seen. I am a *goddess*, and you, *all* of you, you're nothing. I will rip you apart, piece by piece. Take a look at this dead shit right here. He tried to kill me—*me, the magnificent Sentinel 10!* That's a crime that can never be forgiven. Oh, but I'm glad he tried. Because it gave me the Overload. I *belong* in Overload. Cross me, and I will crush you. I will destroy your little clubs; snap you like trees in a hurricane. Any threat to me at all, and I will squeeze your brains out in your sleep. You know I can. As for the Whip and Compass, they're finished. Watch this."

First, she telepathically accessed the W and C bank accounts and electronically emptied them into thousands of random accounts and hundreds of charities. Now the Whip and Compass had no funds, no investments, and no leader.

She listened to the feelings and replies from the others, simultaneously and without difficulty. Mostly, they were in sheer shock. Some sincerely disapproved of W and C's actions. None intended to pose a threat or harm her in any way. They all well knew that a Sentinel 10 in Overload is a psychic bomb unleashed. And nobody wanted a bomb exploding in their backyard.

Satisfied, Amanda released them. She then strode out of the house and headed back to Boston. It was nearly midnight by the time she pulled back onto the country roads, but she still felt no fatigue. The unsettling feeling of having become somebody else returned, at the bottom of her conscious awareness. It changed nothing; it was a mere annoyance. As she drove, her thoughts raced, and she felt no need for rest or sleep. She was drunk with the power surging through her. It was intoxicating, exhilarating. So dark and so much . . . *fun*. She rolled down the window. The night was quiet on the winding back roads, with the fields stretching out like black oceans on either side.

Her force field was still on, its infrasonic waves hugging the ground, and animals fled for a mile around her. "There will be no roadkill on this road tonight!" She screeched with laughter as she accelerated into the darkness. Defiant, euphoric, exalted.

It was nearly dawn when her phone rang, and when she finally looked down at it, she noticed dozens of missed calls, all from Basil Blake. When it buzzed again, she picked it up with a condescending "Hello?"

"Amanda, *thank GOD!*" Basil's voice vibrated with emotion. "I thought I'd lost another one. Thank God you are okay."

"Oh, I am fine, just peachy. *Peachy!*" she suddenly yelled, then laughed.

"Amanda?" Basil called into the phone. "What is happening? No matter what, I love you, all of you. I will do anything to help you."

In her heightened psychic state, Amanda discovered that she could read his thoughts, and feel his emotions—so raw and so sincere, it gave her pause. With the ability to project into his mind, she did not need the phone. She turned off both the phone and her force shield.

"Amanda, you're in my mind. You are not well. What happened, my dear girl?"

She knew he was asking because he had to. She also knew that not only was he aware of her Overload, he'd known the minute it started happening.

"So this is what an Overload is? It's great! Why did you make it sound bad? Here, have a taste. Come on, Basil! Feel it for yourself."

"Amanda, it is terrifying. I do feel it. Please stop yourself. I believe in you, dear girl. I know you can stop it. I've advised dozens of Sentinels over my lifetime, and I can tell you that nobody matches you in willpower and resilience."

His praise and radiating fatherly love suddenly knocked her sane. The runaway train her mind had taken off on was beginning to shift back onto the rails, bit by bit.

"You can do this. You can come back to yourself, Amanda. I know you can. You're even stronger than my daughter. Much stronger."

With the reminder of his daughter came such a vivid sense of loss and unrelenting grief that she almost drowned in it. That tiny part of her old self that was struggling deep underneath the Overload came up to the surface and washed over the madness. The profound realization of what she'd done finally hit her, and it hit her hard. She gasped and pulled off to the side of the highway. "Basil! Oh God, Basil. I did such terrible things. The Whip and Compass. They attacked me. They tried to kill me. They put this bracelet on me with weird hieroglyphs. Before I knew what was happening, I couldn't move. I could barely breathe."

"Yes, the will paralyzer. The bracelet of Jaede. It's Mayan, maybe the last one in the world. It is possibly the only weapon that can be used against a Sentinel 10."

"Santoli put out a contract on me," she told him. "I knew it as soon as the Overload hit. It was to avenge the deaths of his niece and nephew. The deaths the Committee carried out. He hired some street thugs to attack me at the mall, and I killed them all. Oh my God, Basil . . ."

"One minute at a time, Amanda. One thing at a time."

She caught her breath. "He was in the middle stages of Lewy body dementia, you know. It's terminal. He would have been in a nursing home in less than two years . . . God, I know everything about him, and I don't even want to. He begged me not to kill him, but I couldn't listen. Oh, this is horrible. It's so horrible."

She paused. Wincing, she caught her reflection in her rearview mirror. Blood had dried in the corner of her mouth. Her eyes were filled with remorse.

"It's not your fault, Amanda," Basil assured her.

"I'm scared, Basil. What I did. The rage I felt. It wasn't me, and yet it *was* me. One hundred percent, it was me. I would never do such things, and yet there I was. I killed people. I cleaned out their bank accounts . . ."

She felt panic rise within her. "What's happening to me? I'm losing it, Basil. I almost lost *me*. Am I back?"

"Hold on, hold on, let me speak," Basil soothed. "I'm convening an emergency meeting of the Committee. Do you think the Overload is over? Take a breath and focus. Does it feel like it's resolved?"

Amanda wasn't sure what she was supposed to be feeling, but she *was* sure that this emergency meeting with the Committee had already happened, that Basil's worries were intensified by the outcome of that meeting. But she couldn't think about that now. She could only think about this moment. About getting herself out of this state that had changed her so horribly.

"I don't know. No, not really. I mean, sort of? I can still feel it, the rage and the power, pushing and prodding, trying to break through. Oh, I am so scared. Basil, you have to help me."

"I will, I will—" His voice was breaking. "My dear girl, listen to me, this is important: don't go home. Don't go to anyone, don't contact anyone, and don't listen to anyone. Except for me or Alain Proctor."

She couldn't believe her ears. "Proctor? Why? Basil, where are you? I can't read you anymore." But he was gone. She was alone again, in the dark car by the roadside. She stared ahead, not knowing what to do. Then her phone rang.

"This is a good sign," Basil told her. "You're out of my mind, which means you're coming out of the Overload."

She felt sick. "Oh my God, I'm a monster now. I'm just like Proctor. A killer. Is that why you want me to go to him?"

"No, no. Beautiful soul, you are nothing like Alain. You need to seek him out only because he went through the same thing. You need him. And he needs you."

"He needs *me*? I don't understand."

"You will. For now, just know that he will be able to help. Go to him now. The Committee will take care of the rest."

But the Committee had assassinated Santoli's niece and nephew. Is that how they were going to "take care" of her, too—by eliminating her? No, she'd been in Basil's mind. She knew that he cared deeply for her well-being, and he was planning to ask for their *help*. Then why did she need to go to Alain—a killer and stalker?

"There just isn't any way—"

"Just hear me out. Please."

"Okay."

"I spoke with Alain after you and James visited him at his apartment. I'm fairly certain that your presence reverses the damage we did to his mind. When he's near you, he feels normal again. He stops being a psychopath."

Huh? This was pretty big news. Could one stop being a psychopath? She wondered what Lydia would have to say about that. "How is that possible?" she asked.

"You wanted to know why he was stalking you, and now you know. That's why he was following you. He regains his capacity to feel empathy, like a normal person. You make him feel normal again."

I make him feel normal again. She remembered how Proctor's eyes had sharpened and become aware, losing their pale gray color. How he had looked at her with awe.

"He means you no harm, I promise you that. You can trust him if you choose to get him involved. But no one else."

Amanda thought about James. About Matt. About all the new people who had recently come into her world, and about Lydia, her childhood friend; about not being able to trust any of them. So why should she trust Basil?

Because she now knew that she could always trust Basil. She had been deep inside him, had felt his fatherly love, and knew that he was sincere. He wanted to protect her. She needed this sense of security, and she clung to it.

Basil continued. "If I could take this ordeal from you, I would. But for now, all I can do for you is let you know that you are not alone. I'll be in touch as soon as I can."

She didn't want him to go. "Basil? Wait!"

"My dear girl, I must leave you. There's one more thing. The Committee is likely to overreact to this news of yet another Overload, and I'm telling you now that I don't trust them."

He doesn't trust them? "Then why are you—?"

"I'm still going to try to get them to help, but I worry that they won't agree to do so. They're not good people, Amanda."

He was hiding something from her. The realization was coming in faint waves. Suddenly, she saw an image of Basil with the Committee—like a movie reel projected in the corner of her mind. She could still see the dark road in front of her as she drove back to Boston, but she could also watch the replay of the scene.

"Mr. Blake," said the domineering Nourat Halabi. "No doubt you suspect what we're about to say. We cannot have another debacle. It is beyond my wildest imagination that two Overloads should happen so closely to each other, but they did."

Her suspicions were right. The Committee already knew.

"We will not attempt to close this Overload as we did with Alain Proctor's," added Rudolph Wojtek, an overweight man with small, pig-like eyes. "There is no known way to close it or to reliably contain it."

Basil clenched his fists in impotent rage.

"My dear Basil!" Paolo Gioia spoke up. "You are our most respected adviser, and you know that a Sentinel 10 is very valuable. But you know what happened the last time we tried. Try to remember your days as a neurologist. Overloads are just like a terminal illness. There is but one outcome, and it cannot be helped."

They were going to let her die.

Basil collected himself before speaking again. "You know I care for all of them, but Amanda is special. I've been in your service for fifty-five years now. You cannot deny me help with this, Paolo."

"We are well aware of your service to our cause," Paolo replied, raising a conciliatory hand. "But I'm sorry. There's nothing we can do."

Blake's face flushed. "The cause? YOUR cause? Which is what exactly? Get rich and live forever?"

Nourat took over. "We regret not being able to help. I suggest you take the opportunity to say goodbye to her. She doesn't have long."

How long? She pushed down her panic. She now understood why Basil didn't trust them. They didn't value her life. They didn't care that she was going to die. But Basil would keep trying to convince them, and he would try to find other ways of saving her. He was not going to give up. In the meantime, he was pointing her toward Alain Proctor.

The scene kept playing.

"Don't tell me that there's nothing that can be done. You have connections. You could ask."

"Mr. Blake, we're sorry you're so emotional about this," said Rudolph Wojtek. *He was stroking his chin, as if pensive.*

"Please! Someone, somewhere, knows something."

They remained impassive. Gioia shook his head.

"Then you will lose me too. If Amanda dies, consider me done."

She gasped. "If I die? Basil, am I going to die?"

"What?" Basil said, suddenly flustered. He must have realized that she was reading him, that she knew about his experience with the Committee. His tone became authoritative. "Shut off your receiving functions, if you can. In your current state, the Committee could locate you if you use the slightest energy pulse, so don't do that unless your life depends on it. Until they are fully on our side, I don't want them to know where you are. I must leave you now. Don't call me. I will get in touch when I can."

Waves of panic swept over her. Clearly, the Committee didn't care whether she lived or died. She couldn't go home. She placed her head in her hands. She could still see the bodies of the men she'd murdered.

"No, no, no," she told herself. "That was not my fault. It was just like a dream, I had no real control over my actions. There was nothing I could do."

She focused on her breathing. She was in trouble, big-time, but at least the Overload had given her something: a window into Basil and his true intentions; the knowledge and faith that she could indeed trust him. She remembered the waterfall she had focused on in her training, and after a short while, she was able to close off her receiving functions. With that, she managed to close the lid on the remaining Overload. She scratched away the blood that had dried on her face and eased back onto the freeway at a normal speed. She was on her way back to Boston and Alain Proctor was her destination. She gripped the steering wheel. She must trust Proctor, but how could a killer help her survive?

Chapter 21

Conscious of the need to throw the Committee off her trail, Amanda drove to South Station and parked in the public lot. She left her phone in the glove compartment so they couldn't track her via GPS, then got out, went to the kiosk, and paid for a month of parking. She then headed to the bus stop, her legs sluggish, feeling feverish and shivering, as if she were starting to come down with a bad cold.

Thankfully, the bus came quickly, and was almost empty. Just an hour later and it would have been packed with rush-hour commuters heading to work. She chose a window seat in the middle of the bus and stared forlornly into the dawn as it pulled away from the curb.

She didn't want to see her stalker again. But what else could she do? The Committee knew everything about her. Outside, the wind chased ragged shreds of clouds toward the horizon as the bus moved her along to her destination: Alain Proctor's apartment.

Getting closer, she pressed on the yellow tape to make the stop request. She got off the bus and tucked her hands into her pockets, still shivering, as much from apprehension as from the cold.

What are you doing? her mind screamed at her as she made her way to Proctor's building. Part of her knew that he'd help her, yet it made no sense to take refuge with a contract killer who was stalking her. What if Basil was wrong about him? She trusted Basil, but why on earth would anyone trust a man like Alain Proctor?

Then again, hadn't she just been there herself? Her heart sank a little at the thought that perhaps it was the Overload itself, and not the failed attempt by the Committee to rehabilitate him, that had turned Proctor into a killer.

A light drizzle began to fall, sprinkling the pavement, falling on her tired eyes and face, and on her matted hair. Hands thrust into the pockets of her jacket, feeling colder by the minute, she felt sleep deprived, unattractive, and sick. The wind picked up and she quickened her stride. Seeing a coffee shop, she hurried inside. She could hardly take this anxiety anymore; she would have a hot chocolate and give herself one more chance to think.

But inside the coffee shop she felt worse—paranoid, like everyone was staring at her. Watching her every move. As she nursed her hot chocolate, the paranoia intensified. She was also feeling more physically sick by the minute. Her head throbbed to the point where she wondered if the veins in her temples stood out.

She tossed her nearly full hot chocolate in the trash and went outside again. There wasn't a better solution than Alain Proctor. Not only was he the only other human being alive to have experienced Overload, he would also be able to advise her on her symptoms. Maybe he could even help her find a safe place to spend the night.

Amanda steeled her nerves as she entered the condo building. At the sight of the concierge, she hesitated. She had to take a risk, and be quick about it. As she passed the desk he didn't even give her a moment's glance. Safely in the elevator, she breathed a sigh of relief.

Then anxiety rose. *This is the point of no return.*

She stared blankly at herself in the mirrored wall of the elevator as it slowly made its way to his floor. She was not cheered by what she saw: she looked as bad as she felt.

The doors opened onto Proctor's floor, but Amanda hesitated. She still had time to turn back. For one agonizing moment, she racked her brain for another solution, but there was none. There was no turning back.

She stepped out as the doors were closing, and there he was, standing in the hallway, his condo door open behind him, wearing the same damn gray suit he always wore. He looked terribly anxious. So much for the element of surprise.

He took a few steps toward her. "Amanda, it's obvious that something has happened. It must have been extraordinary to make you come here, to me." His voice shook a little as he said the last words.

She neared him, all the while searching for the humanity in his eyes. As she got closer, she was relieved to find it there—they were blue, and full of puzzled concern. She said one word only: "Overload."

His face twitched as if something hit him. He said nothing but took her hand. As soon as he touched her, his breathing accelerated; he paled, then blushed. Amanda cringed and jerked her hand back. This was precisely what she had been afraid of. His interest was physical; it was written all over his face.

"What am I doing? I never should have come," she whispered, turning away. But in so doing, she reeled a little and had to catch herself by throwing a hand against the wall.

Proctor quickly moved to stand in front of her. "Amanda, wait! I'll do whatever you want. No one and nowhere else is safe for you now. *I am safe.*" He peered into her face. "Please, come inside. I will do everything I can to help you, I promise. Just let me help."

Amanda felt weak and dizzy. If she tried to run out now, she would pass out in the lobby or even the street. She *had* to trust him. She had to get over every mistrustful instinct she had and just let go. He sounded sincere, and Basil had told her to trust him.

Fighting waves of nausea, she followed him into his condo.

He shut the door behind them.

"Something's happening to me," she told him. Another wave washed over her, and she immediately sat on the floor, leaning back against the wall and closing her eyes. She was shivering, alternating between fever and cold sweats.

Proctor was immediately by her side. She glanced at him through half-open eyes but was too unwell to worry anymore. He took her hand again, put it to his lips, and kissed it. "You're burning up," he told her. "It's the Overload."

He pressed her hand against his cheek. The sweet gesture touched Amanda's heart on some level, but she immediately ripped those thoughts out of mind. This was not a good man. She did not like him, period.

"Stop this . . . don't touch me." She was too weak to pull away.

After some moments, he let go of her hand. "The Overload is making you sick. You managed to contain it, but it can't be contained for very long. It has to come out."

"Come out? Won't that mean more havoc?"

"It's the only way."

Amanda was struggling. She didn't trust him, but there was literally no other person in the known universe who had been through what she'd gone through in the past twelve hours. If this was going to be the end, there was nothing else she could do to stop it.

She took a deep breath and decided to take the plunge. "Basil told me you went through this. What can I do to stop it?" She looked at him, still finding it hard to focus, both visually and mentally.

He looked concerned. It was so strange to see him like that. She'd only seen the monster in their previous encounters. But now he seemed like he was struggling to find a way to comfort her. She could sense that he wanted to help her.

"It wasn't exactly like this for me," he said, "but I guess it varies. It must come out, Amanda. You must open it and release the energy. Otherwise it will burn you up. You won't last a day. Come, have a seat on the couch." He stepped back and held out his hand.

She shook her head. "But I can't open it up again. I may not be able to close it again, ever. It was horrible—it was like I stopped being myself. I was dangerous. I could kill you!"

"You won't kill me, and you *can* control it this time. In this setting. It's different. Trust me. Release it on me. I'll absorb the energy. It won't hurt me."

"No, no, no," she whispered, her mind reeling, shaking her head weakly. The implications were horrendous: she couldn't contain the Overload by sheer will. Even if she did release it now, how long would it be before it came back? Would she ever fully recover? Tears welled in her eyes. Already she felt a pressure building inside her head, insidious and lethal. Thinking was difficult, but she had to try to analyze the situation. Maybe she was missing something. Maybe there was a different way to go about this.

Basil had explained how Sentinels dealt with power. It would be no good to release the energy into thin air: she would just reabsorb it. During their training in Prague, she'd gathered that the Sentinels' energy bursts were a bit like lightning: they needed a conductor. In their case, it was psychic energy—therefore, the conductor had to be human neurons, and there was no way around that.

She huffed out a quick breath and slowly got up, focusing on keeping her balance. Perhaps the Overload wasn't an end at all. Perhaps it was a new beginning.

Meanwhile, Alain kept staring at her. When she stood up, he suddenly slid to his knees and hugged her legs. He was breathing heavily again. Yet her fear of what he might do was gone. She almost felt sorry for him. Her fear of her *own* feelings for him was not gone, however, and she continued to stomp on them the second they reared their head.

"I've been thinking about you since the moment I saw you," he said. "Thinking of you is all I do, day and night."

He looked at her, as if hopeful. *Hopeful for what?* she thought, suddenly irritated. She swayed, frowning, fighting for control. He pressed his cheek against her thighs, breathing in and out, his eyes tightly closed. "Did you know that when I'm with you—*because* of you—I become myself again?" he whispered. "I've felt nothing for the last three years." He looked up at her. "I can't help what I become when I'm in my altered state."

"I know," she said. "Basil told me what happened to you."

He continued to lean against her, hugging her legs. She didn't protest. She told herself that she needed his help and shouldn't alienate him. *If he likes to fall down on his knees and hug legs, that's fine.*

A bad, sharp pain in her left temple made her wince and gasp. Then it grew worse, like something drilling into her brain. She grabbed Proctor's shoulder and he looked up, alarmed. "Amanda, you have to release it. It will kill you."

"But I don't want to hurt you."

He got up. His hands hovered above her shoulders, at a loss as to how to best make contact. "It doesn't hurt me," he reminded her. "You know that. You've seen it. I like it. It gives me a thrill. Do it! Release it on me."

He seized her shoulders, and just as he pulled her toward him, the Overload opened, perhaps triggered by her surge of fear at being grabbed. She felt the Overload's onslaught distinctly this time. A savage energy, but without rage, perhaps because there was no clear need to defend herself. Proctor's hands tightened then released, and he fell to the floor unconscious. Terrified that she may have killed him, she held back the flow. He immediately opened his eyes again, staring up at her dreamily. He didn't seem in pain, so she had to continue; the energy inside demanded to flow free. She let it flow.

This time Alain seemed to fare better as the energy unleashed itself. He drew himself against the wall and seemed to relish bathing in the power she radiated.

Amanda, too, was starting to feel better. She focused on her breathing and after a few more minutes, shut the Overload down. She realized she was able to do so at will, now that the buildup had been released. It was such a relief to be free of pain, of nausea. Of all that horror.

She turned to Proctor. "Are you okay?"

A look of lust came over his face. "A little too strong even for me, but I'm fine. You can do it again if you need to, my little diamond."

She frowned.

He sighed a little and averted his gaze. "Please have a seat, Amanda," he said in a neutral tone. "You should not fear me, or fear for me. You look so pale. Are you sure you're okay?"

She rubbed her forehead then hugged herself. "I am, but I'm exhausted beyond anything I can describe. I haven't slept for two days."

"Tell you what, I'm going to leave for an hour, and you can shower and rest. There's only one bed, but it's yours."

He pointed the way to the bedroom. Before she could respond he was putting on his coat. He left the condo, locking her inside. This was unexpected. She was all alone in the killer Alain Proctor's condo, which was now the only safe place in the city.

She glanced around, hesitating, taking in the silence of the condo. From here she could see the bedroom, chic and minimalist, with staging that looked like it had been lifted directly from a catalogue photograph. Like nobody really lived there.

"Who *is* this man?" she muttered, then thought, *what if there are hidden cameras?* She winced at her paranoia. "Get a grip, Amanda." She headed to the shower so she could clean up and get a few minutes of rest before he returned.

Chapter 22

Vaguely aware of movement around her, Amanda heard herself moan in her sleep, but she could not wake up. Only a tiny part of her was conscious at all. Her sleep was like a deep, dark well, and she was lying paralyzed at the bottom, outside the concepts of time and space.

She squinted against the darkness. Her mind focused, remembering. She realized that she wasn't in Alain's bedroom anymore, and she struggled to understand where she was. But the Overload effects were too strong, pulling her back into an unnaturally deep slumber. Her eyes closed. Before drifting off into nothingness, she heard him speak.

"Shh. My little diamond... You need to sleep. Don't fight it." Then there was a sound . . . an engine starting. "Everything is fine," he whispered, closer to her, his voice drifting off, and then . . .

Amanda jerked awake with a strangled moan, her heart pounding. Fully alert, she saw that she was in the backseat of a car, and she was wearing nothing but her underwear and bra beneath a bedsheet, which was wrapped around her like a tortilla. At least her arms were free. She lifted her head to see that the car was speeding along a highway, rain sluicing down the windows. The dull light of a rainy day had replaced the darkness.

"Shh. Everything's okay." Alain Proctor was looking at her in the rearview mirror of his gray Mercedes as he raced through the rain. "My diamond rose."

Amanda remembered that she had showered, slipped on her underwear, climbed under the covers, and tumbled into oblivion within seconds. Now she wished she'd gotten fully dressed before getting into bed. Pulling the sheet up a little higher, she looked at him. At least she wasn't afraid of him anymore.

"Enough with this diamond rose business, please. Can you tell me what's going on?" She didn't know where they were headed, but oddly, she felt no danger.

"Contract killers. They managed to find you. We had to leave."

"What?"

"I called Basil Blake. Apparently some of the Whip and Compass higher-ups, all those millionaires you bankrupted when you destroyed the Whip and Compass, decided they had nothing to lose by keeping the contract out for you."

Oh. The bank accounts she had emptied. Amanda wondered just how deep the ramifications of her actions in Overload would be.

"I'm afraid that's not all," Alain said. Her dread intensified. "The Committee was divided about what to do with you. Someone wasn't happy with letting the Overload run its course. So they tipped off the Whip and Compass officials to your location—perhaps hoping that I would get the official blame for your murder. Two birds with one stone. I know that for a while, some of them have been concerned about my, uh, activities. They worry that it will lead back to them if I am ever caught."

"They could tell where I was because I accessed the Overload again," she surmised. "I can't believe that one of the Committee wants me dead." It was jarring to know that someone—anyone, actually—wanted her dead. She was a good person. How could someone hate her so much? From what she remembered of Basil's discussion with them, Nourat seemed the most coldhearted of the bunch, though Wojtek was repulsive in his own way. "Do you know who it is?"

"No."

"And the rest won't help me? But why? What's in it for them?"

She leaned forward, but Alain had no answer. He kept his eyes on the road, navigating the highway out of the city. Finally, he spoke up. "There's some good news: Basil has assured me that the Committee is currently in full agreement to leave you alone and let the Overload run its course."

"That's the *good* news?"

"They won't stand for any attack on their people, as per their policy. They will purge every last one of the Whip and Compass members, down to the last one in their ranks."

Purge. Meaning they're killing them all. When Matt implied we were like the Mafia, it was no joke.

She rubbed her eyes, trying not to let panic wash over her. The windshield wipers beat hypnotically, wiping the rain away to reveal the bleakness of the dawn. She was still exhausted.

"Don't worry," Alain said, his tone softer. "Basil will find a solution to the Overload. With the Committee on our side, there will be no further issues with hired guns. Which is fortunate," he added with a hint of sarcasm in his voice. He glanced at her in the rearview mirror. "Because I don't enjoy strange men surprising me in my condo in the middle of the night."

Amanda was startled. The killers had actually managed to make it inside? She must have slept through quite a fight. Suddenly worried for him, she leaned over the front seat and peered down at his gray suit. He seemed to be fine. Not a drop of blood anywhere. In addition to the usual expensive suit he wore black leather gloves, and in his lap there was a large handgun with a silencer.

"It doesn't look like you think they will stop," she observed, nodding toward the weapon.

"They will. I'll put it away when we arrive." His voice was confident.

"Arrive where?"

"You'll see. Just a quick stop."

She flopped back onto the seat and they drove on in silence. She wouldn't press for more answers now. She would find out soon enough.

Eventually they pulled into the driveway of a small, three-story apartment building in what looked like a seedy area of Boston. "I'll be quick," said Alain. He stepped out of the car and locked her inside without explanation.

She sat motionless for a minute, looking down at her hands. The rain kept drumming on the roof over her head. What had she gotten herself into? How had she ended up with Alain Proctor as a bodyguard? He was a fallen angel of sorts—a contract killer with a sudden return of conscience. But a killer, nevertheless! And here she was, nearly naked in his car, on the run from an ancient secret society, headed to God knows where, with a time bomb in her head and no idea how to save herself.

Holding the sheet up with one hand, she climbed into the front seat. He had taken the gun.

She trusted him not to harm her. At least, she thought she did. But should she? She had to get into his head. There was no way around it. The only way to know if she could trust him was to find out what was really on his mind. The Overload would allow her to do that. It would allow her to do almost anything.

When Proctor returned about fifteen minutes later, he was carrying a bag but no longer wearing gloves. When he tucked his phone into his coat she saw that both hands were bandaged. She steadied herself. Now was not the time to wonder what had happened in that building. She was going to go for it, come what may. He glanced in, seeming unsurprised to see her in the front seat.

As soon as he eased back into the driver's seat, Amanda turned on the Overload again. She wasn't in any immediate danger, so she was hoping she could control it this time. No matter what, she had to be sure of his true intentions. It was worth any risk, and she knew she only needed a few seconds. Still, she hesitated.

"Back in your condo, when we first came in," she began, staring ahead, wondering if the Overload showed in her eyes. "With James. Did you feel something? Did something happen to you? Because I could hear you calling out to me."

Out of the corner of her eye, she saw him looking at her. "Yes, something happened to me. Your presence gave me back my empathy. I could feel again. You opened me up."

She shifted forward, then turned to face him. Her eyes pinned him to the spot. "Well, I'm going to open you up again. In a different way this time, though." And she willed herself into him.

Surprisingly, Proctor struggled, really struggled, against her intrusion. But nothing is a match for a Sentinel 10 in Overload. He gasped, his head tossed back, his eyes squeezed shut. She was in.

As she experienced his mind, he continued to gasp for breath, clutching the steering wheel. She felt a pang at his obvious distress even as she probed his thoughts. Alain Proctor was telling the truth, there was no doubt about that. He'd do whatever it took to protect her. But that's not all she saw. Unexpectedly, she had caught a glimpse of everything: his desires, his need, his despair, his admiration of her, and his hopes. All the components of his love for her.

When she finished, he flopped back against the seat. The rain beat down outside. Finally he turned to her, distress pinching his forehead, and whispered, "Why?"

"I'm sorry! I'm sorry, but I had to. I had to know if I could trust you." She averted her gaze, overwhelmed and embarrassed by what she had learned.

Having taken a look inside his heart and mind, as brief as the intrusion had been, she could no longer barricade herself in the belief that this man was only a murderer with a psychopathic alter ego who lusted after her.

But with that stripped away, her own pull to him became difficult to repress. This was a hurt, lost soul. Proctor wished for purpose and meaning and redemption for his evil. He wanted to become a better man, without having any real idea what that meant. He needed her. He needed her to save him.

She didn't want to like him, but his need for her was a real aphrodisiac. She was finding it impossible to ignore or to deny the connection between them. She couldn't deny how deeply moved she felt after experiencing his mind, how it felt both strange and familiar, as if a part of her already knew him and recognized him as a kindred spirit.

Alain leaned closer to her, as if testing the waters. Sensing no resistance, he closed his eyes and nestled his head on her chest. She didn't pull away. She was surprised at how comfortable she felt with him resting against her. Maybe she felt like she owed him something for her painful intrusion into his soul. As he lay there, resting against her, something else in her stirred, as the heat of his breath touched her exposed skin. Desire. She tried brushing it away. She just wanted to hug him, that was all. Nothing more. She looked over his back, focusing on the world outside. Meanwhile, Alain's breathing slowed down and he shifted just a little, his cheek right above her breast, his arm hugging her seat. The rain had started again, splashing the windshield with shimmering droplets, softly falling all around them.

Eventually he whispered, "You shouldn't have done that. If I were capable of being angry with you, I would be."

Amanda didn't reply. She was uncomfortable with his feelings, but even more so with her own. She was still fighting the urge to hold him. To kiss him. To make him feel better after making him suffer. But that would be so wrong! He wasn't a good man. Why did she want him?

Because now she knew how much he loved her.

Nobody had ever loved her, not even her parents, and she wanted that above all else. Someone to really love her . . . but this! This man. How could it be him, of all people? This was too much to deal with, in the moment. Yet, she really wanted to stroke his hair. To brush it off his forehead. Her hand twitched, betraying her desire to hold him closer against her. All of him.

She caught herself, and gathered her hand into a fist. No, she'd do no such foolish thing as to let him in. She'd be vulnerable; she'd be taking a huge risk with her heart. Being targeted by killers and abandoned by the Committee was bad enough; she didn't need this complication. Maybe she'd think about him later. Much later.

"What happened to your hands?" she asked, clearing her throat.

Barely moving his lips, he replied. "One of the three was more difficult to get rid of than the other two. They certainly meant business."

Amanda imagined what would have happened had he not been there to protect her. She lowered her gaze to the head on her chest. "Thank you."

He pulled away and locked his blue eyes on hers. There was a question in there, but she couldn't guess what it might be and she wasn't about to go digging for answers again. Instead, she reached for a bandaged hand and wrapped hers over it in gratitude and empathy. *Gratitude isn't love*, she thought. *Gratitude isn't admitting to anything.*

At her touch, he drew a sharp breath. Turning her hand in his, he started to kiss it, first one side, then the other. His lips brushed against each of her fingertips. Paralyzed by the strange sensuality of the moment, Amanda couldn't take her eyes off him. He then leaned into her, covering her neck and shoulders with slow, burning kisses while the steady whisper of the falling rain shielded them from the world.

And then, with what seemed an enormous effort, he pulled himself back into his seat. "We have to go," he said bluntly. "Someone might still be after you. Your use of the Overload just now may have alerted them to your location. The Committee will put an end to any potential contracts to kill you, but they can't do it in one day."

He started the car, and they drove in silence for a few minutes. Despite the strangeness of it all, Amanda relaxed. Now that the immediate threat of romantic feelings had passed, she quickly replayed it all in her head, and admitted to herself that it had been nice.

"Where exactly are we going?" she asked, stretching, feeling much more at ease with him.

He handed her his phone. "Basil's expecting your call. He's suspicious of me too. I know he told you to trust me, but he wants to hear from you ASAP. He wants us to join him at his house."

"What was that other place, anyway? Is that where you stash your secret lovers?"

Alain started, turning to face her. He took her hand and gave it a quick peck. "You're joking."

"Of course I'm joking." She waved the topic away. Still shaking her head, she looked out the window then turned back to him.

"Okay, who are you, Alain? Who are you, really? Are you good? Are you bad? What are you?"

He stared at the road ahead. "I'm yours."

Wow.

"Come on," she said, her heart pounding. "Don't be ridiculous. You barely know me. Aren't you supposed to be human when you're around me?"

The side of his mouth curled into an almost-smile. She had the sense that he wasn't used to smiling or laughing.

"I am. When I'm around you. I want you to know that it was the Overload that forced me to kill. I only killed a few people back then, just bad ones. It was out of necessity, and then—"

"Maybe we can talk about that later, okay?" *Maybe never.* She disliked how casually he spoke about killing. "Why don't you tell me about who you were before the Overload. You do have a past, don't you?"

"Everyone has a past, Amanda."

She got the sense that this was all he was going to say. So she decided to try for more simple questions. "How old are you?"

"I'm twenty-five," he answered, without hesitation. "I used to be a paramedic. That was before I became Sentinel 10."

"Wow. I'm surprised by how many of us are health professionals."

"I doubt it's a coincidence; nothing ever is. Do you believe in karma, my little diamond?"

"I don't," Amanda scoffed. "And what is with you and this 'diamond' business?"

"I have a thing for nicknames. You're a diamond rose, Amanda."

"Okay fine, but what does that mean?"

"It means that you're a mesmerizing, natural beauty. A combination of strength and fragility. You have a sort of purity of spirit, a sincerity that is difficult to find. You're everything I'm not, and never was."

Amanda turned to the window again. *Great flattery*, she thought. *But how can he know those things about me if he doesn't even know me?*

He glanced over at her. "You don't like it?"

"It's fine," she lied. "It's hard to believe that just a few days ago, you were stalking me all over the world. And now look at us."

"Crazy," he said.

She shook her head. "Life. I mean, is there any rhyme or reason to anything?"

He glanced at her. "On the contrary, it's all rhyme and reason. There are no coincidences."

She shrugged. She understood that most people needed to believe in some kind of a higher power, and she generally didn't judge them, though she herself was a woman of science and didn't believe in those kinds of things.

The car crossed the yellow line and veered back. He was drooping in his seat. The evening's events must have taken a toll on him.

She didn't want to take the risk that he'd pass out behind the wheel and drive them off the road. Besides, she liked driving. She preferred it. She asked gently, "Do you mind if I drive? You must be tired, and your hands must hurt."

"You don't believe in purpose?"

"I believe in . . . myself. I believe that a purpose is whatever each of us chooses it to be. And speaking of purpose, why don't you pull over? I think my purpose now is to get us to Basil's safely."

After a moment of silence, he said, "I'll stop for gas soon. Then I'll give you my coat to wear, and you can take over the driving."

"Good," she said, relaxing into her seat. Then she remembered, "I have to call Basil. I can't believe I forgot." She reached for Alain's phone. Hers was back in her car, where she'd left it to escape being tracked. She couldn't remember where she'd left her purse. She had no credit cards, no cash, no driver's license. She really was completely dependent on this man.

"Do you want to buy clothes on the way?" he asked.

"No, I'll just ask Basil when we get there. I'd rather not stop unless it's necessary." The fewer risks they took, the better.

Chapter 23

The gray Mercedes eased its way around the curve, nearing their destination. As they pulled up the long, winding driveway, they could see a slice of the lake glistening in the dusk. The rowboat was still moored to the dock, and Amanda could see the quaint thatched roof of the house in the distance. But something was off. Amanda had a strange feeling of unease.

"Something's not right."

Alain straightened up. "What do you mean? I don't see anything."

"No, something's wrong," she insisted, peering left and right. She stopped some distance from the house, her heart racing. "Okay, something is majorly wrong. Where is his security detail?"

Her senses straining, she cracked open the car door and listened. Everything was silent. A calm dusk had settled over the house and surrounding pine trees. A wooden swing swayed on the porch.

"Wait!" Alain cried out grabbing her hand with his own bandaged one. "You're right. I just saw something move over there in the bushes."

"That's it," she said with finality. "Whatever it is, I'm accessing the Overload. We need the shield." She focused and within seconds the shield was on. "Don't move until I come to your side."

He nodded and Amanda stepped out, the ground cold and prickly under her naked feet. Glancing around, she gathered Alain's coat around her otherwise practically naked body and listened again. A cricket song sounded here and there, but everything else was quiet. "Okay, Alain, come out, quickly."

Just as he came out of the car, a group of men burst out of hiding and opened fire on them. After the first burst, the men advanced slowly, surrounding them in a semicircle. If she hadn't put on the Overload they would both have died. But she had already encased Alain in the shield, extending it two feet beyond them in every direction. As the men emptied their guns, each time a bullet hit, it sizzled and dropped to the ground, as harmless as a pellet, its velocity completely absorbed by the shield and converted into energy. The shield was feeding off every shot fired at it, absorbing the energy and getting stronger by the minute.

"Stay behind me." As Alain raised his weapon she arrested his hand. "No, no shooting! No one needs to die. We will handle this my way."

Alain obeyed without a word, tucking himself in close behind her.

Amanda lowered her head and stared straight ahead. The men paused before coming closer, their arms lowered, their faces blank. All at once they unloaded their weapons, threw them on the ground, and walked away. A few seconds later, motorcycle engines revved and six bikers sped away from the premises.

Then everything was quiet again. Just a normal evening in the countryside. Amanda shut down the Overload and put her hands in the pockets of her coat. She felt content. She was positive that she could now control her Overload.

"Was that mind control?" Alain asked from behind her. He placed his hands on her shoulders.

She liked the way his hands felt, bandaged or not, but she wasn't going to let him know that. "Yup. Right now they're heading to the police station to confess to every crime they've ever committed. My programming won't stop until they are convicted. They will plead guilty, and say they have found Jesus." She looked at him over her shoulder. "See, no need to kill them."

He gave her a vague smile. "Found Jesus? Are you serious?"

"Follow the story in the coming weeks. You'll see!" She erupted into laughter.

He looked at her, his eyebrows raised in what might have been awe. "I think you were already a force of nature before you became a Sentinel, Amanda."

"You should have seen me run track and field when I was younger." Giddier by the moment, she leaned on him, chatting as they walked over to the house. Then she noticed Basil and James standing on the porch and pulled away, as if caught red-handed.

"Hi, Amanda," said James. He looked tense. "We came when we heard the shots, but you obviously had everything under control."

"Hello, Alain. It's so nice to see you again," said Basil.

Proctor nodded silently. Amanda watched as he looked at the men on the porch. It was clear he was concerned about James being there. She wasn't sure how she felt about it herself. Basil hadn't mentioned bringing James into the picture.

James gave Amanda a look that made her feel as if he psychically knew about her attraction to Proctor. Then she realized she was in her underwear, with Alain's coat thrown over her. She tried to say something, but her words came out garbled. Dizziness came upon her, and her left arm and leg went numb. James caught her as she stumbled forward. The warm feeling of his leather jacket and the strength of his arms felt reassuring, if only a little.

"Heavens, it's a stroke," said Basil, rushing to her side. Amanda opened her eyes, feeling her face on fire. The fever was coming back, rising by the second. "Can you talk? Can you move? Raise your arms, my dear."

"I'm okay; it was only a brief one, I think," she managed.

James guided her into the house and felt her forehead. "You're burning up. You're not okay at all. What's happening?" he asked Basil.

"It's the Overload," Alain answered, following them into the living room. "Amanda, you have to release it again. It's more extreme now. You don't have a lot of time." He took her hands, plunging his gaze into the depths of hers. "Amanda. Like the other time. Go for it."

Amanda released herself from James's grip and stepped aside. James's face twitched as the other man briefly cupped Amanda's face with his palms and whispered something only she could hear. Words she didn't want to hear. Words she dreaded.

Hurt me.

"No, I don't want to hurt you." Her face twisted into a tearful grimace. "God, it hurts so much. Like a metal rod in my eye." She could barely stand and would have slid to the ground had he not held her up.

"Please. Hurry," he whispered.

"Forgive me," she said and unleashed all the pent-up energy on him. It released like a lightning bolt and blue sparks slashed in Alain's direction. The force propelled him three feet backward. He fell to the floor, out cold.

But she couldn't stop. Not yet. The energy had a life of its own. And she was in pain. It had to go somewhere.

Alain began seizing, shaking all over.

"Stop it. You'll kill him!" James threw forward, trying to push Alain out of the way. Basil reached for his sleeve to hold him back, but it was too late. Amanda turned instinctively, and James became the next target.

Although the Overload was already three-quarters spent, it hit James like a ton of bricks. Terrified, she saw him try to hit back, full force. Arms extended, he groaned, struggling to neutralize the raw immensity of her power, while blue sparks sizzled all over the room.

Finally exhausted, Amanda fell on the couch. Her heart was racing, but she was starting to feel well again.

James reeled and leaned with his forearms on the table, fighting to catch his breath. His jacket had acquired long, sinewy marks, resembling the skin of a person hit by lightning. "Unbelievable," he rasped.

"I am so sorry!" Amanda cried, almost sobbing. She forced herself off the couch and stumbled to Basil's side. "Oh God, how is he? Alain?"

"Alive, coming to," said Basil, his tone grave. Alain's eyes opened and he started blinking. "James, help us get him into bed."

"Whoa!" She turned to see Matt coming through the door, as nonchalant as ever. She could only imagine how it all looked to him: James bent breathlessly over the heavy oak table; Amanda in underwear, wearing a man's coat; Basil leaning over a prostrate man in a gray suit, a shattered lamp by his side.

"Hey, guys! Are you all going to bed? Can I come?"

Despite herself, Amanda snorted. Matt could always be counted on to treat an otherwise grim situation with humor.

"Matthew, come in. Thank you for getting here so quickly." Basil motioned him over.

"No problem." Matt moved across the room and peered down at Alain. "So who's the fallen hero?"

"Alain Proctor," James explained, recovering. "Help me get him upstairs." James lifted Alain's arm over his shoulder and invited Matt to do the same.

"Um, hi, guys?" To Amanda's surprise Lydia was here as well, dragging a shiny compact suitcase. She gaped at her unusually attired friend. "Is everyone okay?"

Amanda wrapped the coat around herself self-consciously. "Stop staring, Lydia. Extraordinary things have been happening. You have no idea."

"Clearly," said Matt.

Chapter 24

Soon the kitchen was filled with activity. Basil was making coffee and tea, while Lydia was placing a couple of frozen pizzas in the oven. Basil had determined that Alain didn't need a hospital so they had put him into a bed upstairs, more or less unconscious.

At Basil's request, Lydia had brought several clothing options for Amanda, and Amanda now traded Alain's outerwear for one of Lydia's dresses, a dark-green leather sheath that hugged her in all the right places.

"Keep it if you like it, Mandy," Lydia told her. "It stopped fitting me about two years ago." Lydia herself was the very picture of boho chic in a crocheted top with boot-cut embroidered jeans and open-heel booties.

For a minute, sitting in the dining room with this crew, eating pizza and sipping tea, Amanda almost forgot her situation. Inevitably, though, her thoughts drifted back to the grim reality of her Overload.

The next time a surge hits, I might not survive, she told herself. *And if I try anything with Alain again, I will probably kill him. Is this the end?*

"I may have found a solution, Amanda," Basil said softly, as if reading her mind.

Her eyes suddenly brimmed with tears, quite against her will. "There's hope?"

Everyone fell silent. Basil lightly tapped her hand. "Someone will be joining us on Skype soon. She's with the Rosicrucians."

Matt let out a gasp.

"I know, I know." He put a hand on Matt's shoulder. "But we have no choice."

"Why do we need help from them when we have our own Committee?" Matt asked with clear displeasure.

Basil lowered his eyes.

"Wait! Are you telling me those assholes aren't going to help?" His uncharacteristically angry tone surprised everyone.

"Matt, how about you put it on ice?" James said. "We're waiting to hear how to save Amanda's life here."

"Okay, sorry." Matt shoved a slice of pizza into his mouth.

Blake switched on the flat-screen TV on the opposite wall. "Hello, Christina-Abigail," he said to the woman who appeared. "It is good to see you again."

"Save it, Basil." The woman appeared to be in her mid-forties; she looked prissy and generally unhappy. "Let's cut to the chase. Here's what I have for your Sentinel. I will explain it in detail for her benefit."

Amanda didn't like the woman's tone, and she fought the urge to tell her to speak to Basil with more respect. However, it was clear that whatever she had to say might be Amanda's only hope. Gioia's words reverberated in her head: *These Overloads are like a terminal illness. There is but one outcome, and it cannot be helped.*

"Have you heard about the Ascendants, also known as the Primordial Archetypes?" Christina-Abigail asked.

Everyone except Basil stared blankly. She continued. "The Ascendants can remove the Overload with no complications or side effects. They did so the very first time it happened. Back when the Rosicrucians and Sentinels were allies."

As if Basil could sense Amanda's confusion, he said, "The Ascendants are difficult to define. They are something of a cross between sentient beings and raw psychic energy. Some believe them to be the result of thousands of years of accumulated psychic residue, before there were any Sentinels to clean up the mess. This residue was gleaned from all living things: humans, animals, plants, even the earth itself. They are powerful, and they are neither good nor evil. Some consider them to be the world's consciousness. A few Rosicrucians have interacted with the Ascendants, some as recently as the 1920s."

Christina-Abigail spoke from the screen. "The Ascendants are the power behind Tarot cards. The querent communicates with them through divination cards, which never fall randomly. They are guided by the Ascendants. Then the querent interprets the cards that come up. Sometimes the reading won't make sense: that's because the Ascendants choose not to talk. In fact, they were the very inspiration behind the archetypal principles of the Major Arcana—the Empress, the Emperor, the High Priestess, the Hierophant, the Magician, and the Fool. It's how they introduced themselves to our explorers. Some texts said they originated in ancient Egypt, although the details are obscure, and our texts do not agree."

"Stonehenge was built to communicate with them," said Basil, jumping in again. "They are referred to as the Judges in the more ancient texts. They probe your soul to determine if you are of worth to this world. Because their power is so immense, so raw, only a Sentinel in Overload can stay alive in their direct presence. Which is why all of these indirect communication tactics, such as the Tarot cards and the standing stones, exist."

"Great. So how do I find them?" asked Amanda.

Christina-Abigail turned a rather cold eye on her. "Ms. Griffith, I must tell you that this information is not complimentary."

"Christina! For God's sake, you—"

"It's not me, Basil. I can't communicate with you without informing my boss. Surely you can appreciate that. He is sympathetic, but we're not friends. We're not going to provide information for free. Sentinel 10, you will owe us."

Amanda could hardly believe it. "Owe you what?" she demanded. "You can't hold this over my head. You've told me enough so that we will find them, I think, even if you don't tell us exactly how."

"Tsk tsk tsk, Ms. Griffith," the lady chuckled. "You must be honorable, or the Judges will have your head instead of helping you."

Amanda felt the cold grip of fear in the pit of her stomach.

Christina-Abigail continued. "However, your reluctance is understandable. I can ask my boss to explain exactly what he requires."

"Please do," Amanda said. The woman simply nodded, then disconnected.

"What a bitch," Lydia said, surprising Amanda. Lydia had certainly been known to have strong opinions and emotions before, but it wasn't like her to throw the B word at a woman she'd had barely any interaction with. "I hope she's not your ex-wife or something, Basil."

"She's my granddaughter," Basil replied softly.

A stunned silence fell over the room.

Blake sighed. "I was born in 1911. The Committee leaders are all several centuries old. Rudolph Wojtek is the oldest and Paolo's the youngest. He's about my age." He held up a hand. "Don't ask; there's so much I can't tell you. Suffice it to say, they recruited me when I was fifty-six and halted my aging. They do this for all of the advisers. Once I retire, in about five years, the hold will be removed, and I will resume aging at a normal rate." He sighed again and lapsed into silence.

"That's it, I'm getting a drink," said Matt. "What do you have, Basil? If you don't have anything I'm gonna run out and get something because I really need to unwind. James, wanna come with? I need to have a chat man-to-man. Maybe I should hang out with Lydia, though, because I feel like I'm going nuts."

"Oh, thank you, Matt, it's nice to feel needed," Lydia joked.

"I'm going to check on Alain," Amanda said.

Chapter 25

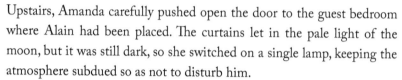

Upstairs, Amanda carefully pushed open the door to the guest bedroom where Alain had been placed. The curtains let in the pale light of the moon, but it was still dark, so she switched on a single lamp, keeping the atmosphere subdued so as not to disturb him.

Alain was on his side, facing the window. He was covered by a blanket, only his pale hair visible in the moonlight. She took a moment to lock the door behind her, then looked back at the bed.

"Alain?" she whispered.

He turned and his face brightened at the sight of her. He ran a quick hand through his hair and sat up in bed. His pants and jacket were on the chair, but he had kept on his shirt. He looked so normal, so . . . good. She smiled and sat next to him. "How are you?"

He continued to look at her, his eyes undergoing their usual change in her presence, growing a crisper blue.

"It is so striking how this works . . ." she marveled. "You really change when I'm here. It's visible. Your eyes . . ."

He shook his head. "I can feel your effects from downstairs. The Overload—it makes me feel your presence at a wider range. So if you see a change now, it's only because I'm very glad to see you."

Amanda suddenly felt on the verge of tears. She lowered her head and reached out to him, stroking his arms and shoulders. "Alain, I can't tell you how bad I feel about putting you through this! I didn't know it was going to hit you so hard this time. I am so sorry."

Emboldened by her touch, he drew her into his arms. His touch was both soft and firm. Flustered by the sensations racing through her, she tensed and turned her face away. She tried to reason with her thumping heart, but didn't try to leave.

"But *I* knew," he said, his voice low and hoarse. "I knew it would be this difficult. Don't forget, I've gone through the Overload before. As a Sentinel, I wasn't killing people because I wanted to. I was doing it because the Overload was killing me. I had to release it." He kissed the green leather fabric covering her shoulder and added, "Don't I deserve a kiss after this?"

Amanda remained silent. Unsure of her feelings, she tried to force her thoughts to stability. To James. Before this disaster hit her, she hadn't seen James in a while. She hadn't even missed interacting with him. Yet when she saw him here, he had once again become the handsome and unattainable hero, and her feelings were more divided than ever.

Because now there was also Alain. A killer. Lustful and hard to understand. Maybe bad to the core. And he was in love with her.

She felt hopelessly mixed up. Yes, feeling loved so unconditionally was exhilarating, but was she in love with Alain? The contract killer? Most assuredly not. Was she in love with James, then? Was it even possible to love someone who didn't love you back? James had had a couple of months now to develop feelings for her, and he'd done nothing to indicate interest. Well, almost nothing. Her mind scrolled through the more intimate moments they'd had together: his flirtatious comments about her eyes, his bear hug after saving her from the oncoming truck, his body against hers during their wild motorcycle ride. She had no idea what she wanted. Or if she wanted either one of them, at all.

Alain pulled her even closer and pressed his face against the silky strands of her hair. She felt the shudder in his breath when he kissed the side of her head. "Amanda, Amanda," he whispered. "You really hurt me this time, you can't imagine."

"Didn't you lose consciousness right away?" she whispered.

He drew another ragged breath. "Won't you kiss me? I'll feel so much better."

He tightened his grip on her and she turned her face to him, to tell him to let go. Instead, she found him so close that kissing was inescapable. She was a bird on a flight path, with no time to change course. He moaned as his lips brushed lightly against hers. Their caresses were as soft as fluttering wings. The gentleness and innocence of the kiss surprised her. She pushed in for more. Pressing her mouth fully against his, she abandoned herself to the moment.

Then the door handle rattled from the outside. Amanda immediately pulled away from Alain, flustered and full of unprocessed emotions. She jumped to her feet, but he grabbed onto her desperately. "Don't go."

"Everyone knows I'm here, Alain. I have to go. But I will see you soon."

She strode to the door and opened it to find James standing there. Her heart dropped. He gave her that look again. Was he jealous? He didn't look thrilled. His lips were set in a straight line, and he was avoiding eye contact. "That woman is back on Skype. I'll wait if you need a minute."

"No, I'm coming right now," Amanda said, making sure to speak in a clear voice. She went out into the hall, closing the door behind her. James walked on ahead down the dimly lit hallway with hardly a glance at her.

He stopped before they got to the stairs. "So, are you an item now with your favorite killer for hire?" he asked, his tone pure snark.

"We are not an item," Amanda said, brushing past him. "But Basil told me how Alain became what he is. He used to be a Sentinel 10, you know."

James followed behind, then paused for a moment before asking, "And how does that change that he's a killer?"

Amanda felt the need to defend Alain. What had happened to him wasn't his fault. "He experienced an Overload. Then, instead of curing him, the Committee botched things up so badly that he became a psychopath. But because I'm a Sentinel 10, he changes back to normal when he's with me."

"How can you stand him touching you?" asked James abruptly, darting a quick glance at her. It was as if he hadn't heard a word she said.

Amanda was taken aback. "Um. Well . . ." She slid a quick hand through her hair, unsure of what to say. "I don't really let him. But he was there for me when no one else was."

James stopped in front of her on the stairs, his eyes level with hers. *God, he is so handsome.* "Amanda, I spent two days and nights driving around the city looking for you, after Basil told me you called in the middle of the night and something was happening. Instead of running to Proctor, why wouldn't you call *me*?"

Amanda suddenly saw exactly how it looked to him, and tried to explain. "Hey, hey, wait. This is complicated. Basil told me to trust *no one* but him and Alain Proctor—because Alain had been through the Overload, and he couldn't be sure of the Committee's reaction."

"I don't give a rat's ass about the Committee, or their reactions. Had they told me not to help you, do you really think I wouldn't? Didn't you see my messages?"

"Actually, I was afraid the phone was being traced, so I left it in my car after I got back to the city."

"I don't understand any of this, Amanda." He glanced at her again, an unidentifiable emotion in his eyes.

"Listen, it was complicated, and now it's even more complicated. Let's talk in a bit, okay? If I am still alive, that is."

Downstairs, Christina-Abigail was standing by on-screen. She waited for everyone to sit down before she spoke, as prissy and arrogant as ever. "I'm sorry, but my boss can't say what we might require yet. I'm sure you can appreciate that this decision is too important to make quickly. Bringing you to the Ascendants would be a huge favor and will require an equally significant sacrifice in return."

Amanda felt overwhelming pangs of fear and despair. She had no choice now but to trust blindly in the mercy of the Rosicrucians? Really? Sitting down, she propped her head on her hands, not listening to the conversation around her.

Suddenly something clicked in her mind. It was as if she regained perspective. *Why should she be at anyone's mercy?* She was powerful, the most powerful human being in the world. In fact, she was so powerful it was killing her. She raised her eyes, focused and angry. With conviction, she stood and moved closer to the screen, fixing it with disturbing intensity. Christina-Abigail shrank back an inch or two.

A Sentinel 10 wasn't here to ask for favors.

"Here's what's going to happen, right now," Amanda enunciated. "You are *most* definitely going to tell me where to find the Ascendants. Because if you don't, *I will burn you alive*, in one last hurrah of the biggest, baddest Overload ever. You tell your boss that. He knows I can. The Overload has no boundaries. Before I die, I'll take you and your boss with me. Consider yourselves chosen. You'd better pray that I make it. That said, I *am* an honorable person, and I will do you a favor of *my* choosing. You can ask me what you wish, and I will consider it. Oh, and if this sort of a decision doesn't earn me brownie points with the Judges, so be it. If they can read hearts, they can't be tricked anyway: I am what I am."

Christina-Abigail said simply, "Your terms are acceptable. No need to get upset. I'm only trying to make the best possible deal for my employers. The Rosicrucians are not a charity network."

Amanda stared back at her, waiting.

"The Ascendants are in a natural cave formation on an abandoned military base in the middle of the Sycamore Canyon in Arizona. I'm sending you the exact coordinates."

"Christina-Abigail, I am ashamed to be your grandfather," Basil said sadly.

Christina-Abigail's face flashed with sudden anger, and she rolled her chair toward the screen. "You told them?" she snarled. "You told your pets your secret? I never thought you capable of it. Decades of keeping secrets, Gramps, is what you do best." Her voice was filled with bile. Amanda wondered what the rift in the family had been; how Basil lost his daughter. How something could have pulled his own child away from him to join an organization that for centuries had worked against them.

Basil's face suddenly looked gray, old, and defeated. Whatever the story there, it must have been painful.

Matt, James, Amanda, and Lydia instantly moved closer to him for support.

"Hey, lady," Matt protested, "we're not pets."

"We're a team. And what you are is not a word for polite company," added James.

"You're one secret I wish he had never told us," Amanda added.

Lydia said nothing, but her look conveyed what she thought of the woman.

Yet Christina-Abigail had regained her full composure. There was something of Basil Blake's dignity to her, after all. "Do you require assistance getting to the base?"

"No, we're good," said James.

"We require you to kindly get out of our faces," Amanda said, and she quickly shut down the Skype connection.

Chapter 26

At the break of dawn, Amanda left with Basil to make the final preparations for the trip to the canyon. James had gone the night before to secure a plane with help from the Committee. Now that Amanda would either be cured or killed by the Ascendants, the onus was no longer on the Committee to deal with her problem. Apparently, they had decided that it was now okay to help. Preparations complete, Amanda and Basil returned to the house to collect their belongings and Alain, and to say their goodbyes.

"Alain, please hurry," Basil said as the chauffeur opened the back door of his Rolls-Royce. Alain seemed immobilized by desire, hungrily running his eyes over Amanda as she said goodbye to Matt and Lydia on the porch.

Amanda knew she looked stunning in the olive-colored, front-zip designer jumpsuit that Lydia had brought. She appreciated that Alain noticed. James never seemed to notice much about her. Until she locked herself in a room with Proctor, and then suddenly, there he was, banging on the door, all jealous! Men. Who could possibly understand them?

She hugged Lydia, then Matt. "Take care, guys. I hope to see you soon."

Lydia swallowed hard, searching her face. "I know you, Mandy, and I know your heart. You will be fine. Please, please text me as soon as it's over." She hugged her one more time, and whispered so only Amanda could hear, "You need to be careful of Alain."

Amanda pulled out of the hug. "Huh?"

Lydia hugged her back then whispered again. "He's dangerous, Mandy. I don't want to get into it now. I just want you to go and get well. But just promise me you'll be careful about trusting him, okay?"

"Okay, fine." What else was she going to say?

Amanda worked to push her trepidation aside and climbed in next to Basil. They headed to the military base where James was waiting for them.

As they drove, she mulled over her friend's words. In the end, she decided to trust her own feelings. What else could she do? And try as she might, she could not feel any danger from Alain.

"Did you know that Sycamore Canyon is the second-largest canyon in Arizona?" James asked. They were now comfortably seated in the plane. James looked confident and natural in the pilot's seat. "It's 56,000 acres of wilderness. No paved roads, no campgrounds. Maybe a hiker or two."

"About as remote a place as it can be," Basil mused. He sat back and crossed his arms, lost in thought.

Amanda spent most of the plane ride taking in the scenery. As they closed in on their destination, the landscape shifted, the ponderosa pines giving way to open spaces and rust-colored mountain ranges. James masterfully navigated the black Pilatus PC-12 plane through clouds and around soaring pinnacles. The cliffs were colorful and sliced with deep gorges. It was a rough and wild place, abandoned to nature.

"Okay, I see it," signaled James.

"That's it? That barely looks like a runway," Amanda said, staring down at the battered path ahead.

"We're going to land soon. Get ready."

He'd probably landed planes in much worse conditions. She had to admit that his confidence and calm was sexy. Yet, as much as she trusted his skills, she couldn't help a little gasp when the wheels of the plane touched down. "We're good, Amanda, we're good," he reassured her, darting her a look. He was keeping everything safe and under control. She liked that.

Once the plane had immobilized, James, Amanda, Alain, and Basil climbed out onto the cracked concrete. The base was definitely abandoned. A rusted bunker squatted in the distance, with birds hovering above it.

Everything was eerily quiet.

James eyed Alain and asked, "Do you even own anything besides suits, pal?"

"I can strip, if you like," Alain replied grimly. Amanda and Basil frowned and tried to ignore the tension between the men. James shook his head and strode ahead.

The air was warm and dry, blowing fine sand and tumbleweeds across the runway. Amanda's hair briefly flew into her face.

She tensed. "Hush!" She realized she was receiving a message, though she couldn't quite make it out. One thing was certain. She wasn't hearing it. She was feeling it. The message came in the form of an emotion, a raw idea that wasn't associated with words.

She extended her palm toward the bunker, her energy a clear match to the feeling emanating from it. The Ascendants. They were beckoning. "I can feel them," she said, narrowing her eyes. "They're in the bunker. Let's go, guys. This thing in my head might blow up any minute."

"I feel them too," James remarked. "They are very powerful."

"They're trying to send me a message," she said in a faint whisper, barely moving her lips. She hurried forward, not waiting for the others.

When they neared the bunker door, Basil stopped. His hand went up to his chest and clutched at his shirt. He was hyperventilating. "I can't come any closer. They are too powerful. They are doing me harm, I can tell."

Amanda didn't want to see him harmed. "Go back to the plane, Basil. You don't look well." She hugged him and tried to smile, but the effect of this unknown force on him scared her. "See you soon."

Behind his rimless glasses, her adviser's eyes were attentive. "My dear girl, you will be fine. Yes, they are strong, but not evil. Much like radiation, their power is deadly if not handled properly. I have to go." He nodded to the men and hurried back to the plane. Amanda watched him get to safety, then turned her attention back to the door.

Alain pulled at the handle. "It's locked."

"Not for long. Step aside." James extended his arm and the heavily bolted doors rattled and flew open.

They peered into an empty room with concrete walls. There didn't seem to be any danger as they entered. Then Amanda shrieked and stopped dead in her tracks. A familiar, severe pain started in her head. "Guys, it's starting again. Oh my God. Please no, not yet . . ."

She became incredibly dizzy. Everything was spinning, while burning pain sizzled through her brain. Both men grabbed at her, but she could hardly feel them. Nobody could help her now.

And then she felt it again . . . the message from the Ascendants. A message that came to her not through words, but through an essence. The spinning stabilized, and through the haze she saw flickering silhouettes in the wall ahead. It was as if the wall had become porous, showing her a glimpse of the other side.

It was time.

"Stay here. I see them," she told the guys. "They're waiting for me."

Silently, stumbling and swaying, Amanda walked toward the wall at the opposite end of the room. But before she reached it, a lightning ball flew out of it toward her, at her side in an instant. It sizzled and hovered, rapidly growing to encompass her in her entirety. She heard Alain cry out in alarm.

A portal opened inside the lightning ball, and without hesitation, she went through it.

Chapter 27

For what seemed like several minutes, she was between worlds. She was a part of the lightning, but she could also make out images and sounds from the bunker where she had left the men. Judging from their body language, things weren't going well. They were squared off to each other, fists clenched. But she wouldn't be any help to the situation until she got better. She had to take care of herself before she could worry about anyone else.

And then the world of the bunker was gone and she was firmly in the other reality. At first it appeared she was in some sort of cave, yet she soon realized it was something else. Something between the physical world and another dimension. Something ceaselessly shifting and merging. Her dizziness stopped, and she felt at peace. It was a deadly calm. Like in the eye of a hurricane.

Rolling walls of cloud-like formations surrounded her, merging into the stone, rising to an incredible height. Looking up, Amanda saw that the cave opened up to a dark, mystical sky, and the rolling walls formed rows in a gigantic majestic amphitheater.

Strange figures loomed ahead of her, vaguely human. Iridescent, then growing dark, then growing white, then back to their rainbow shimmer. In long robes, their silhouettes flickered and undulated as they drifted in and out of this dimension. They were the surreal figures of the Tarot.

There were six of them at first, then three disappeared. After what seemed like a moment of contemplation, one of the remaining figures spoke.

"This penitent looks very strange indeed."

It did not speak out loud. The words were more like a whisper . . . more like a thought that had delicately etched into Amanda's consciousness.

"We have not seen a penitent in a very long time."

Then came a haughty retort. "Silence, Fool. Your foolish banter displeases us."

"Yes, Empress," the first voice replied, as if bowing down to her authority.

"This one is far gone," the Empress declared. "Dead within minutes she'd be, had she not come to us."

"Come closer," the third figure urged, her long limbs slowly flickering into position as she appeared to open her arms. "I am the High Priestess, and I shall read your heart." She shimmered in all colors of the rainbow as Amanda advanced, stopping a few feet away. The figure had no face, yet it exuded a steady and powerful presence that felt human enough.

A peculiar peace took over Amanda, numbing her senses. Nothing mattered anymore. It was as if a wool blanket had wrapped itself around her heart and her soul, anesthetizing her fears, her thoughts, and her desires, while she stood before the ancient Judges. She could have died right there, content and comfortable.

"I can feel your courage, most of all. You are a warrior. Amanda, you are aptly named, 'the one worthy of love.' Your heart is a phoenix. A fiery ball of courage and love, reborn onto oneself. Worthy of love you are, and worthy of life. You shall live, my lovely."

The anesthetizing effects immediately dissipated, and suddenly she could feel again. She could think again, instead of merely registering what went on around her. She felt deep relief. She would live! But why? Her Overload already seemed like a bad dream, but her actions had been all too real. She had killed. What did it all mean?

The figures glided away, as if they were in a telescoping tunnel. "Don't be a fool, Amanda," one of them whispered. "Don't ask yourself what it means. You did kill, of course. You wonder what it might mean about you. But it was not the real you that did it; it was your Shadow Self. All humans have one. The Overload makes one lose all control over the Shadow Self. As in a dream, there is nothing you could have done differently. We judge the Sentinels on their choices. We judge the Sentinels on their hearts. The Shadow Self is beyond anyone's reach."

"So, I'm not evil?" she whispered back.

"The circumstances of your actions were supernatural. You were not your normal self."

The three Ascendants came together. "Hold on, Amanda. You have nothing to fear."

Chapter 28

As a ball of lighting enveloped Amanda once again, a soft yellow glow encircled her, an unfurling wall of light. She could not tell up from down; the glow cocooned her, cradled her, seeped into her mind. Quite dizzy, she reached out to grab on to something to balance herself, but the glow was empty, surreal. It was full of soundless sparks that snapped at her skin, but she could feel no sensation from them, not even warmth.

A wall appeared before her, and she began speeding toward it. Terrified she might crash, she shielded her face with her arms.

But as she peeked through her fingers, the wall seemed to dissipate, and all movement stopped, as if she were suspended outside of time and space. She could see something looming ahead of her, getting closer. Two men. Alain and James; they were still facing each other. Amanda blinked a few times. Her vision was unfocused, as if she were looking through a foggy glass. She even rubbed her eyes. Then she heard their voices, as if coming from a different room.

"Are you in love with her?"

James asked that.

Amanda's heart began pounding, and she listened intently.

"What business is it of yours, Purple Heart?" Alain replied coldly.

"It *is* my business because she's my partner, and I'm looking out for her." James set his jaw and narrowed his eyes. "And she shouldn't have anything to do with a dirty killer like you. Stay away from her; I'm warning you."

Amanda saw Alain's lips moving, but she couldn't make out what he replied. It must have been quite something, though, because in one swift move, James pulled out his firearm and aimed it at Alain, who nearly matched his efficiency when he pulled out two handguns of his own.

"Oh, is that how you feel, handsome?" Alain suddenly betrayed his jealous rage. "That quite settles it, then, doesn't it? Mr. Purple Heart, military pilot, so rugged and manly, you must have crowds of women camping around your house."

James appeared unmoved. "This isn't about me. You're bad news. If you actually care about her, you'll leave her alone."

"It's not about you? Sure. Of course not." Alain made a visible effort to collect himself and settled his lips into a smirk. He pulled his arms apart, revealing his chest. "Come on. You're not going to shoot me in cold blood, are you, Purple Heart? You've never shot anyone in cold blood in your life."

Amanda lost sight of them. She gasped in fear and frustration, her hand instinctively reaching out to the concrete wall now back in place in front of her. What was *wrong* with these two? How long was her transition going to take? She heard something like firecrackers, as sparkles sizzled all around her, and she caught a glimpse of them again. Alain's right arm was extended toward the door while his left arm stayed low, still holding his second gun. Amanda gulped down her fears. She couldn't see James.

Within seconds, the glow dissipated for good, and she was back. She finally felt well. Liberated, in her body and in her mind. Until she saw that James was on the ground, holding his leg, grunting in pain.

Alain saw her and hurried over. "It worked? They cured you?" he asked, anxiously searching her face as he tucked the gun back into his jacket.

"Yeah, I'm fine. But what *the hell* happened here?" Blinking in disbelief, Amanda kneeled at James's side. Then she saw a third party, a dead body near the door, a semiautomatic weapon beside it.

"I'll be fine," James said, pushing himself onto his elbows. Blood rushed out of his left thigh. He had been shot!

"Give me your shirt! Quick!" She frantically motioned to Alain.

"Fine." He started taking off his shirt, but he wasn't exactly rushing either. She could have slapped him! She pressed her hands over James's as they both struggled to contain his bleeding. "There you go," Alain said quietly, finally handing her his shirt.

Amanda immediately made a tourniquet around James's leg. When she got the bleeding under control, she turned to Alain. He just stood there, detached, inscrutable, having thrown his suit jacket back on. "Did you do this, Alain?"

"What?" He now seemed taken aback by her intensity. "No, I wouldn't shoot him. I can't fly that plane. Neither can you or Basil. So we need him alive and well."

He's dangerous, Mandy.

Lydia's words echoed in her mind, and she gave Alain a look.

"It's the truth. We were waiting for you when out of nowhere, that guy forced his way in here and started shooting at us. He hit Purple Heart, and I took him out."

Be careful about trusting him.

She looked at James. "Is that true?"

James grimaced. "That's part of the story, sure."

"That's the part that matters right now," Alain fired back.

"Right," James said.

She glanced at the corpse by the door, a bullet hole clean through the forehead. If Alain wanted James dead, he would be dead.

"How did that creep get here?" she asked, nodding to the body.

"We don't know."

"He must have been hiding in our cargo bay," James answered. "My guess is that Proctor hired him, showed him in, and timed an altercation to enable him to kill me."

"That's insane," Alain scoffed. "Besides, I don't even think there is a cargo bay on your plane."

"I think I know more about planes than you do," James shot back.

Something was definitely off here. "*Did* you do this, Alain? How could you! Why would you?" Nearly hysterical, she struggled to think clearly. She'd been through too much in one day.

"I did not!" Alain said earnestly. He came toward her, but she held up her hand to forestall him.

"Just leave me alone. I need a minute. I don't know what to think." She sat back on her haunches. "We need to help James into the plane. And where's Basil?" Her eyes widened in sudden horror at the thought that something may have happened to him, that the assassin might have gotten to him before charging into the bunker.

"Basil is still with the plane," James said. He nodded in Alain's direction. "And he didn't actually shoot me. Although he probably wanted to."

His snarky tone convinced her he was right. Alain had wanted to shoot James, and James probably wanted to shoot Alain. Men!

But that didn't matter right now. They had to check on Basil, and get James back to the plane. "Help me get him up," she asked Alain. When James protested, she said, "James, please. Enough. I can't handle your weight without him."

James finally relented, and together, Amanda and Alain managed to lift the pilot to his feet. He leaned on them and they stumbled out into the sunlight, moving as quickly as possible. With every step Amanda took, she was filled with horror at the uncertainty of what awaited them in the cockpit. Her Overload abilities were completely gone. She couldn't see Basil, couldn't feel him—he could be dead.

When they arrived at the plane, Amanda saw Basil Blake's limp form, slouched over the seat. She felt like dropping James, jumping over to Basil's side, and unleashing a shock wave of despair, but she fought to keep a calm exterior. He might not be dead. He might just be injured.

"Hold on. I'll check on him." Alain's tone was earnest and firm. He helped her settle James against the plane before leaping into the cockpit. "It's okay. He's fine," he called out. "He's just been knocked unconscious. But his pulse is strong, and he's breathing normally."

Amanda started sobbing, her emotions finally taking over. She slumped next to James on the concrete of the old runway and couldn't stop crying.

Alain sneered and stayed where he was. Then James dropped like a ragdoll. Blood started pooling under his leg.

This was a nightmare. Just when she felt like she'd been saved, she had dropped into yet another nightmare. Amanda stared at the blood that slowly settled into the little cracks in the concrete. She should be doing something. She should bandage his wound better.

"We need to go," Alain said. "He needs urgent medical care. Come on, let's pull him up."

Together they pulled James back into a sitting position. His eyelids stirred, then opened. Amanda regrouped as he regained consciousness. She would stay strong. Without a word, she tightened his tourniquet, and the bleeding stopped again.

"Get me into the cockpit," James said. "We have to get out of here before more assassins show up."

Alain lifted him into his seat as Amanda said, "Can you really do this, James? What if you pass out again?"

He gave a few brief nods. "I got this."

"Okay, let's go then." She and Alain climbed into their seats.

Amanda thought about James's Purple Heart, earned for taking a hit in combat. He must have been through worse battles than this one. Of course he could get them to safety. But as she watched him prepare for takeoff, he appeared to be in a lot of pain—both physical and mental. What kind of memories did being shot bring back for him? Had Charlene also been in the air force? Had he lost her in combat? So many unanswered questions.

She was almost relieved that Basil, the super-empath, was out cold now, because the pain in that cockpit would have been too much for the old man to absorb.

Basil came to about halfway during the flight. "What happened?" he asked.

She told him the Ascendants had helped her, that she was cured from the Overload.

When he asked about James's leg wound, Alain said, "An assassin attacked us while Amanda was being healed. He shot James. I took him out. That's all."

"An assassin," Basil pondered, his confusion evident. "But who would have sent him? And why?"

"My guess is that Proctor here had him smuggled into the plane."

"Right," Alain shot back. "The plane that you procured?"

"I find it unlikely that another person could have been hiding out on this plane with us," Basil said.

"Good point." Amanda couldn't help but think that Christina-Abigail was behind the attack in some way. Yet it made little sense for her to double-cross them. Was the Committee still against them?

"And why didn't he kill me?" Basil wondered aloud. "He had every chance."

They were all quiet as Basil's question hung in the air.

Within a few hours, James landed the plane safely at a military base near Boston. What happened next was a blur of flashing lights and action as Amanda jumped out to meet the ambulance. She rode with James to the hospital, where he was taken in for immediate surgery on his leg. Basil was examined and given a clean bill of health.

Once she knew everyone was in the clear, Amanda took a taxi from the hospital to the train station's long-term lot, where her car was still parked. She drove back to her apartment, immensely relieved that the ordeal was behind her. Exhausted, she took a deliciously soothing shower and climbed into a freshly made bed. She toyed with the memory of Alain's kiss before falling into a dreamless sleep.

Chapter 29

Early the next morning, Amanda texted Lydia and Matt to let them know what had happened. Lydia responded quickly.

Lydia: *I'm so happy everything worked out! So do you have a minute for me later today? I really need to talk to you.*

Amanda: *Sure. What's up?*

Lydia: *I need to speak to you about Alain. It won't take long, and it's pretty important.*

Amanda: *Can't you just tell me now?*

Lydia: *Better we just speak in person, okay? Too hard to explain otherwise. Meet me at the spa around 11?*

Amanda: *OK*

She started feeling unhinged again. What did Lydia need to say about Alain?

But worrying about it was pointless. So she got out of bed, carefully selected an outfit—a cream-colored cashmere dress with a chocolate suede jacket—and dressed. She applied makeup, including a new shade of maroon lipstick she'd been dying to try, and headed to the hospital to visit James.

Before going to his room, she stopped at the gift shop, where her eyes fell upon a charming arrangement of red tulips. She took the vase to the register and paid, then headed upstairs. She walked into his room and placed the flowers on the table beside him. "You like tulips?"

"I'm a dude. I don't have a preference." He smiled at her, yet she couldn't believe how bad he looked post-surgery. His leg was in a cast and his bare chest was covered in bruises. "Oh God," she said, when she noticed them.

How did this man fly us safely across the country with all these injuries?

"I have bruised lungs and broken ribs to go along with the broken leg," he said.

She pulled a chair over to his bedside. He must be in pain; it seemed best to try and distract him. "Well, I have a preference. I grew up with tulips," she told him. "They were my mom's favorite flower." She wondered for a moment why, of all things, she would bring up her parents right now.

"You don't really talk about your parents," he said, as if to echo her thoughts.

She started to ramble, in spite of herself. "My mom was a model and then a photographer. Anyway, she always told me that models are like tulips: the most important part is their head." James laughed, and she relaxed now, laughing along with him. "I can't believe I remember that."

"What else do you remember?"

She didn't like where this conversation was heading, despite the fact that she had instigated it. She turned the focus back on him. "How are you doing?"

"I've been better," he said. "I've also been worse."

He still had his wits about him. So strong, emotionally and physically. She could feel the old draw pulling her to him again. "Well, it turns out I've worked with your surgeon before," she said, trying to regain her composure. "Yesterday I told him he has to make you as good as new—otherwise the U.S. Air Force would have to close shop."

He stared at her, and she could barely catch her breath. "What?"

"You look so happy," he said, smiling. "So radiant."

She dipped her eyes to his chest, and back. "Thanks, yeah, it's good to be alive. But what about you? You're good?"

He stretched a little. "I'm good, Amanda, I'm good. So tell me. What are you up to, today? Plasmid hunting?"

She looked away. "I'm meeting a friend at the spa and then we might head to lunch," she lied. "I could really use a mani-pedi and a mud treatment. Maybe a therapeutic bath too."

It wasn't all a lie. There was a lunch planned with a friend. Alain had asked her to lunch the night before, and she'd agreed. But she wasn't about to tell James that. And she was planning on meeting Lydia at the spa beforehand.

"That sounds nice. My Saturday is all mapped out as well," he said, and winked. Then he reached out for her hand resting at the edge of his mattress. "So when they do these nails of yours"—he carefully lifted each finger in turn—"do they feel the sparks?" His eyes lifted to her lips and back down again.

Amanda froze, feeling shy yet excited. Was he just commenting on her Sentinel powers? Or was he insinuating there were sparks between them? Was James actually flirting?

The moment was interrupted when the door opened. Two young men paused at the threshold, seemingly surprised to see her there. But their hesitation was brief. They barged right in, followed by an older man in a military uniform. James introduced them as his buddies from the air force and his superior officer. They began talking excitedly, and Amanda was suddenly uncomfortable.

"I can head out now." She started to gather her things. James reached for her hand, but she shrugged in the direction of his visitors.

He looked alarmed. "Give us a minute, guys." The men obliged, heading out into the hall.

"You're not leaving already?" he asked her, with a bit more intensity than she was comfortable with. As if sensing it, he switched his tone to levity. "I'll kick these clowns out; I can catch up with them anytime."

"Um, I actually sort of have to go so I don't miss my appointment. Can I give you a call later?"

"Sure, anytime. I want a therapeutic bath, too." It was adorable how awkward he acted about making such a forward suggestion. She had to laugh. On an impulse, she bent over to kiss him on the cheek, her hair brushing his chest. "Did I say thank you enough times? For saving our lives? You are amazing. Absolutely amazing."

He suddenly looked so serious, and so handsome. He reached for her face but his hand stopped midway, hesitating; instead he just took her hand again and gave it a light squeeze. "Will you come back tomorrow?"

"I'll try," she said. "Now get some rest, okay?"

"Sure." She thought she heard him add, "See you tomorrow, beautiful," but of course there was no way closed-off, unattainable James would ever make a remark like that, so she just dismissed it.

As she passed his friends on her way out, they all muttered greetings to her, then noisily barged back into James's room again. As Amanda headed toward the elevator bank, she heard the guys compliment James on how hot his girlfriend was. She smiled. A week ago she'd have been thrilled to have him show interest, but her feelings had become too complicated at this point. And, in her view, James *still* seemed unsure of his own feelings toward her. She'd think about it some more in the comfort of her therapeutic bath.

When Amanda emerged from the hospital, she stopped dead in her tracks. Alain Proctor was standing next to a white Bentley, holding a large bunch of red roses. He was a vision, like that. Instead of his usual suit, he wore a casually chic navy-blue top with a white stripe along the collar, dark khaki pants, and sneakers. He looked young and fit. She had to admit that he was an intensely attractive man, although still not comparable to James in the looks department.

He waited for her to approach, a hint of a smile on his lips.

"Alain? But we weren't supposed to meet until one."

He handed her the flowers. "I couldn't wait." He pulled a single rose out of the bunch a little, just enough for her to notice a brilliant diamond pendant necklace on a delicate gold chain entwined in the velvety petals.

"For my diamond rose." He handed it to her.

While Amanda held his gift, trying to decide how to react, he opened the car door for her.

"Is this your new car?" she asked.

"No, it's not mine. I wanted to impress you."

She almost rolled her eyes. "Wow. Are you flirting?" He didn't answer. He just kept looking at her, and she quickly added, "It's nice! But I prefer Jaguars. That's what I have."

She was desperately trying to hide her attraction to him. She knew that anyone else might have given up on her by now. Anyone aside from Alain, who believed she was his destiny, as she knew from having read his thoughts during her Overload.

With a shrug, she got into the beautiful luxury car, hitching up her dress so that she wouldn't trip. The leather seats were supple beneath her bare legs. In that moment, she decided to cancel her spa visit. Why not spend the day with Alain? She needed to figure out what was going on between them. The massage could wait.

Alain offered to take her to brunch at CLINK, a fancy restaurant in Beacon Hill near the Charles River.

She swiveled in her seat to look at him. "How about we take a walk by the waterfront first? It's so nice out, and we can talk for a bit. We can do an early dinner afterward, if you like."

His voice was pure silk when he replied, "You know I'll do whatever you want, Amanda. I adore you."

Amanda cleared her throat and mumbled something about him flirting again. Then she busied herself with her dress, pulling the cashmere back over her knees. She wasn't used to bold proclamations. She'd never even had a serious boyfriend. How was she supposed to respond?

But Alain didn't seem to mind the silence as he drove. She noticed that he hadn't stopped wearing that mysterious smile since she'd agreed to get in his car.

Once they parked, they strolled down to the waterfront in continued silence, which was now starting to make Amanda feel awkward and on edge. She decided a little small talk would be preferable, so she asked, "So, are you originally from Boston?"

"No," he said, not looking at her. "Iowa, actually. I grew up on my dad's farm."

Amanda couldn't help but notice he hadn't said "parents." She asked, "And what about your mom?"

Her question was met with an unexpected pause, almost like it puzzled him. Either that, or he was emotionally struggling with something. He was hard to read.

"I grew up with just my father," he finally said, his tone quieter than usual. He looked her in the eyes before adding, "I'd rather not say more anything more about it. It wasn't fun."

So Alain didn't have a good father. *Join the club*, she thought. She decided that if she opened up to him about her own "daddy issues," maybe he'd feel more comfortable opening up to her. Either way, they seemed to have something in common.

"I grew up with both parents, but they were pretty much wrapped up in themselves," she began. "My dad was this big-shot surgeon and my mother was obsessed with him. No matter what, he always came first, even if he was barely around."

He gently reached for her hand and brought it to his lips, planting a small kiss on the inside of her wrist. A gesture so simple, yet so intimate. "Tell me more."

Amanda's skin radiated with the warmth of his kiss and sent a pleasant shiver up her spine. She relaxed and let out a little more of her past. "My mother was a model when she was young, then became a fashion photographer. She loved me in her own way, I guess, but she was deeply in love with my dad, and my dad was in love with himself, so it worked out perfectly," she said with a sardonic laugh.

As if sensing her discomfort, Alain slowed down and shifted closer, but she decided that she was finished with the topic. "Wow," she said, "We're having way heavy discussions before dinner. Let's talk about something else! Why did you decide to be a paramedic?"

He put his hand on the small of her back, as if to prevent her from running away. "So I could meet beautiful anesthesiology residents named Amanda," he replied.

Surprised, she stared at him, and soon that smile, Alain's mysterious smile, returned. At that, she burst out laughing. Alain had a sense of humor! It was uncomplicated humor, but humor nevertheless. The important thing was that his teasing was another sign that he was back to normal, back to being good. And that made her happy.

"You are so *not* funny," she managed to say through her laughter. "I bet you talk like this to all the girls?"

The smile fell from his lips, though she noted that his light-blue eyes were glinting, like the sun dancing on the surface of the river next to them. He took her hand and pressed it between his palms. "There are no girls for me, there's only you, Amanda. I'm not embarrassed to say it. I know it. It's just how it is. You are my destiny."

She pursed her lips and looked away, to the skyline across the water, before bringing her gaze back to him. "Alain, we're just getting to know each other. You realize that, I'm sure?" Yet, the highly charged current in the air between them belied the fact that they barely knew each other.

Amanda recalled how he had pressed himself against her body on his knees before her, when she came over to him in her Overload. As if, in fact, from the beginning, *she* was his salvation, and *he* was in dire need of being saved, and not the other way around. It still felt this way, perhaps more than ever.

"Amanda, do you believe in love?" he asked.

The question took her aback a little. What is love, she asked herself, but in the meantime, her mouth was already replying, "Of course I do. I think most people believe in love."

They resumed their stroll. "I didn't know what to believe, before I met you," he replied. "You know I can only regain my full self when I'm with you. Not feeling anything for anyone doesn't feel *wrong* unless . . ." he took a second to find the right words, while she listened intently. "Unless there's a part of you stuck deep within. The real me was trapped within the evil creature I'd become. The real me was still suffering, silent, unable to break free. Until you came into my apartment. Something happened. I know it was supernatural; it was because of your powers. But I knew, I *know*, it was more than that, too. You were like a light that flashed into an abysmal void that held me trapped."

Amanda didn't know what to say. This was the most she'd ever heard Alain talk, and he sounded very thoughtful, very poetic. And she believed him. This was no fleeting passion for Alain.

She'd saved him. And he loved her for it.

In awe at such a realization, she stared at the sparkly mica particles in the asphalt ahead as they walked on, side by side.

"I wanted to become a doctor so I could save people," she heard herself say.

Alain took her hand. "Hmm." His touch was so peculiar; soft, unobtrusive, but undeniably present. It felt as though there was no power in the world other than her wanting him to let go that could ever make him release her. Like he would always be there, no matter what happened.

"My elusive diamond rose." She glanced at him and saw a fleeting smile. "I wondered what you'd reply right now," he said. "Pretty little rose. You're closing off. Running away again."

"I'm not running," she protested, though she knew what he meant, that she was switching topics. Or so it might appear to him. "I'm right here. I'm an open book."

"Uh-huh."

She guffawed. It was funny to hear him say "uh-huh." It was like the intensely dark man had dissolved in the light of day, which was encouraging yet odd to see. "You just have to learn to read!" she insisted. "It takes a little time."

"I have time."

"Okay. Me too."

With one supple movement, he slipped an arm around her waist and hugged her to his side. Quickly releasing her, he didn't say anything, and they just kept on walking.

But she wanted more. She wanted to touch him, to run her hands over his shoulders, his chest. She wanted to know him so deeply, so intimately, that she could breathe for him.

Was it destiny?

As she tried to make sense of all the new emotions coursing through her, she was shocked back to reality by the sound of a man shouting.

"Stupid kid!" he said.

Her attention turned to the source of the voice, and she saw a man standing over a boy who could not have been more than six or seven years old. The poor kid had apparently fallen off his Razor, and he was huddled over the scooter on the ground. One of the wheels had come loose.

The man—Amanda figured he was the boy's father—continued to berate the small child. "When are you going to get this? It's not that hard!"

The boy's shoulders began to shake, and she knew his crying was only going to make matters worse.

"Get up!" taunted the father. "Be a man!"

As the boy pulled himself to his feet, she could see he'd torn his pants in the fall and scraped up his knee. She felt terrible for the little guy.

His father crouched before him, elbows over his knees. His face was angry. "How are you gonna deal with real life if you can't stop crying over every little thing?" he snarled. Then, as if he'd only just realized he was out in public, his eyes started darting all over the place. He lowered his voice. But, even as his tone changed, his words remained cruel. "I don't work myself to death so you can break everything."

Amanda was appalled at the father's behavior.

She turned to Alain to comment and then froze in shock. The look on his face—she struggled to place what it meant. It wasn't anger . . . not sadness or contempt. There was so much wrong with his face, yet at the same time, almost nothing had changed in the way his features were set.

Screaming.

Alain was screaming inside.

That's how it looked.

Stoic and deadly.

"I can't stay here watching this," he said quietly, and turned around to walk away.

Amanda looked back at the father, who seemed to have calmed down. He pocketed the loose wheel and carried the scooter as he gently held on to the boy's shoulder, perhaps using kinder words as they walked off together.

Amanda caught up to Alain. "Hey . . ." she said, taking his hand. "That man was such an asshole! He kind of reminded me of my dad. Was your father like that, too?"

His shoulders sagged a touch. "Something like that, yes."

"Wait, Alain." She held him back. In front of the Children's Museum, they stopped to sit under the draping branches of a weeping cherry tree encased in a planter that acted as a bench. She looked at him, but she couldn't read him. He was so stoic, like the stone upon which they sat. Clearly there was a reason he didn't want to talk about his past. She'd treaded too soon into waters too deep.

Whatever was on his mind, she could feel his pain. She wanted to comfort him, to make everything okay. She carefully moved in to give him a hug, and he let her take him into her arms. She could feel the stone wall inside him start to crumble as she held him, but his body remained hard under her touch. She breathed him in as they sat there, wrapped up in each other. His broad shoulders, his firm back. She couldn't help but imagine how it would feel to hold him like that, his bare skin on hers. She nearly shuddered at the thought.

"Amanda," he whispered. "I'm so happy with you."

Slowly, tenderly, she pressed her parted lips against his. He let her kiss him with her own rhythm, holding her in a comfortable embrace until the only place she ever could imagine herself being was right here, and right now, with him. Wrapped in each other. The branches of the tree above them spreading its leaves like a celestial umbrella over the promenade. Protecting them from the world; sealing them in this perfect moment.

When the kiss ended, Amanda pulled away gently. Her lips tingled from his touch. This was unlike anything she'd ever experienced.

"You must be starving, little diamond," he said.

She let out a breath she hadn't realized she'd been holding. "You have no idea."

Arriving at the Liberty Hotel, where the chic eatery was located, Amanda was reminded of bygone grandeur. The hotel used to be a jail in the late 1800s, but the impressive stone exterior with its large windows, tall towers, and intricate moldings looked more like the old estate of an eccentric upperclassman. When conservationists renovated it into a hotel, they kept all of the architectural charm, including the original iron bars on the windows.

Inside, Amanda was stuck by the luxury of the atrium. The exposed brick walls soared up three stories; large iron chandeliers dripped from the high ceilings; and groupings of wingback chairs and tables were scattered throughout. It was a unique building, much like Alain, Amanda mused. They both seemed stony-faced on the exterior, but upon closer inspection, they were warm and inviting on the interior.

They were shown to a table situated right next to an old jail cell door. As soon as the server arrived, Amanda asked for the wine and dessert menus in addition to the regular menu.

Alain was looking at her intently now, and leaning forward. "I like it when you take charge."

Alain sipped his water and began looking at her like she was on the menu. She didn't blame him, but she didn't know how to respond. She found herself talking about traveling, which seemed as safe a topic as any, until the server came back to take their order.

Amanda ordered smoked mussels and Alain added, "I'll have the same."

There was something about the way he said those words that made her feel connected to him. *The same.* He understood what she wanted. He wanted what she wanted. He made it a point to connect with her.

Suddenly she knew exactly why he had nicknamed her the diamond rose. She'd felt like a frozen rose, and he'd provided the warmth she needed to recover and blossom. His love soothed the old wound in her heart. She had a deep longing to be special, understood, needed, and protected, and no one had ever made her feel as loved as Alain did. James had started to show interest, maybe, but she was tired of his uncertainty. Her time with Alain made James seem like a distant memory.

While they dined, she told him more about her parents. She told him how she felt like an accessory in their lives, something they could flaunt and then forget whenever they felt like it. She told him about how they perished in a mountain-climbing accident and how she stayed with her maternal grandmother until her grandmother's stroke.

They talked for hours, though he never circled back to his own life story, and Amanda decided not to press him.

After their meal, they made their way to the pier. The moon shone like a quarter in the dark pink of the evening skies; the stars glistened on the harbor. As they walked, the conversation died out, but her connection to him intensified. They were almost back to the parking lot. She wrapped her arm around his and leaned closer, her cheek touching his shoulder. Alain immediately drew her close. He kissed her again, passionately. It was all too much. When she stepped away from his embrace, he took her hand and said, "Let's get you home."

"Do you know where I live?" she asked, before remembering the night he'd waited for her outside her building.

He kissed her again.

"Of course you know where I live," she continued, as he opened her door and she slid inside. "You were stalking me."

"I wanted you to notice me. I wasn't trying to hide."

She snickered as he climbed into the driver's side. "You were so creepy. You gave me nightmares. This is so strange." She took his hand and felt the scab on his palm—a remnant from his fight with her would-be assassins. "How did we end up here, Alain? I'm glad we did, but you know what I mean."

Alain started the car. "I know. I just didn't know what else to do back then. You were the only person who could make me feel. Make me human again. That's why I need you, but that's not why I lo—" He cut himself off.

"What?" she asked softly. He turned to her again, the angles of his face highlighted by the glow of a passing car, but said nothing. His light-blue eyes were so thoughtful. So enticing. She reached out and traced one of his eyebrows with her fingertip.

He took her hand and kissed it. "Let's talk when we get there," he said, and they drove in silence to her building.

On the way, she remembered she had promised Lydia she'd text her back about rescheduling their plans. But she didn't want Lydia to tell her anything that could take away from the perfection of this night. She would get back to her. Eventually . . .

Upstairs in her building, she turned the key in her door. She'd felt so comfortable making out with him this evening, under the moonlight by the water, but now she was starting to have second thoughts. She'd known him less than two weeks. And he was an assassin . . . at least some of the time.

But she'd killed, too, hadn't she? Under the same "spell" that he'd been under. And she wasn't really a killer.

Was he?

She opened her door. "Why don't you make yourself at home," she said, dropping the keys on a tray by the door. She then headed to the kitchen to get a vase for the roses and to take a moment to collect her thoughts. She trimmed the stems and set the flowers in a lovely crystal vase, which she set down on the kitchen table. She was about to head back to the living room to join Alain, but all of a sudden he was there, behind her.

"Is this okay?" he asked quietly as he placed his hands on her hips.

Her doubts evaporated. The feel of his hands on her was sublime, both erotic and safe. She turned to face him, caressing his arms and shoulders.

"Hold on." He stepped back and immediately took off his shirt. He was very well built and more muscular than she would have suspected. He leaned in and kissed her, slowly, tenderly.

"Can I undress you?" He slid to his knees and gazed at her.

Was she really doing this? She closed her eyes and just stood there, paralyzed between hesitation and pure desire.

Alain's hands pressed against her legs and slowly glided up under her dress, lifting the fabric as they trailed her curves. He rose to his feet and lifted the dress over her head, revealing her perfectly toned body. Hearing his breathing accelerate, she opened her eyes and was startled to see his lustful face, making her think of the stalking sociopath with the photos of his victims in his condo.

Be careful about trusting him.

He soothed her. "Shh. It's still me." His hand tentatively touched her cheek, then smoothed her hair. "I don't want you to be afraid."

Reassured, she pushed Lydia's words out of her head and relaxed as she watched him remove the rest of his clothes. Once naked, he drew her toward him.

"You're all mine, my little diamond."

He put his lips close to her mouth, hovering there for a second, as if gauging her reaction once more. He then pulled her into a passionate kiss while he took her hand and guided her to touch him. He drew a deep breath, then scooped her into his arms and carried her to the bed.

She was pinned underneath him, his body warm and heavy on top of her. But she wasn't afraid. She saw his eyelids lower as his mouth returned to hers, and she closed her own eyes, paralyzed with desire, excited by his passion for her.

Alain soon paused and lightly traced the contours of her features, then planted soft kisses on her eyelids, cheeks, ears.

"Hurt me, Amanda," he asked suddenly.

Her eyes flew open. Had she heard him properly?

"You have to punish me. I love the energy pulses. Not the ones during the Overload, of course, but like the one you gave me the first time we met. I want to feel how powerful you are."

"I should have known you were into kinky stuff," she sighed. She was taken aback, but only slightly.

His eyes looked shamelessly into hers. "This is my only kinky stuff, I promise. Nothing else. I'll do whatever you want. Please. Just one time."

She sat up and tentatively zapped him with an energy pulse.

He bit his lip. "Oh, stronger than that," he begged. "Just one good one."

She gave him a larger pulse, quite strong, and he groaned in ecstasy as the charge pulsated throughout his body. He opened his eyes, and there was that glimmering lust again. He threw himself onto her, pinning her arms, holding her under his weight, and whispered in her ear, "I know it's your first time."

How could he know that? No one knew that.

Her heart fluttered with surprise, maybe even fear. "How—?" she started to say.

"Shh . . . I love you. More than any words can say. You're my beautiful rose." Her lips parted, but he stifled her replies with a kiss. "No more talking. Just let me taste you."

He covered her body with kisses, inch by inch, going lower and lower, his hands trailing closely behind, skimming her neck, her breasts, teasing her nipples, settling over her hips while he kissed her stomach. She enjoyed it, yet her body tensed up, especially when he lifted her leg to kiss the inside of her thigh. She told herself to relax.

Suddenly the kisses stopped and his touch disappeared. Alarmed, Amanda opened her eyes.

He was on his knees next to her, watching her, his eyes soft and attentive. Leaning in, he briefly pressed his forehead to hers. "Let me make you happy, Amanda," he said, and with that she lay back and let him do whatever he pleased.

Chapter 30

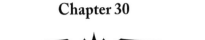

Amanda awoke unexpectedly. It was dark in her bedroom, and Alain was asleep by her side. She remembered all the pleasure he had given her, and she wanted to kiss him, to caress his body, to make him feel wanted and loved. But that could wait. He looked at peace, for once. All that intensity seemed lifted from his body. She didn't want to wake him.

Quietly, she slid out of bed and stood in front of the floor-to-ceiling windows, looking over the city lights. In the pale glow of the moon, the curves of her body were outlined against the darkness.

She opened her palm, and the crystal pendant he had given her sparkled, as if glowing from within. Stretching out her arm, she set the stone against the window, looking at it, lost in thought.

"You're like a moonstone, Amanda."

She turned to find Alain awake and propped up on a pillow.

"Moonstone now? I used to be a diamond; are you downgrading me to moonstone?"

"I love your sense of humor." He climbed out of bed, his naked body emerging from the amalgam of pale and dark. He touched her again with his mesmerizing caresses, sliding his hands all the way down from her shoulders. He then pulled her toward him by the waist and took the necklace from her hand. Once he had it secured around her neck, he kissed her again.

"I'm in love with you, Alain," she blurted out. "I'm in love with you."

He froze. "You're *in love* with *me*," he slowly repeated, looking down. "You shouldn't love someone like me, my little diamond. It's wrong." He smiled mischievously. "Now I have to punish you."

He lifted her legs around him and propped her against the window. The crystal shone between her breasts.

She smiled. "You don't believe me?"

Alain didn't answer. He wrapped her in his arms and nibbled on her breasts while she cried out with surprise and desire.

"Do you want me?" he asked, looking up, breathless from his hunger for her.

She leaned toward his lips and whispered against his cheek. "Yes."

With a sudden burst of passion, he squeezed her against him and swiveled around, then tossed her onto the bed. Before she knew it, he had climbed on top of her, his body heavy and forceful, ready to deliver his kind of punishment. It was hard and sudden; she gasped and grabbed fistfuls of his hair. He pinned her arms to her sides. "There's my little rosebud," he whispered. He pushed himself in again, hard, tearing a shriek from deep within her throat. Completely helpless under him, Amanda gasped as she took it all, again and again. There were no more kisses; only his movement deep inside of her, holding her down, making her take it. She tightened her legs around his hips and screamed into the ceiling as waves of pleasure rippled through her.

His mouth found the side of her neck, and his strong arms tightened around her again. Only her legs were free to move, and she spread them wide open. He pressed into her with intense, drawn-out strokes. She wrapped her legs around his waist, and he held her in a tight, all-body embrace. When he released her a little, she dug her nails into his back as deeply as she could, and whispered, "Oh God, Alain, you have me."

He slowed down his lovemaking. Panting and nipping at her neck, he whispered back, "This is how I have wanted to take you, ever since we've met." More pleasure erupted inside of her. He paused, letting her recover, but he did not let her rest. His passion reached new heights, getting increasingly rougher, more possessive. Groping her breasts, he suddenly clutched the necklace into his fist, as if he wanted to rip it off. But then he released it and kissed her again with desperate, wild abandon.

After two orgasms Amanda was more than satisfied, but he showed no sign of slowing down. She squirmed. Finally she cried out in discomfort and pushed at his chest, begging him to stop. He paused, a dangerous glint in his eyes.

"Make me," he growled. "I'm not stopping until you make me."

"No, no," she panted. "I can't. I don't want to hurt you."

"You do."

Hearing a change in his tone, she opened her eyes, and saw his lips curled up in a lustful smirk. "What?"

"Last chance, beautiful. Or I'll make you want to hurt me."

She was startled at the sight of his face, his pale eyes. It definitely looked like the bad Alain was back. She also found this thought horribly exciting. His smirk grew. He brushed a finger over her lips, then started his lovemaking again, rough and forceful. There was no getting away from him, so she really zapped him, with more than half her strength. Alain cried out in a long moment of ecstasy and fell exhausted next to her, reaching for her with weakened arms.

"Amanda, Amanda . . ." he whispered, as if savoring her name. "I would die for you, Amanda. I love you so much."

He wrapped her in the warmth of his arms and the sweat of his skin, making her feel loved and safe. She had never experienced such an intimate moment.

"I love you so much," he repeated. She could feel his heart pound against hers. Everything was hot and wet; she was limp in his arms, but her right hand weakly stroked his shoulder blade, and he softly kissed her neck, as if grateful for her effort to reciprocate his caresses.

After a moment he pulled away, glancing at her face. Barely moving her lips, she asked him to hold her closer. He complied, kissing the side of her head as she nuzzled against his neck, trying to press every inch of her body against him. His touch was gentle again, his hands gliding back and forth over the curve of her waist and bottom.

She was already half asleep when she heard him say, "You're my anchor, Amanda. My love for you is the only good in me. I can't live without you anymore. Stay with me. Please, please stay with me."

This statement seemed strange to her, but she chalked it up to his past and all the trust issues that must have plagued him. She guessed that some of those issues stemmed from the betrayal of the Committee members, whom he had trusted to heal him, and who had ultimately ruined him.

"I'm not going anywhere," she replied, and she heard him sigh. "Why would you say that?"

He didn't answer.

"Alain?"

"Shh."

"Are *you* going somewhere?

"Of course not," he said.

They stayed in bed the entire next day, watching movies and ordering takeout. In between more lovemaking, movies, and snacks, the phone rang. She saw James's name spring up on the screen. Amanda could feel Alain watch her intently as she let it ring.

"Aren't you going to answer?"

"This is awkward," said Amanda. "I told him I might visit the hospital today."

He put his hand over the now-silent phone and threw it under the bed, far away from her. He then kissed her again. "I know you have to interact with James. I know you're partners, and you'll obviously continue as a Sentinel. I would never prevent you from doing your job. But right now, I'm going to be selfish. I want your attention to myself."

Something bothered her. She would "*obviously* continue as a Sentinel?" Did that mean he would continue on his path as well? Panic reared its head, but she told herself to remain calm. "And what about you? Are you going to continue your work as an assassin?"

A silence hung between them for a few moments as they stared at each other, propped up on their elbows. He touched her cheek and smiled. "Can you still read my mind?"

"No, that was only during the Overload," she said with a deep sigh.

"Well, I'll just tell you, then. I'm trying something new. I'm becoming a real estate agent. Basil said he can hook me up."

Amanda felt such relief she could have cried. She clasped her arms around his neck.

"It's not going to be a nine-to-five, everyday thing, though."

"What do you mean?" she asked.

"The houses are not local. I may be gone for a day or two at a time."

This did not sit right. Realtors didn't sell things in other cities. They worked locally. Assassins, on the other hand . . .

"I know what you're thinking, and I promise you it's not that. I'm targeting wealthy clients who have real estate all over the country. Besides, with your effect on me, I can't possibly kill. I imagine what it's like for them, and I feel horrible. I know it's hard for you to believe, my little diamond, but with you, I am not that man."

"Okay, but don't you need a license or something. I mean—"

"Basil is pulling some strings. You trust Basil, don't you? Why don't you just call him?" A deep sincerity tinged his words.

"I trust Basil, but I also trust you. I don't need to call him." She pulled him close and she spoke into his chest. "Exactly how many days are we talking here?"

He gave her a squeeze. "Not that many. I don't need to sell a lot of them, and you don't mind being the primary breadwinner, do you?"

"Ha ha. We haven't even moved in together yet!"

His hand fell. "Aren't we going to? You don't want me?" His eyes became suddenly bleak.

She immediately straddled him. "I *do* want you. But I think we need some time before settling in a new lifestyle."

He caressed her legs. "Okay. I'll do whatever you want."

Her phone rang again, and kept ringing. Alain switched on the TV.

"You know, he tried to save you," Amanda said, feeling the need to mend the rift between Alain and James.

"What?" he barked, startling her. He softened his tone and said, "Sorry, what?"

"James. When you were seizing on the floor as I was expelling the energy from the Overload. You had lost consciousness. He saw you were seizing and directed the rest of it onto himself. He thought you were dying."

Alain smirked, angrily flipping channels with the remote. "The great hero. Did you know that he had a girlfriend he didn't save? She died three years ago. I suppose he's always looking for ways to compensate for that failure."

Amanda couldn't believe that everyone seemed to know more than she did about this woman James had loved, had been engaged to. This woman he'd lost. Who'd died . . . Was it James's fault? Alain wasn't the one to get this information from—if she even wanted to know any more.

Instead, she cupped his chin and turned his face toward her. "You are madly jealous."

"I am. I feel like he could take you from me."

She felt the emotion in his voice. She snuggled against him. "No one can take me from you. I love you. I could have loved James, but now I have given my heart to you." She pulled away and gazed up at him. "And I have no other heart to give."

She settled in his arms, her head under his chin. She couldn't believe how natural he felt against her. Like their bodies had been designed to fit together.

"I know you love me. But *you* don't know it yet, not even now," he said suddenly.

Amanda pulled away just enough for him to see her face, giving him an expression of exaggerated dismay. "That is the weirdest thing I've ever heard."

He remained serene. Pensive, even. As she settled back against him, he spoke to her softly. "When we met, you were hiding behind a thousand walls, completely shut off. You're so afraid to trust. To fully embrace your feelings. Now it's only a couple of walls, and you're peeking out at me from time to time." He pulled her in for a long kiss. "But I always knew who was behind those walls, and I knew you were my destiny. Purple Heart is finally starting to see you for who you really are, and—"

"Wait. Never mind James," she interrupted. "What did you mean by knowing who was behind the walls?" She worked very hard to not let anyone see behind her walls. How had he seen her?

He smiled. "I read people very well. I always have. But it was more than that. Back when we first met, at my place, I felt *you*. I don't know how, and it hasn't happened again. When your presence triggered this change, this . . . awakening, in me, it also let me see within you. I caught a glimpse of your heart, I . . . bathed in your soul. It was so beautiful. Like a warm tropical lagoon. And I knew right then and there I was gone. Gone forever." He looked into her eyes. "That I was yours forever."

Amanda remembered the strange sensation she'd experienced that first day. The look of awe on his face, which she later attributed to his rediscovering his normal self in her presence. So that's what it was. She had awakened his humanity, touched his soul. He'd seen inside of her, and he was awed by what he saw. He loved her. He was hers.

"I'm yours too," she told him. "Forever." She slowly approached his lips. "I love you so much. I will never leave you."

Chapter 31

Alain stayed at Amanda's condo for the next several days, and Amanda continued to avoid texts from Lydia and calls from James all the while. The closer she got to Alain, the less she wanted to know anything about him that wasn't perfect. Because he was perfect. He was perfect for her.

And James . . . She knew she wasn't going to be able to hide from him forever. He was hospital-bound. What else did he have to do but call her—which he did, several times a day, leaving terse messages at first, like "James here, call me back." After a few days, he'd just hang up without saying anything when she didn't pick up. She never answered; she simply couldn't bring herself to tell him about her relationship with Alain.

She couldn't help but feel somewhat guilty about it. But why? It wasn't as if James ever showed interest in her. Well, maybe they'd had a flirtatious moment or two, especially at the hospital. Maybe she felt guilty because of what she'd heard James say to Alain when she was with the Ascendants: *if you care about her, you'll leave her alone.*

Was that why James had left her alone? Because he knew he was still in love with his dead fiancée, and he didn't want to hurt her? That didn't matter anymore. She no longer needed him to adore her. She had Alain.

Yes. She was being honest with herself: she realized that secretly, she'd always longed to be admired. And it didn't matter that she had an MD degree, that she was a knockout, or that she was the most powerful super-psychic of her generation. None of that could heal the wound in her heart that her parents had created, first by their narcissism, then by their deaths. Alain was exactly what she needed. He understood everything. And he loved her unconditionally.

Still, she wanted James as a friend. Deep down, a part of her felt hurt by his absence and was slightly ashamed of being with this other man.

After a few days of ignoring James's calls, she finally picked up. Alain was away on business, and she knew she couldn't ignore James forever. She'd have to face him eventually. They were partners, after all.

"There you are," he said.

"Sorry, James. I've been a terrible friend. I've just been a little busy."

"Sentinel stuff." His tone was tense and skeptical.

Now she felt guilty again.

"I know about you and Alain," he said abruptly, startling her.

"I'm sorry?"

"Basil told me."

Hearing him say that he knew, knowing that he hadn't learned it from her, stabbed at her. "I don't know what to say."

"There's nothing to say," he said curtly. "It's your life. Sorry I can't be around to protect you from him, though."

"I don't need your protection."

"Look, I learned something about Alain that day at the bunker."

"What?"

"Why don't you just ask him," he said, hanging up abruptly. She tried to call him back a few times, but he never picked up.

After about a week, Lydia's texts about "needing to talk" had gone from once or twice to several times a day. Finally, after going on a much-needed grocery shopping trip, Amanda texted Lydia to reschedule their spa visit.

The Sky Spa was on a rooftop, and few people made it there on an early Saturday morning. Lydia was already sitting inside a steaming therapeutic bath when she arrived, dressed in a shiny electric-blue bikini. She waved at Amanda when she saw her.

Amanda made her way to her friend, carefully stepping over the shallow puddles left by the morning rain. The wooden floor of the terrace was warm to the touch of her naked feet. She wore a black mesh one-piece, strategically embroidered with blue flowers, and she was carrying flip-flops in one hand. In the other she held a cardboard tray with a juice for Lydia from the adjacent snack stand and a "green goodness" mix for herself. She placed the tray at the side of the pool and eased into the bubbly warmth of the bath.

"Okay, now you have to confess," Lydia said. "What is going on with you? I have not heard a word from you since you came back. What gives?"

Amanda sipped her drink. "I got myself a boyfriend," she finally confessed.

Lydia's eyes lit up. She looked like she wanted to applaud, but she was holding her drink. "Ooh! This is so great. Finally, you and James got together. I'm so happy for you guys!"

"Um, it's not James. It's . . . it's Alain, actually."

Lydia's smile died. "What?" Her dark eyes stared in disbelief.

Amanda just shrugged. She hadn't expected anything different. She finished her juice, put down the cup, and lowered her body farther into the water, up to her chin. "You're judging me, but you clearly don't know him at all. I mean, those things you said to me, before I went to the Ascendants—"

"The warnings, yes. I was serious."

"Seriously *wrong*. I think you're jealous!"

"Mandy, what possible reason could I have to get in the way of you finding true love? It's what I've always wanted for you. Just not with this guy."

Amanda frowned at her. Lydia the psychiatry resident. She thought she understood everything. Meanwhile, what about the mess of her own love life? What about her seriously bad judgment about Hank? No, she didn't know what she was talking about.

"Yeah, well, Alain loves me," Amanda said defiantly. "He understands me like no one else can. He's my soul mate."

"No, he's not. Listen to me. I understand he has some charm, a sort of virile magnetism. But he doesn't love you, Mandy. He can't love you. It's not in his makeup. This is what I've been trying to talk to you about, but you just disappeared. Look, I had a long talk with Alain at Basil's house. He walked in when I was making breakfast."

"You psychoanalyzed Alain?"

"No. It wasn't like that. We just talked, and he said some things. Some flags got raised."

Amanda didn't want to hear what Lydia had to say, but in a way, she knew she needed to hear it. "So?"

"He told me that after his Overload, he couldn't feel anything except a desire for fancy things, like his designer suits and his Mercedes. But even that faded in time. He remembered his childhood, when his father forced him to hunt and kill things. He realized that he could actually feel something during those hunts, and he was desperate to feel anything. Can you imagine the kind of monster he is? That the fear and pain of his victims is thrilling to him?"

Amanda looked away. It was too much to imagine.

Lydia didn't relent. "He told me that killing became addicting because he couldn't feel anything else."

Amanda looked away, studying the foam swirling on the water's surface. While Lydia's information was news, it didn't really change her opinion. She was talking about the "bad" Alain. The one he was without her. But he wasn't like that anymore. She knew he could *feel* now, having spent all those days alone with him. He needed her. She trusted in his love. It was all she'd ever wanted.

She looked at her friend. "Lydia, hold on. Everything you're saying, yes, it's horrible. But it's not who he is anymore. With me, he's different. Even Basil says he is."

Lydia shook her head. "No, no, no. People don't change. Not that dramatically. I love you to bits, Mandy, but if you think that he somehow changes because of you, you have some narcissistic traits yourself."

Amanda rolled her eyes. Lydia would never understand . . . There was so much good in Alain. He was the sweetest yet strongest man she'd ever met. She saw it so clearly; she just wished her friend could see it too.

She tried a different argument. "Did he tell you that he was a paramedic before his Overload? Before he became a Sentinel? That's a pretty selfless line of work, don't you think?"

Lydia cocked an eyebrow at her. "Oh yes. Sure. We talked about that, too. I asked him why he became a paramedic, and do you know what he told me?"

"What?"

"Because he wanted to help people."

Amanda's heart was flushed with relief. So Lydia was seeing there was more to Alain than she wanted to acknowledge. "See?"

Lydia shook her head. She looked away for a moment and then back at her friend. "We call that a *reaction formation*."

"Meaning?"

"In his case, he was having a reprehensible impulse and feeling discomfort about it, so he subconsciously decided to do the opposite. Meaning that he felt the reprehensible impulse to kill people and twisted it around in his sicko psyche as an impulse to help people."

"That's nuts."

"*He's* nuts. You need to stay away from him. Do you know what else he told me?"

Amanda didn't want to know any more, but she also didn't want Lydia to think she was immune to reason. "Sure. Tell me."

Lydia held her nose and went all the way under water. When she emerged, her chestnut hair soaked and her long eyelashes glistening, she looked balefully at Amanda. "He talked to me about advertising his services on the dark web. He compared himself to the other killers who offer their services out there, and he said that if a victim could pick their assassin, he'd be the best choice. I could not make this up! He said, 'If I had to be killed, I would rather have someone like me do it, quickly and professionally. So many of the others are horrific perverts.' I mean, like he's not a horrific pervert! He creeps the shit out of me. Just to look at him, there's something so creepy about him."

"Hey!" Amanda jumped to his defense, though she wasn't completely able to deny that there was something horrifically perverted about Alain only being able to finish if she zapped him. If he *forced* her to zap him. No. She wasn't going to equate these two things.

"Oh, and him telling himself that killers exist, so it might as well be him, because at least he's not cruel? We call that *rationalization*. He's a textbook narcissist. In fact, it's more than that. He's a classic psychopath."

"Alain is not a narcissist. He'd do anything for me. This is all crazy."

"Mandy, I don't want to upset you, but I have to warn you, as your friend. You're not safe with him. One way or another, he's going to hurt you."

"Lydia, stop it. *He loves me.* Do you even know what love is? What it's like to have someone actually in love with you? Everyone says things like 'here's my partner,' and that's exactly what they are: partners, friends with benefits. I'm talking about *real* love. Do you know what love is?"

Lydia gave no answer, but her eyebrow twitched.

"I know you don't believe me, but you don't know him like I do. I was in Alain's head during the Overload. I saw inside him! What he feels for me is real, and completely pure."

Lydia reached for her juice again. She gulped it down, then spoke quietly. "Amanda. Listen to me, please. Let's forget my own impressions. Let's go back to the basic facts. He's been killing people for the last three years. Aren't you horrified? Disgusted?"

"But he's not a killer anymore! My love has saved him." She knew the words sounded ridiculous, but they were true. She knew Alain was human again when they were together.

Lydia threw her hands up and scoffed.

"It's true, Lydia! My psychic powers reverse the damage that was done to him. Just by being in my presence, he becomes normal again. Even the color of his eyes changes. He told me he feels terrible about what he did in his alternate state."

Lydia looked at Amanda forlornly, despair in her eyes.

"Don't give me that look, I know I'm right. Everything is different now that he's with me." Amanda was losing patience. "I remember meeting him for the first time, and that man was completely different— devious, lustful, uncaring. But Alain is nothing like that now. He is bold, direct, unafraid of his feelings. You know, he's good now, and he adores me. Do you really expect me to give that up? To betray him? To leave him when I know he needs me in order to remain human?"

Lydia sighed deeply and dragged both hands across her face. She took a good long look at her. "Amanda, I'm saying this because I care so much about you, and I see that you're involved with a dangerous man. I see it so clearly. He idealizes you, Mandy. It's not love, it's just a recipe for disaster."

Amanda wrinkled her forehead. Idealizing? What was Lydia even talking about? Her head was swimming with the psychobabble.

Lydia didn't wait for her to reply. "First they idealize, then they start hating the object of their fantasies."

"Okay, seriously. Alain will never hate me. I don't think we're ever going to see eye-to-eye on this, Lydia, so let's stop discussing it, okay?"

Lydia sighed, then closed her eyes. "I can only hope that I'm wrong and you're right. I want to be wrong, Mandy. I really do." With that, she sank beneath the water, letting the bubbles envelop her.

Chapter 32

Amanda struggled over her conversation with Lydia for the next couple of days, while she waited for Alain to return. The way Alain was with her, the way they were together . . . No, Lydia was wrong. She just didn't understand what she and Alain shared. It wasn't that her friend was jealous. She was just, well, ignorant.

After shopping one day, Amanda returned home to find that the lights and television were on. Alarmed, she put her bag down, then she heard "Amanda?" from the other room.

Alain appeared in the foyer. His lips twitched into a small smile and she gave him a hug, pressing her head to his chest, caressing his shoulders. She took a deep breath and just relaxed in his arms.

"How is my little diamond?" he whispered, holding her.

"I missed you," she said, while he softly stroked her back.

"Are you hungry?"

She wasn't thinking about food. All she could think about was how wonderful it felt to be in his arms, and how absolutely wrong Lydia was about him. She pressed him against her one more time before stepping away. "Not really. Are you?"

He took her hand and led her into the living room. "How would you feel about something light? Some tea and cookies?"

"That's just what I wanted. How did you know?"

"I know you, Amanda." He brought her over to the couch. "Sit down. I'll make us some tea. You have so much tea stuffed in those cupboards, I feel like you live on it."

She took a seat on the couch while he went to the kitchen.

"What were you watching?" she asked, when he returned with a steaming mug to go with her cookies. He sat beside her, and she leaned on his chest, wrapping her arms around his waist.

He reached for the remote and switched off the TV. "The news." He picked up his plate and munched on one of his cookies. He looked almost . . . happy.

That warmed Amanda, but his behavior was so unlike the usual intense Alain. She was also a little surprised to see him so enthusiastically engaged with the cookies. She raised an eyebrow. "Okay, I think you are actually hungry," she ventured. "I've never seen you go at food like this before. Are they laced with some special ingredient?"

He smiled and handed her the plate. Plain sugar cookies. "The secret ingredient is childhood memories," he announced.

Amanda bit into one. It was soft and sweet. "So these remind you of good things?" she asked, happy that he might share some small joy with her.

He took a long sip before answering. "I, too, was an orphan of sorts, Amanda." His voice hadn't changed, but she felt him tense up. She realized now that this wasn't going to be a warm and happy anecdote, but instead, a sensitive discussion. She stroked his arm, an invitation for him to feel comfortable with her and to trust her.

Eventually he set the cup back on the table. He glanced at her. "I only got sweets at school. Our teacher would bring us treats sometimes. Mostly cookies like these, homemade."

"You never got cookies at home?"

"I never got anything," he answered, his tone neutral. "Home was the place where—" he cut himself off, as if struggling with something. He looked away. "I'm sorry, Amanda. I don't want to talk about these things. Bottom line is, I had no mother and I had a monster for a father, but now I have you, and it's all behind me. Just kiss me."

Amanda leaned in and gave him a quick kiss. She stopped him from kissing her again by placing her fingers over his lips. She wanted to probe a little further. After all, there might never be a better time to ask. "Can you please tell me something more? Anything about yourself. Who you were growing up."

His face pinched as if with pain, but only for a moment. He traced her collarbone with his finger. "You're so beautiful, my little diamond. Let's go to bed."

"Alain . . ." she whispered, taking his hand, trying not to show her annoyance. "Don't be like this."

He sighed. "Why do you want me to remember? I want you to make me . . . forget." He pressed his hand against the back of her neck and pulled her in to his kiss. He sucked on her lower lip, then deepened the kiss. She released his fingers, and his hands slid right under her silk blouse, reaching for her breasts. "My angel," he whispered, leaning over her.

"Stop. Just . . ." She pushed him away a little. "Just stop." She grabbed his shoulders and held him at arm's length, looking him in the eye. She took a breath and got brave. "I think it might help you if you told me something about your past. It would make me feel like our relationship was—well, a bit more normal."

He narrowed his eyes. "We don't have a normal relationship?"

"What is up with you tonight? You're really testy." *Or afraid? Or upset?*

He looked down as if he were ashamed.

"Talk to me."

He didn't budge; he didn't make a sound.

She sighed and jerked her head toward the window, frowning. Was she ever going to get in without the Overload? Was he ever going to let her?

Just then, she heard him shift. Slowly, he lay his head and shoulders on her knees and wrapped his arms around her. He stayed like that for some time. She stroked his hair and forehead, and soon he closed his eyes.

He looked so vulnerable and sad, clinging to her as he was.

"I love you," she whispered.

He raised himself on his elbow and repositioned his head on her breasts, never releasing his hold. "I adore you," he answered softly. He closed his eyes again, and she continued stroking his head.

"I can hear your heart beating, my love," he added. "I love your heart. It's so strong and pure. I could die like this, and I wouldn't even notice." His hand skimmed over her breasts and released one button on her blouse.

"Alain, come on. Wait for bed," she chided, but he unbuttoned another, and another.

"Shh. Just a taste. Nothing more." He loosened her bra and freed one breast. He closed his mouth over it.

Tiny twinges of pleasure rippled through her. "Alain," she tried to protest, completely unconvincingly. She wanted to give in to him, but she was struggling with why they could never finish a conversation without it ending in sex.

"I can tell you one thing," he announced at length, tucking her breast back in.

"Yes?"

"One thing, and no further questions?"

"I guess." She needed to focus, which proved challenging, given that he had nearly driven her to a small climax. "Does it really hurt you to talk about it?"

"Yes it does. You can't imagine."

"Then don't tell me. I don't want you to hurt."

"But you asked me for one thing. I can do that."

He lay back in her lap, and Amanda resumed stroking his head. He cleared his throat as he struggled to begin. "It's harder than I thought." He shifted closer to her body. "It's like I can't get the words out."

"I love you. I'm not—"

"Shh . . ."

He kept his eyes closed. "Anything related to my past is hard. Any reminders."

"But you liked the cookies."

"But I didn't like talking about them. As soon as I started talking about them, things came to the surface. The memories. I felt very angry."

She sighed. "I feel so bad for you, my darling."

"The hair," he suddenly said. "My hair. Why I bleach it. It's because he had the exact same color hair. Every time I looked at myself in the mirror, I was reminded of him. So I bleach my hair so I can see only me."

"Your father . . ." she began. It was hard to know what else to say.

He took a deep breath then kissed her knee before sitting up again. "I'm going to bed." He gathered the plate of cookies and the empty mugs. Amanda watched him dump the cookies into the trash.

"I'll come with," she said.

Alain shook his head as he placed the mugs carefully in the sink.

"Please. I want to be there for you."

"I'm not a child!" he shouted, his eyes flashing with sudden, inexplicable irritation.

She was taken aback. He'd never yelled at her. "Whoa. What the hell was in those cookies, Alain?"

He swallowed hard and crossed his arms. "I'm sorry. These memories, they really stirred things up. Things that I don't need. That I don't want. Things that I'm not."

She approached him cautiously. His eyes were almost normal, but not quite. They were still blue, but he clearly wasn't okay. It dawned on her that her effect on him made him almost good, but not all the way. Not when he was lost in the past, in horrible memories. Would she ever be able to help him fully heal?

Poor Alain. He must have been through something awful.

"I'm going to get ready for bed," she said, but he didn't acknowledge her. He didn't even stir. Amanda turned and headed into the bedroom, where she changed into a white satin nightie. As she turned around to head back out and say good night, she saw him standing in the doorway.

"Amanda," he said, pulling her into his arms. She sighed against his shoulder.

"Are you okay?" she whispered.

"I am. I'm a little damaged, Amanda, I'm sorry. I can't say that it won't happen again, but I can promise it won't happen very often."

"Alain . . ." She cupped his face. "Don't hold out on me, okay? I'm here for you, if you need to talk. About anything."

He tilted his head to kiss her wrist. "I'm not a weak man. You won't see that side of me often, I promise. Now, will you wait for me in bed?"

She rolled her eyes. "Yes, Alain wants sex. I know."

"No, Alain just wants to hold you." He wrapped his arms around her waist and pulled her against him, his eyes glimmering with desire. "And he wants to taste you. My beautiful rose."

"I love when you call me a rose," she whispered, her eyes dipping from his eyes to his lips, and back. "I used to hate it, but now I love it."

He brushed his lips against her ear as he spoke, his voice sending warm tingles all over her body. "You're my diamond rose, sweet and strong, always and forever."

He headed to the bathroom and she slid under the cool sheets. She pressed her face into the pillow he used, on his side of the bed, and breathed him in. Lying there, waiting for him, after what she'd just experienced with him, after what she now knew, there was no way Lydia knew what she was talking about. She was forcing answers to align with her studies, just like she always did. Alain was broken, for sure. But he wasn't any of the things Lydia accused him of being. She could fix him—with her love.

Chapter 33

The following Sunday, Amanda was driving along the riverbank promenade on her way to yet another routine cleanup mission. Not that she needed any exciting assignments right now. She wouldn't want to travel or be away from Alain too long. Even though he was away on business, he'd soon be back, and that was all the excitement she needed.

The past two weeks or so with him had washed away any lingering doubt that he was good, or good for her. Just two days prior, Alain asked her if he could please move in with her. She hesitated but a minute before agreeing. Why bother keeping two places, when he was at her place most of the time anyway? And she missed him when he was away. She wanted to fall asleep in his arms every day. Sure, he had issues, but he wanted to be better. They loved each other, and everything was fine.

She had no idea that the day was going to end in a dramatic change. Would she ever have left her bed if she knew?

It began with a phone call from Lydia, which she eagerly picked up. "What's up?"

Lydia was probably calling to say that Basil wanted her to join Amanda for the cleanup. This thought made her happy. Though Lydia had been overly psychoanalytical about Alain at the spa, Amanda understood that her heart was in the right place. She knew Lydia was just looking out for her, as she always did. Plus, Lydia had a tendency to psychoanalyze everyone and everything. That was okay. That's just who she was: her passion for her work meant she was going to be great at it.

But there was nothing about Lydia's tone that sounded happy. "Amanda, we have some news. Basil is here with me. We have something important we need to talk about. Can you come to Cargolan Storage right away?"

Amanda frowned for a moment, but she wasn't going to let Lydia's tone bring her down. "Okay, sure. I just left there, but I'll turn around. I'll be back in about twenty minutes. Does that work?"

"Yes."

This was weird. Lydia was usually more talkative. "Hey, is something wrong?"

Lydia didn't reply. "Lydia? Hello?"

"Yes, yes, I heard you."

Amanda began to panic. "What's wrong? Is it James?"

"No, it is not about James. We're here. Talk soon," Lydia said and disconnected the call.

Amanda gripped the steering wheel as she turned the car around and headed back to the storage facility. She tried not to get too worried, but Lydia's tone and reluctance to speak were a little terrifying. Something in her friend's voice had shattered her peace of mind.

James was okay, and Basil was okay. Who else could it be? Was it Matt? Or maybe something was up with the Committee. She drove back to the facility and toward the mysterious news, trees rushing by as the wind chased the white foam on the river and a few joggers ran along the promenade. Try as she might, she could just feel it. Something ominous was going on.

God, what happened?

Gravel scrunched under the wheels as her car skidded to a halt in front of the facility. She headed inside and walked along the short familiar hallway into the conference room. Her long coat billowed to the rhythm of her steps.

Lydia and Basil were seated at the table. He was wearing a plain black sweater and looked older than usual, as if he had not slept. He'd probably flown in from Vermont in a rush. Lydia was nervously clenching and unclenching her hands. A closed folder lay between them on the table.

Basil spoke first. "Amanda, please sit down."

She complied, silently looking from one to the other. Her friends just stayed quiet. They wouldn't speak. She felt herself grow pale before she got up the courage to ask, "What's going on?"

"My dear girl, I don't know how best to tell you. Something terrible has happened." Basil wouldn't look her in the eye. He lowered his head and made such a mournful groan that it tore at Amanda's very soul.

"Oh my God, who died?" she cried out. Nothing other than death could have prompted this somber scene. She was filled with panic. It wasn't James. It wasn't Matt.

Oh my God, Alain. Is it Alain?

Lydia finally spoke up. "People have died, Amanda. Innocent people. Alain is still killing. He's still working as an assassin for hire. We know you didn't know about it."

Amanda sprang up so abruptly that her chair crashed to the floor. "No. No, you are wrong. You are lying!" She moved back, her hand held in front of her as if to hold back their words, to protect her heart from the truth.

"Amanda, my dear girl. Alain Proctor has killed two people over the last four weeks."

"NO!"

Basil pushed the folder toward her. It stayed at the edge of the table. Amanda's eyes slowly filled with tears. She closed them to blink the tears away, but the folder was still there when she opened them again.

Lydia's hands were squeezed together so tightly that her fingernails were white.

Amanda took a step forward to pick up the folder. She did her best to steel herself before opening it. Inside were crime scene photos. Homicides. One photo in particular arrested her attention, a blond woman lying among broken furniture. There was a close-up shot of her crushed windpipe, finger marks around it. A photo of another victim, a man, revealed a clean shot to his forehead. Just like the intruder at the bunker. Alain's signature shot.

She looked up at their somber faces. "Who . . . who were they?"

"As far as we can tell, they were innocents," Basil said in a quiet tone, as if trying to soften the blow of his words. "They certainly weren't connected to any of the secret societies. The two victims may have been having an affair. Alain may have been hired for a revenge killing. That's my best guess."

An inhuman sound filled the room as all the air left Amanda's lungs. She stumbled backward and dropped the folder as if it were on fire. She backed up to the concrete wall and slid down its rough, cold surface.

She had let a brutal murderer into her bed and into her heart. She pressed her head into her hands and let out gasping sobs—the sounds of a soul coming apart. Basil rushed to her side and hugged her tightly. Lydia was not far behind. Amanda screamed and furiously fought off their embrace, knocking Basil's glasses off his nose. A long while passed before she could formulate any words.

"When? *How?* My God, no, please no. I don't— I don't believe it!" She stared at them, clinging to a desperate thought. "It's a mistake. It has to be. He didn't do this. How can you *possibly* think Alain did this?"

Basil's mournful eyes met hers. "My dear girl, I would give everything I have for it not to be true, but there is no doubt as to who took the contract and who fulfilled it. I am so sorry."

"But you told me I changed him. You told me he was different when he was around me! Why, Basil? Why did you lie to me?"

"I didn't lie to you, child, and it is true that he does change when he's with you. It's when he's with the rest of the world that the beast returns. I'm working on a solution to help him control those impulses. I promise you that I am."

Amanda didn't want any of Basil's solutions. Beside herself with rage and grief, she slapped him on the chest. "Why do you always meddle? Why?" Her voice broke pitifully. Then all her strength escaped her and she crumpled the rest of the way to the floor. The concrete was dusty and stone-cold beneath her cheek, but she didn't care.

They tried to help her up, but she wouldn't budge. She lay there for hours, almost catatonic from grief. Even as the sun began to set against the promenade, she was still curled up next to the wall, wrapped in her long coat. She could not interact with her friends, who sat back at the table, helpless. She could only listen, though she found their words almost impossible to absorb.

"Basil, I can't take this anymore," Lydia finally said. "I don't do well without food, and I feel like I'm going to pass out. Like, soon."

Basil's voice came out hoarse. "We can't just leave her. God help us! I don't know what more we can do."

Lydia stood up, her hands flat on the table. "No, I'm done. I'm calling James. And Matt. I'm going to call the police and an ambulance. I'll have her admitted to my psych ward, if it comes to that! I'm sorry, but we can't do anything for her here."

"I asked you ten times already to just go and let me be. I'll be fine," Amanda whispered, staring blankly ahead. But Lydia paid no attention. She extracted her phone out of her bag. All Amanda could do was to watch and listen.

"James," Lydia said into the phone, her voice tired. "Basil and I have just spent the day watching over Amanda. Proctor has been killing again, and we had to tell her. She's out of her mind with grief."

She paused for a minute to let James reply, then continued. "I don't know what to do. We're at Cargolan Storage. Basil is almost as broken as she is. I can't physically drag her out of here, and I'm so exhausted I feel like I could faint. What should we do?" After another pause, she said, "Okay. I'll call Matt to bring us some things in the meantime. See you soon. And thanks."

Amanda's phone vibrated in her bag, lying next to the table where she'd dropped it. She didn't respond. She hardly cared. When the vibrating stopped, Lydia reached in to see who had called. She immediately locked eyes with Basil. No telepathy was needed: her expression told everyone who the caller was.

Alain.

Amanda stifled another sob. Her torment was only beginning. She couldn't see herself talking to him ever again. What was she going to do?

Some time later, Amanda heard footsteps in the hallway. Matt raced into the room, stopping when he spotted her limp shape near the wall. "Whoa! Is she okay?"

"Hush, Matt. She is not well," Basil warned.

Lydia silently reached into Matt's gym bag and fished out a water bottle. She unscrewed it and immediately gulped down half. She pulled out two more bottles, one for Basil and one for Amanda.

Basil handed Matt the folder. He scowled as he flipped through the photographs, then slammed the file onto the table. "That piece of shit. That piece of shit! If I get my hands on him . . . !"

"What. You'll kill him?" Amanda asked, suddenly coming to life, her voice raspy and low. For once, Matt seemed at a loss for words.

Her phone rang again. Seeing their expressions, Matt seemed to catch on that Alain had been calling her, and that Lydia and Basil kept letting the calls go to voice mail. "That piece of shit!" he said, grabbing Amanda's bag, but an energy surge immediately forced it out of his hands.

Amanda sat up against the wall, slowly lowering her arm. "Sorry, Matt. I have to deal with this on my own."

The sounds of more steps came from the hallway. James pushed the door open. Amanda turned her face away from him. She could only imagine how terrible she looked from crying all day. Then she felt foolish, to be thinking of her looks at a time like this. She glanced over at him again, wondering why he was just standing there. "Amanda?" he asked tentatively.

"Can I have a water, please?" she asked him, then closed her eyes. She wasn't just ashamed about her looks. She also couldn't bear to look at him after all that had happened. After the choice she'd made.

Matt quickly handed two bottles of water to James, who nodded a brief thank-you.

James looked at the group. "Guys, you're tired. I'll take it from here, okay? Just go home, and I'll text you an update when I have one."

Lydia immediately wobbled out of the room, lacking the stamina to say or do anything else. Matt quickly followed, but Basil stood his ground. He shook his head. "I can't leave."

"Please go. I don't want to see you right now, Basil. Please." Amanda rested her head against the wall wearily.

The old man hesitated then glanced at James. When James nodded, he picked up the folder and left quietly. Amanda finished drinking the first bottle of water, then slowly poured the second over her face, soaking her neckline. She didn't care.

James sat down next to her, his back to the wall. "Hey, partner," he said gently.

Her lips trembled, and she started to cry again.

"Amanda, we can't stay here. I'll drive you home. Come on. Let's go."

She kept on crying, silently. She had no fight left in her. He must have sensed that as he carefully took the bottle from her hand, then pulled a small Kleenex package from the back pocket of his jeans. "You're a bit of a mess, partner. Here," he said, and pressed the tissues to her face, drying it. The gesture was persistent and awkward, but it started to put Amanda at ease. "Better?" he asked.

"No. Never. I don't see how this will ever get better," she whispered.

James sighed and pressed his head against the wall. "Ah, but it does get better," he whispered back. "I promise you it does. I guarantee it. Come on. It's already eleven. You can't keep a wounded man sitting on the concrete for this long. It's time to go home. Give me your keys?"

She hesitated, but he had a winning approach, and her pain relented. She started to get up, stumbling on the length of her coat. She reflexively grabbed his arm, and met his eyes—steady, compassionate, attentive. Hers felt almost swollen shut.

"Let's go." He gently guided her out of the building and into her car.

As James drove into the city, Amanda looked ahead, indifferently registering the quickly moving lampposts and changing streets. "When did you get out of the hospital?" she asked him absently.

"A few days ago."

"You didn't call me. I thought you might call me when you got out."

"Yeah, well, you've been busy," he said. He didn't sound happy about it.

As they drove in silence, Amanda's thoughts turned to the scene she'd returned to after meeting with the Ascendants. James on the ground. Alain with a gun in his hand. She was filled with a sense of hot dread.

"James?" she said.

"Yes?"

"What really happened in that bunker in the canyon? Before I returned."

James let out a deep sigh. "Do you really want to know this now?"

She was frustrated that he was giving her a hard time, but she was also a little scared about what he might tell her. This was the time, though. She needed him to tell her.

"I do."

He cleared his throat. "Well, when you went into the light and the portal closed, I sort of went on the attack. I asked him point blank if he was in love with you."

She knew this already because she'd experienced it between worlds. But she didn't fully know why. "Why did you ask him that?"

"What does it matter now? Don't you want to know what he said? Or does it matter what lover-boy says? You'll always take his side anyway. It's like that, isn't it?"

"It's not like that. Where is this anger coming from?" she asked, and it was his turn to be silent. Her heart stung now, but she wasn't altogether sure why. "I'm sorry, James. It's just been such a long day. Of course I want to know what he said."

He set his jaw, as if focused on his driving. "He said, 'Amanda's mine. Or at least she soon will be.' You should have seen the look on his face. It made me pull my gun on him."

She was sick. Alain had already decided she was going to belong to him, no matter what.

James continued. "He pulled his guns on me too, both of them. I told him again that he'd better stay away from you. That if he really cared about you, he would stay away."

If he really cared about me, he would stay away. Did he ever care about me? Did he only care about himself? Lydia was right all along.

"Then the other guy came in and opened fire."

"The other guy. We still don't know where he came from."

"Well, that's about all I can tell you. And look, we're here now."

When he pulled into her parking lot, she asked, "James, how are you getting home? You left your bike back at the facility." Part of her wanted him to stay with her. To protect her. From what, she didn't know. Alain wouldn't be back for another couple of days and by then, she'd know what to do.

"That's okay. I'll park here and get a cab back," he said. "I'll tell the others you're home safely. But first let me walk you inside so I'm not lying to them about it."

He parked the car and helped Amanda inside. She was dazed, her head throbbing. It was only then that she realized he was limping, and her heart went out to him. He must still be in pain, yet he put his own pain second to hers, made sure she was okay. Was that because he was military? Or because he truly cared?

With each step they took, she pictured more clearly what being home was going to be like without Alain. She could manage it, of course. But it would be very hard—haunted by happy memories she would never have the chance to make again. She turned to face James. "I'm sorry to impose like this, but do you think you could drive me to a hotel instead? I can't stay here tonight."

He examined her face. "Are you sure?"

"I am. I'm also concerned he might show up. He keeps calling. I don't know how to deal with all of this right now."

"Okay, let's go."

He took her back to the car then drove to a nearby Hilton. He checked her in and then handed her the keys to her Jaguar before walking her to her room. When they got to her door, she gave him a soft kiss good night on the cheek. His stubble against her lips sent a current through her. One she was not in any shape to analyze or address.

"Good night, James," she said, giving him a quick hug, breathing him in.

"Be well," he said, and she watched him limp down the hallway to the elevator. Then she went in to the room and closed the door behind her.

Minutes later, while she was staring out at the city, trying to feel normal, her phone rang again. Alain's name glowed on the screen. She couldn't avoid him forever. She accepted the call.

"Hello, beautiful. Is everything okay? I keep calling, but you haven't been answering."

She couldn't get the words out.

"Amanda?" Alain asked, his voice alarmed.

Silence still.

"Amanda!"

She finally found the strength to reply. "Yes. It is me."

"What's happening?"

"How could you?"

"What do you mean?"

"Murderer."

Now it was his turn to be silent.

"Were you killing them before you came to see me, or after? Did you think of them while we were in bed?" Her voice turned shrill. "Beast from hell!"

"I can explain. I won't lie. I'm not denying it, but I can explain. All those people were after me for helping you. I need to see you."

"Oh God. Liar! Demon liar. Stay away from me!"

"Amanda, I need you. I can't live without you."

"What you did makes me sick. *You* make me sick. We are done. Done! I cannot possibly be with you after this."

"Amanda, please don't. Please don't leave me."

She ended the call. It was all she could do.

That night Amanda cried herself to sleep and the next day she stayed in bed until checkout time. She returned home in the afternoon and walked straight to her bedroom, dropping her bag on the floor near the entrance. She was no longer worried he'd walk in on her. At some point, she'd have to get the locks changed.

She half-opened the blinds and the light of a dying day crept in. Her own face floated on the glass, flat and tired. She dragged herself to the bathroom, but taking a shower was beyond what she could bring herself to do. Looking at herself in the mirror, she undressed. She could see that all light had been extinguished inside of her, and she didn't care. She tied up her long hair, returned to the bedroom, and climbed under the covers. Then she cried bitterly, with heart-wrenching sobs, welling up and dying down, at times writhing in torment, until finally, she fell asleep again.

While she slept, she dreamed of him—he was in her room, standing over her while she slept, bending over her body and kissing her lips, speaking, saying to her, "I love you. Until the end of time, my diamond rose."

Amanda stirred. She heard the words, felt his kiss. In a dreamy daze, she saw his face over her, then he became a shadow, quickly leaving her room. The front door opened and closed. She sat up in bed, but by the time she could understand that she hadn't been dreaming at all, he was long gone.

Chapter 34

Within a couple of days, Amanda was starting to feel more normal. She knew she had to get over Alain, and she was trying to be strong.

However, one evening when she was on the phone with Lydia, an odd, alarming sensation came over her. A jolt shot through the middle of her head, behind her eyes. A feeling of doom.

"Amanda, are you listening?" Lydia asked.

She wanted to answer, but she was distracted, trying to connect to this sensation, this feeling, this event, to some sort of meaning.

"Amanda?"

"Lydia, listen, I feel something. Something terrible is happening."

"What do you mean?"

"I think it's a premonition. Do Sentinels have premonitions?"

"I have no idea. I don't think so. I never got one, I don't think it's our thing." Lydia paused, as if trying to decide how to respond. "Are you sure it's not indigestion? You just had your first real meal in three days."

Amanda waved impatiently at the phone. "No, it's not that. It's nothing like that. And I don't feel it anymore."

"Okay, humor me. What made you think it was a premonition?" Lydia asked.

Amanda walked over to the window and looked over the city. "I can't say for sure, but I got the impression that something terrible was happening. Something irreparable and dire, that sort of thing."

"As a psychiatrist, I can tell you that a feeling of impending doom might signify a panic attack. Are you having any shortness of breath? Is your heart racing?"

"No, nothing like that." Amanda stared straight ahead, then swiftly turned around. She was sure she'd heard Alain call her name, and she ran into the next room to see if he had let himself in. But no. No one was there.

"Amanda? What's going on?"

"I heard him, Lydia. Alain. He was calling my name. As if he were here, right in my condo. He called my name, clear as day. But of course he's not here."

"You're having auditory hallucinations now? Well, you have been under a lot of stress lately. Don't worry about it, it happens. People can also dissociate during panic attacks, so maybe you just—"

"Lydia, please. Something is wrong. I need to call Basil. I'll call you later, okay?"

"Good idea. Talk soon." Lydia disconnected the call.

At that precise moment, a call from an unknown number came through. She picked it up. "Hello?"

The voice on the other end of the line was garbled and unintelligible, unrecognizable. It sounded as though it was coming through miles of static.

"Hello?" she repeated. Then the line went dead.

She was still puzzling over the mysterious call when her phone rang again. This time it was Basil.

"Amanda, we must meet tomorrow. At Lydia's house."

"Why? Did Lydia tell you about my premonition? Basil, what's going on?"

"I can't get into it right now. I have something to do first, and it's late. Tomorrow at Lydia's at noon. Okay?"

His voice was firm. She knew she wouldn't be able to budge him. Strange, that he wasn't interested in her premonition. "Sure, no problem. Does Lydia know we'll be there?"

"Not yet. Would you mind letting her know? Thank you, my dear. Have a good night."

Basil ended the call and Amanda looked at the time. He was right. It was late. She texted Lydia, hoping she wasn't waking her. Then she removed her makeup, brushed out her hair, and slipped into her silk nightie. It wasn't long before she drifted into a deep sleep.

That night, Alain visited her in her dreams again. He wore a white suit and was waiting by his car, like the time he'd met her at the hospital.

Something was different in his face, though. Something surreal. Something innocent.

"Alain?" Amanda hurried toward him, but even though she was straining to reach him, she wasn't getting any closer. She stopped and looked down, seeing that instead of a road, she was walking on old wooden boards. Then she looked back up at Alain and heard his voice, coming from far away. His lips did not move.

"Remember, my little diamond. Until the end of time . . ."

His Mercedes now flashed ambulance lights, shedding colorful circles all around, blinding her. She squinted against them and lowered her eyes.

At her feet, a white cat lay on its side, looking up at her, half its body mangled and bloody. The ground was now black, full of volcanic bubbles. She looked up again, and she was standing at the edge of Sycamore Canyon, and the sky looked like a massive iron shield.

Amanda jerked awake. The blinds were open and dawn was breaking. She was alone in bed. She burst into tears. She knew what had happened. Once she collected herself, she picked the phone up from her night table and dialed Basil. He answered immediately.

"He's dead. Alain is dead, isn't he, Basil?"

"Yes, he is. I am so sorry."

"You're not going to ask me how I know?"

A short silence. "Yes, I should ask you."

"I had a premonition last night, and then I dreamed of him in all white, and there was . . . well, I just knew. What happened?"

"Car crash. They think he did it on purpose."

"Suicide?" whispered Amanda.

"He came to see me yesterday."

"Why?"

Basil hesitated and Amanda could sense that whatever he was going to tell her, it wasn't going to be the full story. "He was angry at me. Upset over what you knew. Over what you'd been shown."

"The pictures of the people he killed."

"Yes."

"Basil, did he try to kill you?" She asked the question, but she already knew the answer. Deep down inside, she knew. Anyone who tried to take her away from Alain had to be eliminated—that was just the way Alain's twisted mind worked.

"I don't think knowing the truth will help."

"Basil?"

He paused for a moment. "I had a plan for him to live in voluntary confinement, except when he was with you. He came to see me at my house. He held a gun to my head. He engaged the chamber."

"No, that can't be," she said, even though she could picture the scene clearly.

"Even while I stood there, with my life in his hands, I could feel him. His emptiness. His need." He paused for a moment and Amanda thought she could hear him sniffling on the other end. "So I hugged him, Amanda. I hugged him."

Amanda couldn't imagine the fear Basil must have felt, and despite it, his incredible empathy was there.

"I'm not sure how to define what he felt. It derailed him, in any case. He pushed me away then turned to leave. That's when I told him about my plan. I laid it all out for him. Essentially, the Committee would arrange a kind of house arrest when he wasn't with you. They would keep him sequestered so he couldn't engage with anyone else or harm anyone else."

"What did he say to that?"

"He said he could live with that, because he could not live without you."

Her heart sank. Then why had he killed himself? She was so confused and so torn. Before she could ask for more information, he spoke again. "He did not have the best life, Amanda. His childhood. His monster of a father. I tried to be a father to him, but that made him even worse with me."

"He felt something for you, Basil. He appreciated you very much. I'm sure of it."

"Yes, in his own way. Yet he tried to kill me."

His words tore through her and hit right at her heart.

"But he agreed to your plan," she said. "To live only with me." She let the gravity of this sink in a bit.

"Yes, he agreed. I called Paolo to confirm and then Alain left. He said he was headed out to meet the Committee. And then . . . he crashed his car against an overpass. Against the supporting columns. It was a brutal collision, head-on. Not an accident. It was clear he intended to do it."

"Oh God," she said, all the breath leaving her body.

"But he did love you, Amanda, with everything he had. I felt it. Whether he was good or bad, he loved you. I don't know if that makes it better or worse for you."

"Better, Basil—if there could be such thing as better right now." If only she had called out to him or had run after him when he came to see her for the last time. "Is it my fault?"

There was a pause. "What do you mean, dear girl?"

"My fault. For telling him I'd never see him again. For calling him 'a beast from hell.'"

"Amanda, who can blame you, after what he did? You didn't push his car. Whatever he did is on him. All of it. I am so, so sorry."

She dropped the call and put the phone down. Slowly she let her head touch the pillow again.

Why did this have to happen? Just when she had put her insecurities aside, and trusted that he loved her. Her parents had never loved her. No one had ever loved her. Maybe Lydia, but that was different. She had trusted Alain completely. She'd let that knowledge soothe and bathe her heart.

She froze in a sudden understanding. Her grief for Alain reminded her of how she'd felt when her parents had perished; how she'd blamed herself for not being good enough to make them stay. Her parents' death was final proof that they didn't love her. Somehow their passing had crystallized that painful understanding. They had left her. They had betrayed her. They had abandoned her, and they died not caring. Their death was the ultimate rejection.

Now she felt that way about Alain, too.

It was exactly how she felt about his death. And just like with her parents, underneath it all, she blamed herself. For not saving him. For not being good enough to become their salvation. Because she couldn't save any of them, she was left alone. So it was her fault.

Amanda sobbed into her pillow.

Knowing that she was being irrational did not change how she felt.

Chapter 35

Basil's chauffeur was biding his time in the Rolls-Royce on the other side of the street when Amanda arrived at Lydia's. Matt's SUV was parked in front of the garage. As Amanda got out of her car, Lydia appeared on the porch and came flying down the stairs. "Hi, Mandy," she said, hugging her tightly. "Come in. I am so sorry for what you're going through."

Amanda followed Lydia inside. Basil and Matt were sitting in the living room, a tray of untouched appetizers on the coffee table in front of them. Apparently the situation had caused everyone to lose their appetites—even Matt. But the will to eat wasn't the only thing missing.

"Where is James?" Amanda asked.

"He's on assignment in Ohio, an absolutely urgent situation," Basil replied.

Amanda had little reaction. She sat next to Basil, poured a cup of tea and stared into it, watching the tiny tea leaves turn in slow circles. Her tears started again, and she was grateful to her friends for their silent respect for her pain.

"We were so close to saving him. I can't believe he's gone," Basil finally said.

"You can't save someone who doesn't want to be saved," replied Matt.

His words enraged Amanda but she tried to remain cool and rational. "He wanted to be saved."

Matt got quiet, but Lydia clicked her tongue, making Amanda want to lash out. Lydia's next words intensified the urge. "Amanda, please. Matt has a point. I know how much you cared, but Alain . . . he really was a psychopath. A clinical case. They feel nothing. They're not really human. Even their brains show abnormal activity."

Amanda couldn't hold back any longer. "No, he was *not* a psychopath. Not with me. My presence made him human again, every time. Just ask Basil."

All heads turned to their mentor, hunched over his coffee, looking more like an old man than he ever had before. He raised his head and said quietly, "She's right, Lydia. It made perfect sense that it should be so. Her energy compensated for the removal of his own."

Lydia gave in, begrudgingly. "It still makes very little sense to me, but maybe I'm wrong. What's the Committee's take on all of this?"

"They haven't really weighed in."

"I'm sorry. What?" Amanda demanded, unable to control her outburst. "After what they did to him? After what they made him? How they destroyed him?"

"They're busy with other things at the moment," Basil said, placing a hand over hers. "Remember that they agreed to help, to keep him confined when he wasn't with you. But I guess he changed his mind about that. He was such a complicated man." He sighed. "You can take as much time as you need before jumping into the next assignment, Amanda. That's all the Committee ever offers: time off." He sighed with some frustration.

"Anyone want coffee?" Matt asked out of nowhere. Amanda had almost forgotten he was there—he'd been uncharacteristically silent. It was strange to see him tread more carefully now that she had rebuked him.

"No, thank you, Matt," Basil said. "I'm afraid I must take my leave now. There are preparations to be made."

Before he stood to leave, he took both of Amanda's hands into his and looked her intently in the eyes. "My dear Amanda, anything you need, you know you can call me anytime. Anytime. I'm so sorry about this sad ending, I am. I really thought we could save him."

"I should have done something. I just wasn't strong enough."

"No, my dear. This was about him. Perhaps he decided it was better this way, as terrible as it is. Perhaps he could no longer stand the monster he'd become. Perhaps he felt himself slipping farther and farther into the darkness—so far that not even your light could save him."

Everything he'd just said sounded like random words to her. "Thanks, Basil, but I'm afraid there's nothing anyone can say that will make me feel better."

"We'll talk soon." He patted her on the shoulder and left the room.

Amanda lowered her face into her hands. "I thought I knew him, Lydia. I really did." Lydia just sighed.

She pictured him driving into the concrete pylon. He'd agreed to be with her forever. He loved her. Why would he want to die? A thought struck her then, so powerfully that she jumped out of her seat. "What if the Committee killed him?"

"No way. They agreed to help him," Matt said matter-of-factly. He softened his tone. "Plus, I saw the police report. It was clearly suicide."

"But Alain said that someone on the Committee wanted me dead and him out of the way. Plus, we've investigated psychic assassinations before. Remember the skydivers? Those were made to look like suicides!"

"That wasn't on the Committee, Amanda. That was the Whip and Compass, remember? The twins."

Lydia placed her arm around Amanda's shoulder. "Mandy, I'm sorry. I know you want to believe that Alain didn't leave you by choice, but that's not what happened. I'm sorry to be blunt."

"But why choose suicide? He'd be sequestered from the world, but he'd still have me. Would death really be better?" She looked at her friends imploringly.

Lydia looked sympathetic. Matt looked uncomfortable. "I, uh . . . I left something in the car," he said, and put down his mug. "BRB!" he called as he ran out of the house.

Amanda stood and looked out the window. "I miss him so much, Lydia." She watched as Matt maneuvered his red SUV onto the street and took off. She wasn't surprised he was leaving, and she didn't care. She heaved a sigh. "There's this longing in me . . . I can't explain it. There's a part of me that doesn't care that he was a killer. I saw the real him, the human part of him, not the monster. I saw him in a way that no one else could. And he saw me for who I really am."

"Maybe the monster in him wouldn't let him live," Lydia mused.

"Or perhaps it was the man," Amanda replied.

Lydia stayed silent. Looking over, Amanda saw that she was frowning and biting her lip.

"What now?"

"Mandy, I have tremendous sympathy for *your* feelings, because I know they're real, but . . ."

Amanda tensed up. "What?" She steeled herself for Lydia's reply.

"I'm just going to say it like it is: I'm so glad he's gone."

"Oh, here we go again. You know, Lydia, your relationship with Hank was never perfect, but I tried to support you when you decided to get back together with him. And I never wished him dead!" Though in fact she had—for a very brief moment—wished just that.

Lydia kept her cool. "I can't say I'm glad he's *dead*, of course. But I am glad he is *gone*. I think we should all count our blessings that this terrible man is out of our lives."

Hot rage rose in Amanda. "You had no idea who he was! You never gave him a chance."

"I gave him the benefit of the doubt until our conversation at Basil's house. After that I knew he was dangerous. Amanda, I can't be more clear: he was a clinical case. Thoroughly antisocial, callous, unemotional—a complete psychopath. Oh, he had charisma, I'll give you that. But psychopaths are notoriously charming. He was also reckless, a liar with no empathy, and he enjoyed his kills. It even makes sense that he couldn't deal with the breakup—and that's why he killed himself. He was narcissistic, with borderline tendencies."

A deep and heavy silence settled between the friends. Did Lydia even understand that she had just blamed Amanda for Alain's death? Grief flooded her, grief burdened with guilt.

"Mandy," Lydia said softly from somewhere behind her in the room. "That's not what I meant."

"You just told me that he killed himself because of me."

"He killed himself because of *him*. He failed to possess you completely. I have read so much about psychopaths. I wish you could just trust me."

Amanda stayed silent. She didn't know what or whom to believe anymore. "Maybe the Committee did kill him," she said after a while, coming back to her previous point.

"You can't believe that."

"Why not? When the Overload happened, the Committee refused to help me. They were fine with me dying. They had no qualms whatsoever."

Lydia pressed her lips together.

"And like I said before, one of them hired an assassin to finish the job more quickly—at least, that's what Alain thinks happened."

"As we've established, you can't trust Alain. The Committee refusing to help you is one thing, putting a hit on you is another thing entirely. I think you are vilifying the wrong people."

"Whatever happened, I just don't believe he'd commit suicide." Amanda paced from the window and back. "Once I learned what Alain had done, it destroyed my feelings for him. But when I found out he'd agreed to be sequestered, that redeemed him. It proved he didn't *want* to be a killer. What he did in his altered state was not what his normal self would ever do. Can you try to understand that?"

Lydia looked directly at Amanda and spoke like a clinician, not a friend. "There's no such thing as multiple personality disorder. It's a myth. None of the younger psychiatrists believe it. There is little evidence it is real, but, like any outdated concept, it will disappear only once its proponents die out."

"Lydia, will you just *stop* lecturing about psychiatry? Look outside your box and see that there's a whole world of other explanations."

"That may well be, but I can't buy this whole 'miracle transformation in your presence' thing."

Another silence extended between them. Lydia was never going to understand what had transpired between Amanda and Alain. And maybe that was okay. She took one last try anyway.

"In our last conversation, I called him 'a beast from hell.' I don't blame myself for saying so, because what he did was monstrous. But the man, the man within the monster . . ."

Lydia sighed with exasperation. "Will you please stop crying about this psychopath?"

Amanda gaped at her. "That has got to be the harshest thing I've ever heard you say. Why are you being so utterly cruel? Has the situation with Hank shut you down emotionally—so much so that you can't even sympathize with my pain? You insist that I deserve better, but is that your way of telling yourself that you're better off without Hank?"

Lydia frowned. "This conversation is not about me and Hank." She walked quickly to Amanda and wrapped her in a deep embrace. "I just thought . . . I have been scared for you, Mandy."

Amanda returned the hug. "I know you're just trying to be a good friend. But you can't take away my pain, Lydia. I have to suffer through it."

The two women separated. "I'm sorry," Lydia said. "I apologize for being insensitive, and you're right. I didn't know him. I'll even attend his funeral, okay? You've convinced me. I love you. I only want what's best for you." She patted Amanda's arm. "May he rest in peace."

Chapter 36

A cold drizzle was falling at the cemetery when a small group came to lay Alain Proctor to rest. Basil, James, Lydia, and Amanda were the only mourners present. Alain Proctor had no relatives, no friends. Absolutely no one. Basil had paid for everything, but Amanda had chosen the line written on the headstone: *Till the end of time.*

Basil gave an impromptu eulogy, his eyes moist. "I remember when you came to us, Alain. I could feel your heart. All Sentinels are special to me, but you were different. You were in a fight against the inner pain that was eroding your humanity, even before the Overload happened. I did my best to guide you away from it. You listened to me, and many times I saw glimpses of such good inside of you. If only we hadn't run out of time . . ." He trailed off as Lydia and James each took an arm. "Rest in peace, Alain."

"Rest in peace," Lydia echoed, and James nodded at her words.

Amanda couldn't speak. She simply placed a white rose on the ground. They stood in silence for a while. Finally, James said, "Should we go?"

Amanda touched his sleeve. "You go. I just need a few more minutes. I'll meet up with you guys at the restaurant."

Once everyone else left, Amanda crouched in front of his grave, staring at the inscription she had left. His words would stay forever with her. *Till the end of time.*

The wind stirred dry leaves and swept them over the stone. Her leather-gloved hand picked up the rose, and she briefly touched it with her lips. "I had an ocean of love for you, Alain. But it wasn't enough. Why couldn't I save you?"

When she heard footsteps behind her, she whipped around. It was James, heading back toward her. The drizzle had turned into snow; tiny dot-like snowflakes were falling and melting on his dark hair and wool coat. Maybe he'd forgotten which restaurant they were meeting at. With a sigh, Amanda turned away from him, once again focused on the grave.

She was too numb to be upset, but she wasn't exactly happy about being interrupted.

"Hey James, I need a second," she warned as she felt him approach. The next thing she knew, his arms were around her.

He hugged her from behind, resting his chin on her shoulder. "I'm not letting you go this time."

Amanda tensed up, unsure what to do or what to think. All she could do was feel. Warmth came over her, from the inside out. She leaned into him. "It's not easy, James," she managed to say, straining to keep her voice steady. "This man loved me."

"*That* is not very difficult to do," he said, his voice deep and soft and close. He lightly kissed her on the cheek, and Amanda's heart began to race.

"You know I have courage, Amanda. You know I do. Just not when it comes to relationships. When I lost my fiancée, I lost all hope for love. Charlene was my high school sweetheart. We had been together since we were sixteen. I never dated anyone else, before or after she died. No one."

He turned her to face him. Snow was gathering on his hair, melting into the thick dark strands. "If I can be honest . . . I also didn't know how to handle you. There's something about you. About your strength. It's sort of, I don't know. Intimidating, maybe? You were so powerful, and so closed off. I felt useless around you—and I lost all courage. But as I got to know you, I saw your heart—how beautiful you are, deep down inside." He gently placed his hands on her shoulders. "I think we've always had something, Amanda. I just couldn't open my heart. It's taken me three years to get over Charlene. Now you've lost someone, too. You understand what that means. We both know what it's like. I can wait for you."

He looked so handsome, so serious. Would things have been different had he not hesitated for so long?

But she realized that she was intensely grateful for this second chance.

"I didn't choose you," she said as she peered into his eyes, her voice breaking. "You won't hold that against me?"

He shook his head. "You need time to heal. No one understands that better than I do. I will be here for you. When you're ready."

Chapter 37

Amanda went back to her work at the hospital but remained on a break from Sentinel assignments. Her grief made that kind of work impossible. She and James met regularly, but dating was out of the question. She couldn't bear the thought of trusting someone with her love and losing her heart again. As it was, any reminder of Alain Proctor brought fresh tears to her eyes. Why hadn't she succeeded in saving him? Had he suffered? Had there been something more she could have done, *should* have done? These questions continued to plague her.

On a cold Sunday in late February, when a blizzard watch was in effect and the streets were empty and buried in snow, Amanda was up early and looking forward to having the day to herself. She turned on the electric fireplace in her living room and spent a few minutes quietly watching the blue flames flick up the sides of the brick walls. In a way, they reminded her of her Sentinel powers, and she found the effect almost hypnotic. She could stare at the flames forever, lost in meditation.

Eventually, she stretched and headed to the kitchen, where she made herself a large hot chocolate with whipped cream. Then she opened the curtains and gazed at the snowcapped city below. She was happy about the blizzard. The world looked so peaceful right now, as if it were sleeping.

Cozy and content, she finished her hot chocolate and soaked in a warm salt bath. Afterward she donned a bathrobe, brushed her hair, and put on lipstick. She considered inviting James over to spend the afternoon with her, watching movies. She was still thinking it over when there was a buzz at her intercom.

"Yes?"

"A package has just been delivered for you, Dr. Griffith."

Who would brave this weather to deliver a package? And on a Sunday, no less. She put on jeans and a white sweater and went downstairs to the front desk, where the concierge handed her a small package.

"It's not an anthrax bomb, I hope," said Amanda, joking—and yet she was a bit wary of the mysterious package. She turned it over and saw that it came from a post office in South Africa—no return address, no name.

"Who delivered it?" she asked the concierge.

"A young man. No uniform. He just handed it to me and left."

Mystified, she headed back to the elevator, tearing open the package as she went. It contained a small box and a letter. She opened the box and stared at the gorgeous pair of diamond earrings inside. She blinked and paled, then quickly opened the letter. As soon as she read the first line, her heart jumped in fear and surprise.

If you're reading this letter, it means our story didn't have the happy ending we wanted, my beautiful Amanda.

She dashed back to the front desk, clutching the box. "Which way did he go?"

The concierge pointed left. Amanda ran into the street without a second's hesitation. She gasped as the cold threw what felt like ice needles into her face, the wind tugging her hair in all directions. Her breath quickened as she ran to the corner, frantically looking around. There was no one in sight.

She stood for a while with an insane hope in her heart. Empty storefronts looked back at her. A city bus went by, the wind picked up again. But there was no one.

She hurried back inside. The concierge stared at her as if waiting for an explanation, but she had none, not even for herself. Rubbing her hands, she said, "Can you tell me what he looked like?"

"Young guy, maybe twenty. Tall, with short black hair."

Amanda turned on her receiving functions and applied mind control, in case he was hiding something. But he wasn't. She headed back to her condo, sat down on the couch, and read the note, her heart beating furiously in her chest.

If you're reading this letter, it means our story didn't have a happy ending, my beautiful Amanda. I'm sitting here beside you in your apartment, but you're fast asleep. You don't know that I'm here. I want so much to be close to you, but I know I can never be close to you again. I'm listening to you crying in your sleep. I feel like I'm destroying you, my love. This life, I had it rough. I would have done anything to keep you. Anything except change. I tried, but I cannot remove the monster inside me. I can, however, save you from it. I can save you from the heartache the evil within me is causing you. I don't know what I'll do in my altered state outside of your presence. And that is bad news.

I wanted to give you these earrings. I got them at the same time as the necklace. I had a ring, too, but I guess that wasn't meant to be.

Have you heard about the multiverse theory? Maybe there is a parallel universe where there are no Sentinels. A place where there's only a young boy from Iowa, who was separated early enough from his deranged father so that he could build a stable life: become a paramedic, meet a beautiful anesthesiologist, and fall in love with her.

I still believe in karma, my little diamond. What is meant to be will be, and there must be a reason for it all.

Don't grieve for me. I am at peace, wherever I am. Be happy, and remember the good in me. Or, better yet, don't think of me at all.

Amanda closed her eyes. Tears ran down her cheeks, but her emotions were a mix of pain and a relief. A relief to know that he wasn't blaming her. That he wasn't angry with her.

She sat on the couch for a long time as random memories flashed in her mind and the tears streamed down her face. Eventually, the pain subsided. She smoothed her hair, took a deep breath, reached for her phone, and dialed.

"Basil, it's me. Good morning. Yeah, lots of snow here, too. We're all boxed in for the day." In a calm and even tone, she told him about the letter. "It came from South Africa, and it was delivered by a stranger. I mean, he makes it clear in the letter that if I'm reading it, he's gone. But how could it have been sent from South Africa if he died here in Boston in October?"

"Amanda, I'm sorry. I know you want to believe that he's still alive, but I promise you that he isn't. I saw his body." Basil spoke slowly and steadily. "I personally made his arrangements. He is dead. I don't have an explanation for how he got the letter to you. Perhaps he hired someone to deliver it in the event of his death. Listen, the point is, he has released you. He wrote this note to release you from him. And Amanda, there's something else you should know. I think it will help you let go."

"What is it?"

"The way you kept him human . . ."

"Yes?"

"That started to change after the Ascendants cured you of the Overload. I could feel it. The ambiguity was flowing back and forth in him. He was drifting back and forth between being a psychopath and being himself, and he was becoming more unpredictable."

Amanda was shocked. She'd had no idea her effect on him was getting weaker. Alain had never mentioned it. "No, you must be mistaken."

"I'm afraid not, my child. He told me that it was happening to him. He wondered whether being sequestered would be enough."

Amanda could feel her heart in her throat. "He must have decided there was no hope."

"It would seem that way, my dear. He wanted to live, to be there for you. But ultimately, maybe he realized the plan was not going to work."

Every word fanned her grief. Why wouldn't he at least try? But then . . . She held the letter closer to her eyes. There was something in his words, here. "You're right," she quickly agreed, peering at it. "Alain is gone. I don't know what I was thinking. Talk soon."

She was focused on the letter. She'd noticed something: the last paragraph looked different—like an addition, as though it had been written in a different ink at a different time. There could be no reasonable doubt that he was dead, yet . . . was someone imitating his writing?

"I'm losing my mind," she whispered.

She sat for a very long time thinking, then went back to the window. The snow still fell softly, the wind swirling crystalline flakes around the roofs and street signs.

She had not saved him. With all her new, incredible powers, she could not save him from the evil lurking within him. She could fight any number of supernatural challenges, but none of that had helped save the man she loved. If there were answers to the mystery of the letter, only time would tell. Either way, there was no point torturing herself when the matter was entirely out of her hands. The end of their story would always be the same. Alain had released her. One way or another, this letter was Alain's final goodbye. He hadn't wanted to leave her, but he'd known that staying would destroy her. He'd done it for her. He wanted her to be happy, with or without him. This thought made her cry again, but these tears brought her relief.

Slowly, tentatively, peace came over her heart. She looked at the earrings sparkling in her hand, a testimony of his love for her. Reaching out, even from beyond the grave, because he cared. She had awakened love in his heart, and she had loved him, and that was all anyone could ever do. The battle against the evil within him was his own. She couldn't have fought that battle for him. No one could. He'd tried, and he'd lost. Good doesn't always win, but it will always do its best.

She had to turn the page.

Slowly, as if afraid that any sudden movement would disturb the peace in her heart, she put the earrings back into the box and reached for her phone. She let out a sigh, and texted James to invite him over for an afternoon of movies and takeout. They'd take it slow and see if they still had a chance together.

Lastly, she phoned her adviser again. "I'm ready, Basil. Sentinel 10 is back on board. When's my next assignment?"

Acknowledgements

My deepest thanks to my amazing editorial goddesses: Jessica Moreland and Francine LaSala from Brigid Book Works LLC and Pat Dobie from Lucid Edit. This book would never have happened without your talent and patience. Many heartfelt thanks to Lyda McLallen of Talk Plus Tell and my Book Sherpa, Gail M. Kearns.

I began writing this novel in July 2017 after my return from Prague, where I'd gone to attend a forensic psychiatry conference. The story came to me like a movie. Each scene or chapter unfolded in my head as I flew back to Canada. Once set in motion, the wheels of creation kept on turning and resulted in the Sentinel 10 series.

Looking back, the original idea appeared twenty years ago while watching Buffy the Vampire Slayer. Amanda was the first character to form in my mind—a strong female character—though her background story would develop later. James was created at the same time. But the world of the Sentinels really started to take shape while I was in Prague. Most importantly, that's when Alain transformed into the exact character he is now. The conference was about psychopathy, and it triggered the detailed creation of his persona and his background story. Prague also inspired his demeanor and looks. In fact, he wears a gray suit and drives a gray Mercedes because the taxi drivers in Prague dress that way and drive Mercedes! When I arrived, I was met by such a driver, outside the airport. My hotel had sent him to pick me up.

Lydia was spontaneously concocted when I began writing and putting ideas to words. The same went for Matt, but mark my words, I have big plans for this character. His transformation will start in the fourth book. Every character—Amanda especially—will grow throughout the series. Change doesn't happen overnight; as a psychiatrist, and as an individual working to better myself, I know this truth firsthand. I'm currently finishing the eighth book of the series. *The Diamond Rose* is only the first chapter in Amanda's hero's journey!

I hope you can join me for the second chapter, *The Crystal Skull,* which will be released in 2021.

Yours truly,
Daniela Valenti